DROPS
of GOLD

OTHER BOOKS AND AUDIOBOOKS
BY SARAH M. EDEN

CHRONOLOGICAL ORDER OF ALL RELATED
SARAH M. EDEN GEORGIAN- & REGENCY-ERA BOOKS

DROPS
of GOLD

A JONQUIL BROTHERS
ROMANCE

FROM *USA TODAY* BEST-SELLING AUTHOR

SARAH M. EDEN

Covenant Communications, Inc.

Published by Covenant Communications, Inc.
American Fork, Utah

Printed in the United States of America
First Printing: January 2013; Second Edition: April 2021

30 29 28 27 26 25 24 23 22 21   10 9 8 7 6 5 4 3 2 1

ISBN 978-1-60861-569-8

To Dad
for every dance recital, every set built, every
badminton game – for believing in me

PREFACE

I ABSOLUTELY LOVE DELVING DEEP into research, immersing myself in the study of a time period and a way of life. Occasionally I come across a source of information so invaluable I can only sit back in grateful awe. In formulating this story, I discovered two such works and feel the need to recognize them here:

Commentaries on the Laws of England: In Four Books; with an Analysis of the Work, by Sir William Blackstone, Knt, published in London in 1836, and *Commentaries on the Liberty of the Subject and the Laws of England Relating to the Security of the Person*, by James Paterson, Esq., MA, published in London in 1877.

The astoundingly great information and commentary in these two books added an authenticity to this story I could not have claimed otherwise and have already sparked ideas for many stories yet to come.

CHAPTER ONE

Nottinghamshire, England, December 24, 1814

"But which way is Farland Meadows?" Marion shouted into the biting wind. She hadn't anticipated being left on an empty public road.

The coachman pointed directly behind her before cracking his whip over the heads of his team, sending the mismatched beasts into a frenzied run. The mail coach rattled and swayed at the abnormal speed.

"Typical," she muttered to no one in particular. Being abandoned in a part of the country she'd never set foot in fit perfectly with the unpredictable nature of her life lately.

Two days earlier she'd been hired sight-unseen, based on nothing more than a single recommendation, to fill a position for which she knew she was completely unqualified. She swallowed back a lump of guilt. She not only hadn't earned that recommendation, but she had also written it herself under an entirely fictitious name—though, she thought with pride, she'd done remarkably well disguising her handwriting. If her current occupation proved unsuccessful, she could seek her fortune as a forger.

Forging was probably wrong, she reflected, especially the references she'd created for herself. That lie was not nearly as white as she would have liked. Lamentable. *But starvation is also lamentable*, she reminded herself. A clear conscience was a poor substitute for a full belly.

Watching the hasty retreat of the mail coach and its two passengers, Marion could do little but review the journey and determine what to do next. Since she'd changed mail coaches at Southwell, Marion's fellow passengers had been a middle-aged spinster of the working class and the woman's nearly blind father of exceedingly advanced years. They'd struck up an easy conversation, something Marion had feared for months would never happen again. She'd resigned herself to a myriad of depressing fates. If her imagination hadn't had a tendency toward the absurd, she might very well have submitted to an interminable bout of blue-devils.

"'Ave you family in Collingham, child?" the woman in the mail coach had asked.

Marion had reminded herself that age could be a relative thing. At nineteen, she was hardly a child. But compared to the octogenarian seated beside the woman, Marion was an infant.

"No," Marion had replied, keeping her eyes on her folded hands and, with some difficulty, her voice low and submissive. "I've found a position."

"Don't sound like a servant," the older man had observed gruffly.

Ah, furuncle! She'd need to practice more. She had repeated her words silently, trying out a few different inflections.

"Don't *look* much like one either," the woman had added. "Though I s'pose ye can't 'elp yer looks."

A few miles of blessed silence had followed, in which Marion had tried to devise ways to make herself look more like a servant, although she wasn't sure what particular features screamed "servant" and why she seemed so entirely without them. Perhaps red hair was frowned upon for a member of a household staff. A generous amount of walnut rinse might darken it. Marion had pictured her reflection in her mind. A *very* generous amount would be needed—even when caked in dirt, carrots were orange.

Maybe she should frown. Were frowns more servant-like than smiles? Perhaps a pout would help. She'd have to think on it and see if she could find a mirror to practice in front of.

"An upper servant?" the male traveler had then asked, his overly loud voice making Marion wonder if his hearing was failing as well.

"Most likely." His daughter had shown not a hint of confusion, though Marion hadn't the slightest idea what the two were discussing. "She's too young to be a governess."

"I *am* a governess," she'd responded with a smile after realizing they were talking about her.

The woman had seemed shocked for a minute then had slowly nodded her perfectly round head in approval. "There are several large estates not far from Collingham. Lampton Park. Finnley Grange. Sarvol House. Carter Manor . . ."

Marion had smiled. None of these apparently grand estates even sounded close to the paradise for which she was destined.

Farland Meadows.

It sounded straight from a fairy tale. She'd amassed a wide collection of fanciful mental images of what the picturesque estate must look like. It would be lined with stately trees, she was certain. Rolling hills. Meadows, of course. It would be positively overrun with meadows filled with flowers and bright grass. Perhaps a stream trickled through one end of it. Farland Meadows would be perfect. It simply had to be.

"And where are you 'eaded to?" her curious companion had requested.

With a broad smile, Marion had said the name that had been at the forefront of her mind the past two days. "Farland Meadows."

Even before she'd finished the idyllic words, her companions' faces had fallen.

"You've been 'ired up to the Meadows?" the woman had asked, her voice a tense whisper.

Marion had nodded. She'd felt her smile slip.

"'Ave you nowhere else to go, child?"

Marion had shaken her head.

"Won't last," the older man had grumbled loudly.

The woman had sighed almost mournfully. Neither she nor her father had spoken again.

Nightfall had been imminent, and if Marion hadn't missed her mark, so was a snowstorm, when the coach had come to an abrupt and unexpected halt. The door had opened, and the coachman had motioned Marion to step out.

"The Meadows ain't no place for ye, child," the woman had whispered fervently as Marion had climbed down.

Wind whipped furiously around her skirts and had threatened to pluck her well-worn bonnet from her head. The coachman had handed Marion her handleless valise.

"Good luck to ye," he'd muttered and climbed back onto the coach.

"This can't be Collingham," she'd called out, looking around at the uninhabited copses of trees and empty, open fields around her. A low wall separated the road from the land surrounding it, but there was no other indication of civilization nearby. Collingham, she understood, was a small but relatively busy town.

"Less of a walk for ye," the coachman had answered, settling himself onto the driver's bench.

When she had called out for direction to her new place of employment, the strength of the wind had made his reply impossible to hear. But he'd pointed.

And now the coach was but a little silhouette against the increasingly dark horizon.

"Typical," she muttered again, shaking her head. If she weren't so cold, the situation might have been amusing. She could easily have been the heroine in some ridiculous gothic novel. All she lacked was a handsome rescuer to come riding up on his noble horse to sweep her off the ground.

Marion looked up and down the road. Empty. "Typical." She laughed at herself.

What am I waiting for? Marion demanded of herself. She spun around to face the direction the coachman had pointed and began walking, holding her small valise to her to block the wind, which bit and gnawed at her face.

The stinging cold rid her of any weariness her long days of travel had created. Thoughts of Farland Meadows warmed her. Such a peaceful name. It would be a wonderful place, she felt certain. Beautiful grounds. Warm, loving family with an angelic child.

The Meadows ain't no place for ye. The woman's words wouldn't leave Marion's mind. She was wrong, Marion insisted. Absolutely wrong. The Meadows would be perfect. How could a position that was so obviously a direct answer to her most fervent prayers be anything but heaven-sent?

With her customary smile determinedly on her face once more, Marion began walking again. Now that she thought back on it, the driver had been uneasy when she'd told him her destination. Three people in one day concerned for her at the very mention of Farland Meadows? Curious, to be sure.

Marion shook her head and dismissed the incidents as an odd coincidence. In a matter of minutes, she reached a set of open iron gates leading into a thick stand of trees cut through by a carriage path. *Farland Meadows?* she wondered. The gatehouse not far distant was visible despite the setting sun, but no lights glimmered inside. Four knocks went unheeded.

Cold seeped through her skirts and threadbare coat. Marion glanced down the carriage path that cut through the bare-branched trees then glanced back up at the road. There was no way of knowing if this was, indeed, Farland Meadows.

"I could at least ask for directions." Marion was an old hand at talking to herself, something that had always made her mother laugh and her father shake his head.

With a shrug, she followed the carriage path. The grounds of the still-unnamed estate felt undeniably peaceful. Marion rounded a corner on the path and, mouth hanging open, stopped in her tracks. The red light of sunset reflected off the facade of a perfectly wonderful home, well-kept and obviously cared for, with just enough wear to give it character. She couldn't have been more pleased with the house if she'd designed it herself.

Marion smiled. This had to be Farland Meadows. It absolutely *had* to be. She took a deep breath of pine-scented air, the cold nibbling at her features. She hugged her handleless valise to her and smiled up at the home straight out of one of her dreams.

Perfect.

Too happy to merely walk, Marion ran and even twirled once or twice as she circled around to the back of the house. The life of a governess wouldn't have been her first choice, but taking a look at the picturesque setting, Marion knew she couldn't have hoped for a better outcome.

She stopped in front of the servants' entrance, bonnet hanging limply around her neck. Marion had no desire to arrive for her new position with her flame-red hair flying about in complete disarray. She tapped her bonnet back in place and tucked as many of her loose locks inside it as she could manage without a mirror or a single hairpin. That would simply have to do. Marion knocked hard at the door and waited.

After several minutes, the door opened. A girl of no more than fourteen stood just beyond and gave her a questioning glance.

"Is this Farland Meadows?" Marion never had been able to dampen her natural enthusiasm. She didn't imagine she sounded much like a servant.

"Aye." The maid nodded.

Marion felt like hugging the girl. She managed to restrain herself. "I am Mary Wood." Marion had already decided Mary was a more appropriate name for one in her situation. "The new governess."

"Governess? We didn't hire a governess."

She closed the door, leaving Marion in stunned silence on the doorstep.

CHAPTER TWO

Layton Jonquil stood in the midst of his six brothers. They'd already honored an hour's worth of requests from their extremely enthusiastic mother. Layton didn't feel particularly in the mood for caroling—and hadn't for years, in all honesty. But this was Mater. Layton would do anything for his mother.

"'God Rest Ye Merry, Gentleman,' I insist."

"Oh, Mater. Not that one." Charlie, the youngest, groaned lightheartedly.

What Layton wouldn't give to be sixteen again, the only weight on his shoulders that of pleasing a mother overly fond of holiday traditions.

"I did not give life to a gaggle of gentlemen only to have them object to such a fitting carol." Mater gave them a look with which they were all too familiar. Since their childhoods, she'd had the uncanny ability to shame them into behaving with a single glance. She hadn't lost her touch.

Philip, the eldest, made some flippant comment. Layton heard the laughter around him just before the others began the first strains of "God Rest Ye Merry, Gentleman."

Layton's thoughts turned to Father. That carol had been a favorite of his. Layton continued singing mechanically, even as his memories took him miles, years, away. He could remember distinctly where he'd been when news of Father's death had reached him. Cambridge. Philip had told him in a stuttering, thick voice, obviously trying to be the strong, unshakable head of the family he'd suddenly found himself required to be.

Philip had been so young—he couldn't have been more than nineteen. Layton had only been a year younger. There'd been no warning. Father had never been ill. He'd been as active and fit at forty-nine as most men half his age. No one anticipated a failing heart.

It still seemed so senseless. Layton glanced at Mater as the carol continued around him. Nine years, and she still wore the blacks of full mourning.

Oh, tidings of comfort and joy . . .

The words lodged in Layton's throat as memories flooded his mind: carefree moments of childhood, talking with Father as they walked the grounds of Lampton Park, long discussions about life and family, a smile sneaking across Father's face as he tried not to laugh at yet another of Layton and Philip's pranks.

Around him his brothers began the second verse, and Layton closed his ears to it. That horrible afternoon at Cambridge: riding to Nottinghamshire with Philip, watching him struggle with his composure, Mater's tear-streaked cheeks, Father's bleak funeral.

Layton didn't know how he'd reached the window. He had no recollection of dropping out of the carol or of leaving his brothers, but there he stood, staring at an empty landscape.

He took a deep breath. It didn't even feel like Christmas, not the type of Christmas he'd known. No Father. No Caroline. No Bridget.

"I had hoped Mater would leave that particular selection off the list." Philip spoke lightly from directly beside him then added more somberly, "It always makes me think of Father."

"Me too." Layton tried to force thoughts of funerals from his mind. There'd been too many in the past nine years.

"He'd have enjoyed being here for Christmas." Philip sounded regretful.

Regret. Layton chuckled humorlessly, soundlessly. He knew regret well.

"And he would have adored Catherine," Philip added, indicating their hostess.

"True."

Their best friend, Crispin Cavratt's, new bride was a particularly adorable woman. Father had always had a soft spot for females. He'd wanted a houseful of daughters. He sired seven sons.

"That means seven daughters-in-law," he'd once said with that smile of his that pulled his nose to one side.

He didn't live long enough to see a single one. He never saw his sons grow into men or his beloved wife enjoy being a grandmother.

"It has been good . . . having you here . . ." Philip stumbled over his words. The two of them never used to be awkward. "I wish you could stay longer."

"I can't." He only wanted to get back home, where he could be alone.

"You know you can talk to me." Philip laid his hand on Layton's shoulder. "About anything."

Layton shrugged free, keeping his eyes firmly fixed ahead. "There's nothing to talk about." The time for talking had long passed.

Philip didn't press the issue. The next moment, he left the room, followed shortly thereafter by a lady for whom Layton suspected his elder brother had developed a partiality. If he didn't miss his mark, that connection would grow into something permanent. Layton was happy for his brother, even though watching the budding romance left a decided weight in his stomach.

The Jonquil brothers had dispersed throughout the west sitting room and were chatting with the Kinnley guests. Layton watched each of his brothers in turn. The family resemblance was ridiculously strong. They all had the same golden hair and blue eyes. Each of the brothers was tall and slim, except for him. He alone was built like a prizefighter.

Layton sighed. That minor physical difference had never bothered him before. But lately . . . It was just one more reason he didn't fit into his own family.

He made an undoubtedly unnoticed exit but stopped only a few feet from the door. Layton could hear Philip's voice from the back corridor, his words made indiscernible by echoes. It was just as well.

Layton made his way to the front staircase and up to his bedchamber. Jones, his valet, would be celebrating Christmas below stairs with the rest of the servants. Layton draped his coat over the back of a chair then sat on the edge of his bed.

Spending time with his family wore on him. Spending time with *anyone* had worn on him the past few years. Layton untied his cravat and unwound it, letting his breath slowly escape. The square of linen dropped into a crumpled heap on the bed beside him. He closed his eyes and deftly unbuttoned his waistcoat.

"God Rest Ye Merry, Gentleman" echoed in his heavy mind, the feelings of loss and emptiness it inspired clinging to him like a wet shirt. Layton shook his head in an attempt to clear it. When had Christmas become such an unpleasant affair?

He dropped onto the bed, staring up at the heavy canopy. Why had he agreed to come to Suffolk? Surely Mater would have understood if he'd declined, if he'd insisted on staying with Caroline. Yes, she would have understood, but she would have been disappointed.

Layton closed his eyes and draped his arm across his forehead. *Disappointed.* Was there a person in all of England he hadn't disappointed? If Mater wasn't already on that list, he certainly didn't want to see her added to it.

He would leave in the morning. In mere days, he'd be back home.

His breathing grew more even, his arm resting more heavily on his head. Sleep approached, and Layton dreaded it. He could postpone the inevitable if he rose, paced his bedchamber. Perhaps he could throw open the window and allow the cold winter air to awaken his dulling senses. In the end, it would do no good. Sleep would come eventually, whether he wished it to or not.

The uncomfortable sensation of sleep slid slowly over him. For a moment, nothing. Then came darkness and the fuzzy images of dreams.

He was frantically flying down the corridors of the house he'd lived in for six years. He was lost. Lost within the walls of his own home.

Layton threw open the first door he reached: an empty bedchamber with pale-blue bed curtains, plush cream carpeting, and sunlight filtering through thin draperies. His heart began to race. He ran on, jerking open the next door only to find the same empty bedchamber.

On and on he ran. Every door opened to a duplicate scene, but every door was wrong. Layton ran harder, his breath coming in gasps. Somewhere in the distance a sob pierced the air.

Layton tried unsuccessfully to push his legs faster. Each door led to the same serene scene as if mocking the desperation of his search. The echoing sobs grew more harrowing as fog drifted into the unending corridor. Layton opened countless doors, no longer stopping to look over the repeated scene.

The crying grew louder.

He was close. So close. If only he could find the right door.

The fog became suddenly thick, the air bitterly cold. Layton stood frozen before a doorway. The sobbing had stopped. Only the sound of his uneasy breathing rent the silence.

The door he faced opened on its own. It led to the same bedchamber, but this one was dim and cold. Layton closed his eyes as he stepped inside.

"No," he whispered, shaking his head.

Not a sound penetrated the darkness. He opened his eyes to study the eerie scene. Heavy drapes covered the windows, not a ray of light breaking through them. Four walls of pale-blue curtains enclosed the bed.

Layton inched closer, his heart never slowing.

"No," he whispered again, stinging pain grasping his throat as he fought back the urge to fill the room with his own sobs. "Too late. Too late."

A single candle burned low on a small table at the head of the heavily curtained bed, casting a shivering glow. Layton stood frozen beside it, not wanting to pull the curtains back but knowing he must.

His fingers grasped the front curtain—it crumpled soundlessly—then clenched it in a desperate fist. Still he stood, unable to move, unable to pull it back. He'd come so far. Yet there he was, one movement from retribution.

He took two slow, deep breaths. He couldn't even hear his own breathing now, as if the very life had been sucked from the room.

Layton clenched the heavy fabric tighter. In one swift motion, he flung the curtain back.

"No!"

Layton sat upright in his bed, sweat dripping from his forehead like rain. His pulse raced. His lungs struggled to gasp for air. His eyes fought to adjust to the darkness of the room.

That dream.

He mopped his face with the bedsheet as drops of sweat stung his eyes. How many years had he been haunted by the same dream? He could not recall the last time he'd slept an entire night without it.

Layton dropped his head into his hands and tried to force the lingering images from his mind. He felt closer to seventy-seven than twenty-seven, and yet, a lifetime stretched out in front of him, decades of dreams he couldn't escape, living with heavy regrets and guilt he had no right to wish himself free of.

CHAPTER THREE

SHE'D RECEIVED AN ODD WELCOME, to say the least. After the young maid, whose name she'd discovered was Maggie, fled the doorway, Mrs. Sanders, the housekeeper, showed Marion inside, muttering all the while about servants putting on airs. Every member of the small staff watched her with more than a hint of wariness. Several of the faces she'd briefly encountered regarded her in much the same way one would a cut of fish that had turned.

Curious, to be sure.

Not a single smile could be seen on any of their faces. The entire house felt somber. Marion half expected to find the windows and doors draped in black. Mrs. Sanders spoke little beyond a few grumbled words indicating the room that was to be Marion's.

Mrs. Sanders turned at the door and looked Marion over. She squinted through her assessment, something Marion would not have guessed she'd been physically capable of doing, considering she wore her silver hair in a bun so tight the corners of her eyes pulled from the strain.

"The last one left in something of a hurry," Mrs. Sanders said. *The last governess*, Marion guessed. "You'll have time in the morning to straighten. Duties will be cut back in honor of the holiday."

"Yes, Mrs. Sanders."

The house was indeed silent as Marion plaited her overly red hair and twisted it into a bun at the nape of her neck. Papa's pocket watch read five thirty. The household staff, she had been told, broke their fasts between half past five and six o'clock every morning.

"Five thirty," she had repeated upon being told of the ridiculously early breakfast hour.

Looking back, Marion smiled at her perfectly subservient tone. She'd practiced, after all. Keeping the enthusiasm and cheerfulness from her voice was difficult but not entirely impossible. Perhaps she would make a decent governess.

But then, she had yet to try her hand at teaching children. Suppose she discovered herself completely inept. Marion smiled, imagining herself tied to a tree somewhere on the grounds while a bevy of wild-eyed children wreaked havoc on the peaceful Farland Meadows. What a mess that would be!

Marion choked down a laugh as a knock echoed from the door of her room.

"Come in," she called out, a hint of amusement still obvious in her tone.

Maggie stepped inside, a tray in one hand, a candle in the other. "Yer breakfast, Mary." She brought the tray to the table where Marion sat.

"My breakfast? But why—"

"Mrs. Sanders says how yeh're to take yer meals here." Maggie set the tray down. She kept her eyes diverted. "An' how I'm supposed to leave the tray by the servants' door in the schoolroom. But this bein' Christmas Day, I thought yeh'd like it brought to yeh."

"I would much prefer to eat below stairs." *With people.*

Maggie looked a little uncomfortable, still unable, or unwilling, to meet Marion's eyes. "But 'tis a real treat up here. Havin' it brought to yeh an' all."

"Oh, I know," Marion quickly reassured the young maid. "It just seems an awful lot of extra work. And for a governess, of all things. It—"

"Mr. and Mrs. Sanders says it's best that way." Maggie spoke as though the couple claimed a level of authority equal to the prime minister's himself rather than the butler and housekeeper they were.

"It seems like a great deal of trouble," Marion pressed.

Maggie didn't relent. "Jus' the way things are."

Marion twisted her mouth and pondered the declaration. *The way things are.* Well, things could always change. She fought down a satisfied smile. She'd never failed to make the best of a situation.

"When does Miss Caroline awaken?" Marion asked, changing the topic to the child she'd been hired to look after.

"Not for another hour, a' least." Maggie walked to the door.

"Happy Christmas," Marion called after her with a bright smile. Farland Meadows could use a touch of joy.

Maggie's countenance didn't lighten at all. In fact, the girl seemed distressed. "'Taint much happy 'bout today, holiday or no. 'Taint much happy here 't'all," Maggie said. "Master's rather somber, he is." She disappeared into the darkened schoolroom.

Marion let out a long, deep breath. The housekeeper and butler had banished her to the nursery wing. Her employer, apparently, was ill humored, and the entire house shared in that defect. The happy, cheerful house she'd expected felt suddenly cold.

"Only because there's no fireplace," Marion told herself. Her stomach grumbled, reminding her of its empty state. She smiled, amused at her own body's antics. "And because I'm hungry."

The biscuit and preposterously weak tea she'd had in Newark the previous afternoon had long since proven insufficient nourishment. She eyed the toast and porridge Maggie had brought her. She hadn't eaten porridge since her childhood. *Appropriate*, she thought. If she must be relegated to the nursery wing, being fed on child's fare was exceptionally fitting.

After two bites, Marion decided she much preferred the watery tea. Perhaps Cook had been given the day off. She forced down the remainder and carried her empty bowl and crumb-strewn tray out of her room and across the dim schoolroom to the servants' door, setting it on a nearby table. She hummed a Christmas carol from her childhood, the tune doing wonders for her outlook.

Using the candle from her room, Marion walked the perimeter of the schoolroom and opened the many curtains. The earliest hints of sunrise penetrated the cloudy sky as a light dusting of snow settled on the ground below. How she loved freshly fallen snow! She watched for a moment as flakes drifted aimlessly about, a quiet peacefulness enveloping the landscape.

"Quit dawdling," Marion told herself after one last lingering look outside. She had work to do.

She spun around to survey her surroundings, and her jaw dropped. Toys and crumpled papers lay scattered in chaotic piles. Books were strewn about unnoticed and unheeded. Had no one bothered cleaning? Certainly the last governess hadn't left such a deplorable mess, hasty departure or not.

Her own room required very little attention, so Marion relegated it to another time. 'Twas always best to tackle the difficult things first. She set herself to cleaning, humming as she did. Child-sized fingerprints smudged the pages of the scattered books. Miss Caroline, it seemed, had at least looked at her books before discarding them. Nearly every wadded piece of parchment had been scribbled on, the lines thick and almost dashed as if she'd used a charcoal pencil in dire need of sharpening. The toys sat haphazardly about the room, but not a single one was broken. The child did not seem naturally destructive but simply insufficiently looked after.

"Your hair is pretty." The voice was no larger than a drop of rain and clearly belonged to a child still half asleep.

Marion turned toward the sound, uncertain of what she would find. The child who stood before her could well have been an angel. Her ruffled white nightdress nearly glowed in the morning sun spilling in through the windows. A mess of blonde curls framed her face in something of a halo, her enormous blue eyes wide in innocent anticipation. The girl couldn't possibly have been more than four or five years old. *Too young for a governess.* Marion pushed the thought from her head. This was, undoubtedly, Miss Caroline's younger sister.

"Hello," Marion greeted the child, her smile emerging naturally. She dropped carefully to her knees, pulling her dress free at the last moment. She could scarce afford to replace her gowns should she manage to wear knee holes in them. "What is your name?"

"Caroline." She scrunched her eyes in the bright sunlight.

Miss Caroline! Her charge was a tiny child, the appropriate age for a nurse, not a governess. There must be a mistake!

"Are you my new nurse?" Miss Caroline did not look entirely sure of the arrangement.

"No," Marion answered carefully. "I am . . ." *Well? What am I?* "I am to be your governess."

"What's a gubness?"

Don't ask me. But Marion smiled. "A governess teaches and tends to children."

"Sounds like a nurse."

"Except I will teach you to be grown-up."

The girl stood frozen, obviously scrutinizing this newest arrival into her small world.

"Do you know how to curtsy, Miss Caroline?" She kept a cheerful tone in her voice lest the child think she was scolding.

Miss Caroline offered an awkward dip then watched Marion uncertainly for her evaluation.

Marion smiled more broadly, something she didn't think she could have prevented herself from doing. "Very well done. You are quite a young lady, I see."

A smile tugged at the girl's mouth. That was the right approach, then. Most little girls wished to be thought of as grown-up.

"How old are you?" Marion sat back on her feet, trying to seem unconcerned.

She held up four dimpled fingers. *Four! Furuncle.* Four was definitely too young for a governess. What was going on?

"Oh my!" Marion allowed her eyes to widen. This mess wasn't the child's fault. "How old do you think I am?"

Miss Caroline studied her for the better part of a minute, her eyes alternately narrowing and widening, her mouth pursing and twisting as she pondered the puzzle. Adorable!

"Ten?" Miss Caroline guessed.

"That is very nearly correct," Marion replied. "I will be twenty years old in only a few weeks."

The girl's mouth formed a perfect *O* as her eyes grew wide once again. Marion nodded her agreement. Twenty must seem positively antiquated to a child of four.

"Are you leaving too?" Obvious uncertainty colored Miss Caroline's tone.

"Leaving?"

"Everyone leaves," Miss Caroline said quite matter-of-factly.

Not I! For one thing, Marion had nowhere to go. For another, she had already begun to adore the fair-haired angel standing before her.

Marion used her best pondering face, going so far as to tap her lip with her finger. "I had planned to stay here for some time. Would that be acceptable, do you think? Or would it be better for me to leave?"

Miss Caroline shook her head so vehemently her curls bounced about.

"Then I should stay?"

"Forever and ever!" Miss Caroline declared before running across the room and throwing her arms around Marion's neck.

Pulling the girl onto her lap, Marion held the angelic child in her arms. It probably was not very governessy, but it felt right. How terribly lonely the girl must be to take to a stranger so quickly, so desperately.

"Did you know today is Christmas Day?" Marion asked her armful. The girl nodded. "What shall you do with your family today?"

"Oh, they are all gone."

Again, the unemotional explanation of an unusual situation. Perhaps Miss Caroline did not even realize that a household where "everyone leaves," as well as having her family gone on Christmas Day, was an unexpected situation.

"Where have they gone?" Marion wanted more information about this unusual household. If she knew more, she might discover the reason she'd been hired as governess to a child far too young for the schoolroom.

"Papa is in Stuckfolk," Miss Caroline said.

Fighting down a laugh, Marion corrected, "Suffolk."

"Mm-hmm. With Grammy and all the boys."

"Boys?" Mrs. Sanders hadn't mentioned any boys in the household. Perhaps she was to teach them. They ought to have tutors though. No. Mrs. Sanders's letter specifically said she was to be governess to Miss Caroline.

"Papa has lots of big boys," Miss Caroline said.

"Do they live here?" Perhaps she'd been hired under false pretenses.

"No-o-o." Miss Caroline pulled back enough to look Marion in the face. "They live lots of places." She began counting off on her dimpled fingers. "With the horses." *A groom?* "With the books." *Hmm.* "With all the blue." *What does that mean?* "At Painage and Beatin'. And Flip lives all over."

"Ah." Marion nodded her head as if the explanation was perfectly clear. "That sounds . . . exciting."

Miss Caroline smiled brightly.

"I've brought you a ribbon for your hair. A Christmas present." Marion was glad she'd chosen a blue ribbon during her wait for the mail in Southwell. The ribbon would nearly match the color of Miss Caroline's eyes.

"Will my hair ever be like yours?" Miss Caroline asked, her eyes plastered to Marion's ruler-straight fiery red hair with something akin to envy.

"Why would you wish for hair like mine?" Marion asked amusedly. "Especially when yours is so lovely."

"Harriet said it was fuzzy."

"Harriet?"

Miss Caroline shrugged. "She left. She said my hair was fuzzy every time she brushed it."

"Curly hair can be fuzzy when it's brushed." Marion remembered vividly a childhood friend plagued with the same problem. "One must *comb* curls."

The child pouted. "I do not have a comb."

"Perhaps your mother does."

"Mama is gone too," Miss Caroline said. "Papa said she won't come back."

Had Miss Caroline's mother passed on? Or were her parents estranged? She would not question Miss Caroline on such a potentially delicate subject.

"Well, *I* have a comb. It belonged to my papa. I think it will work well until we can ask your papa for one of your own."

"Oh, could we really?" Excitement lit her eyes.

Marion nodded.

One half hour later, Miss Caroline was dressed, her hair carefully combed, the cobalt-blue ribbon tied in an adorable bow over one ear. Over the course of the ministrations, Marion learned that Miss Caroline had experienced the departure of at least six nursemaids (*she* being the only governess so far), none of whom stayed long, by a child's reckoning, at least. Her father, though away at the moment, had been present enough to make a favorable impression on his daughter. Miss Caroline spoke highly of him and the time they spent together. Such a contrast to the less-than-flattering description Maggie had offered earlier.

"Papa is wonderful!" Miss Caroline explained as they crossed the schoolroom to the child-sized table. "He doesn't call me Miss. I like that."

Marion attempted to explain. "Your father need not call you Miss. The servants do so because they respect you."

"Couldn't they like me instead of 'specting me?"

Marion hated to disappoint her, but the girl needed to understand how these things worked. "I do not think that would be a good idea."

"Can you not call me Miss? I don't want you to. Please!"

Marion sensed an aching loneliness behind the protest. "Perhaps when no one else is present."

Caroline nodded eagerly. "What should I call you?"

That was a good question. If she were a nursemaid, which would be more fitting, she would probably be called Mary. As a governess, she would be Miss Wood. But Caroline was so young and so obviously lonely.

"Perhaps 'Mary' would do when there is no one else around. But Miss Wood otherwise."

"I like you, Mary." Caroline smiled so brightly, Marion had to smile back.

"And I like you, Caroline."

"You will stay, won't you?" Caroline looked quite intensely at Marion. "You won't run away?"

"Why would I run away?" Marion asked with a slight smile.

"All the others did." Caroline was perfectly serious.

As Caroline ate her breakfast, Marion pondered her words. *All the others ran away. Ran away.* Why would Caroline believe her other nurses, for surely that was who she kept referring to, had fled and not simply left? And what exactly would have driven them away?

Curious. Very curious.

CHAPTER FOUR

AFTER THREE DAYS ON THE road, Layton desperately wanted to be home. He'd opted to ride from Newark-on-Trent. A few hours on horseback was precisely what he needed after the confinement of the carriage.

As he approached Farland Meadows, the scent of pine hung heavy in the air, an aroma he would always associate with his childhood. It was strongest at that time of the year since everything else was stripped bare by the cold of winter.

Bridget had left him in the summer when the smell of flowers mingled with grasses and herbs, when one scent was impossible to distinguish from the rest. So many aromas were now associated with her. Pine was one of the few that did not immediately bring to mind that horrific summer. It made Farland Meadows bearable. Pines and Caroline.

As he turned onto the carriageway that led to his home, Layton heard a squeal, a childish, delighted squeal. His mouth turned up ever so slightly. *Caroline.* Layton pressed his mount to a fast trot. He'd missed her terribly. She was the sunshine in his dark existence.

As he emerged from the thicket of trees surrounding the carriageway, a second squeal met his ears, followed by the most wonderful sound he could imagine.

"Papa!"

In less than a moment, Layton dismounted and wrapped his gelding's reins around an obliging branch. Two long blonde braids beneath a knitted woolen cap bounced across the snow-covered lawn toward him. Smiling as only his little angel could make him, Layton held his arms out and scooped Caroline off her feet, her joyful giggles filling his ears.

"Papa, you're home!"

He laughed. "Of course I am, dearest. I told you I would be."

"I am better now, Papa." She smiled, her dimples deep and charming. "Not a single spot."

"Not a single spot." He mimicked her declaration with a chuckle and tapped her wee nose. "Grammy missed you and wished you could have come."

"And Flip?" Caroline's enormous blue eyes grew ever larger.

"And Flip," Layton acknowledged. "And Corbo and Chasin'. Stanby. Charming." Caroline's butchered versions of his brothers' names had always been endearing.

"Holy Harry?" She smiled wider.

"You know he doesn't like to be called that." Layton pulled her closer, loving the smell of childhood that always surrounded her.

"You and Flip call him that," Caroline reminded him.

Layton set Caroline on her feet once more. "We shouldn't, but Flip is a troublemaker."

Caroline giggled and slipped her tiny hand inside his. He readily admitted he was a doting father. He couldn't imagine being anything else.

"What have you done while I was gone?" he asked.

"We have had ever so much fun." Caroline's gaze wandered from him. She giggled and squealed then pulled her hand free of his. "Mary!" she called out as she laughed and ran back into the yard.

Layton stood empty-handed and confused. Caroline was usually so clingy when he returned from even a short absence. He'd been gone for nearly two weeks and back for less than five minutes, yet Caroline was already gone.

He watched her scamper away, braids flying behind her. A mere few seconds without her, and he was lonely again.

Caroline giggled, the very picture of childish enthusiasm as she paused to scoop snow into her two tiny mittens. Cheeks plump and pink, she ran again, snow slipping through her fingers.

"Press it together so it sticks," an unfamiliar voice instructed.

Layton couldn't tear his eyes from his daughter. Something had changed in Caroline. Some of her shyness, her reticence, had slipped away in the ten days he'd been away from Nottinghamshire. She'd pulled away from him without a backward glance. Caroline had never done that before.

He was sorely tempted to call his daughter back to him.

Magical, musical laughter rent the air, laughter as pure as a child's but not juvenile in the least.

"A direct hit," the same mysterious feminine voice declared, laughter bubbling at the ends of her words. "You have slain me!"

"Oh no, Mary!" Caroline cried. "It's only snow. Snow can't hurt you."

"Then you think I will live after all?"

Layton studied Caroline, her innocent features clouded by the pensive expression he too often saw on her face. Who was this stranger pressing thoughts of death on his child? Could she not see the girl was upset by it? Layton strode determinedly to where his daughter stood.

"It's only snow," Caroline repeated.

"And you have had enough snow for today." Layton's tone left no room for argument. He lifted Caroline into his arms once more, his contentment returning in an instant.

"It's only snow, Papa." Caroline looked intently into his eyes as if searching for confirmation. "Mary will be fine, won't she?"

"Mary"—He couldn't help the edge in his voice, for he heartily disapproved of this Mary—"will suffer no ill effects. From the snow." Yes, he meant that to be a warning.

"Oh, Papa! I am so glad!" Caroline threw her tiny arms around his neck and nuzzled his face. Layton smiled despite his perturbation with the still-unidentified Mary. "I never want Mary to go. Ever! She is ever so much fun. And she made my hair not fuzzy. She laughs and laughs. And we sing songs. And she tells me the most wonderful stories. And—"

"Good heavens, Caroline!" Layton chuckled in spite of himself. "You are a fountain of words since I've returned. Is this what spots do to four-year-old girls, or did you just miss me?"

"Oh, I did, Papa!" Caroline tightened her arms around him. Her head dropped almost wearily against him.

Layton breathed deeply of her, happily forgetting all around him. This was home.

"Miss Caroline should sleep well this afternoon." That same unfamiliar voice interrupted the moment.

Layton grasped Caroline a fraction tighter and turned his attention to the woman he'd not bothered to look at yet. Now, his daughter securely pressed to him, he took a good, long look. The woman stood confidently before him in a tattered black coat and poorly mended gloves, her fiery red hair flying in every direction while her bonnet—"serviceable" was the closest thing to a compliment it could be given—hung limply behind her.

"Who are you?" Layton rubbed Caroline's back to keep her warm.

"Mary Wood, sir." The woman curtsied. "I am the governess."

"We do not have a governess."

"I was hired only recently, sir. I replaced the nurse."

The nurse. Layton vaguely remembered the woman, a mousy thing who hid in corners and mumbled under her breath from beneath the nursery windows.

"Hilga or Hattie or something of that nature," he muttered.

"Harriet, Papa," Caroline mumbled, her face pressed into him. "She left."

Layton eyed his newest employee with more than his usual criticism. She'd set his back up, though he could not rightly say why.

"Yes, sir," the governess replied, though her tone was anything but meek and subservient. "I've been here but three days."

"Hmm." Why did she smile so much? She seemed far too cheerful to be a servant.

"Caroline is rather young for a governess," Layton said.

"And yet, here I am." Was that annoyance he saw flash momentarily through her eyes? So there were limits to her cheeriness.

"I'm not too young for a gubbyness, Papa." Caroline's voice clearly communicated her growing sleepiness. "She is teaching me to be a diggyfied young lady."

"*Diggyfied?* That was, I imagine, *Miss Wood's* exact phrase."

"Right-o, guv'nuh," Mary said, sounding precisely like a London street urchin. "The Li'l Mizz needs a right bit o diggyfyin' iffen ye're asken Mary Wood. Righ' she does, guv'nuh! An' a righ' hot bath, sez I. Jus' leave it tah ol' Mary Wood!"

She offered a military-style salute and spun on the spot before sauntering up to the house. Layton didn't know whether to throttle her saucy neck or laugh. Both proved strong temptations. And he *never* laughed.

"Mary is silly." Caroline giggled groggily as she snuggled closer to him.

"Yes, apparently she is." The corners of Layton's mouth twitched as he watched the obviously offended governess walk toward the house, chin held high, hair flying in complete disarray, turning at the last minute to the back and the servants' entrance. He was certain he would never forget the way she'd tapped her nose as she'd called him "guv'nuh" or the triumphant gleam in her eyes as she shot him a mocking salute.

He had every right to dismiss her for her impertinence. It would probably be the wise thing to do. A servant who had no qualms about mouthing off to her employer could set the most well-run household on its ear. And Farland

Meadows, regrettably, was far from well run. Yet he found himself strangely reluctant to dismiss this Mary.

"Should we go in and ask Cook for some hot chocolate?" Layton asked his daughter, walking toward the house.

"Mmm."

"Do you like Mary, Caroline?" He spoke as casually as he could manage, at a loss to understand why he hoped she didn't while also hoping she did.

"Oh yes." Caroline mumbled. "She likes when I talk, Papa."

"I am sure everyone likes to hear you talk," Layton replied. She so seldom did that it was a treat.

"Harriet said I was agmavating." Caroline shifted her head on his shoulder.

"Aggravating?" Layton asked, feeling himself tense. Had her last nurse really said such a thing? To *her*?

Caroline nodded. It was a *very* good thing for Harriet that she had left.

"But Mary says what I say is 'portant." Caroline yawned. "And she listens when I talk."

"She is kind to you?"

"Mary is wonderful."

"Then we should keep her?"

"Forever and ever." Caroline's head grew heavy on his shoulder as he walked up the front steps.

Layton had never been able to deny his daughter anything. So Miss Saucy would be keeping her position, it seemed. But only after she'd been reminded of her place, something he supposed *he* would have to do.

Why couldn't the household simply run itself and let him be?

CHAPTER FIVE

SHE WAS ABOUT TO BE let go. After that horrid display outside, Marion certainly couldn't blame Mr. Jonquil. She'd been insolent and saucy. Had she actually saluted the man? She knew she'd called him "guv'nuh" more than once.

"Oh bother," Marion muttered under her breath as she approached the door of the library, where Mr. Jonquil had requested she meet with him. Caroline was soundly asleep upstairs, the nursery straightened beyond what was strictly necessary. Marion had no valid excuse for postponing this meeting any longer.

Caroline had described her father as a giant. She hadn't been far off the mark. Of course, being nineteen instead of four significantly decreased the impact of his stature. Still, he was quite decidedly broad shouldered and must have stood six feet high or more. Compared to Marion's five feet two-odd inches, Mr. Jonquil was quite tall. Something in his air was overpowering, something that had little to do with his size. If he weren't so ridiculously handsome, he'd have been positively frightening.

Marion took a deep breath at the door. What was the worst thing that could happen? she asked herself. If he dismissed her, she could always beg. She certainly wasn't above such tactics. Perhaps an abject apology would help. On her knees? Marion considered the idea but found it so absurd she broke into a grin. What a picture she would make. She might be able to conjure tears if she worked at it . . . or pinched herself really hard. Then again, if he fired her, she'd probably cry without even trying.

She knocked.

"Come in," a deep masculine voice called from within.

For a moment, Marion contemplated walking in with her hand clutched dramatically to her heart, tears dripping sorrowfully down her cheeks. Maybe even falling onto the floor in front of her employer, sprawled in a heap of humanity. She had to bite back another smile as she stepped inside the library.

She should have anticipated the smell of leather and aged parchment, and yet it took her entirely by surprise. She felt her smile fade almost instantly. Would the smell of books always remind her of Papa?

"You wished to see me, sir." She managed a far more subservient tone than she ever had in the past. 'Twas amazing, the dampening effect thoughts of unemployment and death had on one's spirit.

Without so much as glancing up at her, Mr. Jonquil waved her inside from his seat at his imposing mahogany desk. She was really in deep this time. *Well done, Marion!* There was nothing for it; she would simply have to grovel.

Marion took a fortifying breath and moved across the room until she stood in front of the desk. No time like the present, she reminded herself. "Mr. Jonquil, sir?"

Her employer glanced up from a stack of papers, and for a fraction of a moment, Marion held out hope that he'd miraculously transformed into a hideously ugly elderly man. With several missing teeth. And enormous spots. And nose hair.

"Ah, furuncle," she muttered under her breath. He was still gorgeous. Could a man be considered *gorgeous?* she wondered. If one could, Mr. Jonquil was just that. His thick, wavy, golden hair curled at the nape of his neck where it had grown a little long. She'd thought his eyes a simple deep blue but saw at that distance that they were, in fact, blue flecked with chocolate and emerald. No hint of shoulder padding filled out his extremely well-fitting coat.

Yes. The man was gorgeous, and that was intimidating. Intimidating and entirely unfair.

The clearing of a masculine throat brought Marion to her senses. Oh heavens! She was staring! Staring at her employer! If the man didn't already find her impertinent, he'd soon be convinced she was completely attics-to-let. It was not the best way to make a positive impression.

Please let me stay, she could almost hear herself say. *Raving lunatics make wonderful governesses.* A smile tugged at her mouth as she imagined what Mr. Jonquil must think of her mental state.

"Perhaps we should postpone this interview to a more convenient time for you, Miss Wood," Mr. Jonquil suggested dryly. "You seem rather distracted at the moment."

That succeeded in wiping every hint of a smile from her face. "I am sorry, sir." She quickly pushed on before she lost her nerve. "I must apologize also for my behavior earlier. I know I was impertinent. Worse. I was . . . flippant and . . . disrespectful . . . and . . . um . . ."

"Saucy," Mr. Jonquil inserted.

Marion nodded. She *had* been saucy. Mr. Jonquil seemed to be expecting further confession. "And . . ." How many more synonyms could she conjure?

"Outspoken."

"*Well*-spoken," Marion countered. Immediately, she slapped her hands over her mouth. She felt her eyes fly wide open. Mr. Jonquil's only acknowledgment of her outburst was a raised eyebrow. Marion let her arms drop to her side and dug her toe into the carpet in frustration. "Double dungers," she muttered.

"Double dungers?" Mr. Jonquil repeated, that eyebrow arching higher yet. "Is that a common phrase amongst the *well-spoken*?"

A look of challenge showed in Mr. Jonquil's captivating eyes, along with something disturbingly condescending. She had the feeling he meant to put her in her place. For a person who had been on the verge of begging only moments earlier, Marion felt that old, familiar fight bubbling inside. She might be a servant without even a guinea to her name, but she had pride.

Marion mustered every ounce of dignity she possessed. "Oh, yes, sir. *Double dungers* is quite *au courant* among highly educated linguists."

That one golden brow dropped, the other joining it in a look of confusion—disapproval, almost. Apparently Mr. Jonquil felt she was being impertinent again.

She let out a whoosh of breath. This was going to be more difficult than she'd anticipated. "I'm sorry, sir." Her eyes dropped to the scuffed toes of her boots. He miraculously hadn't discharged her yet. She couldn't afford to be a failure.

"Now, Miss Wood." Mr. Jonquil's stern voice sent a wave of panic through Marion's body. The time to grovel had obviously come.

"Please, sir." She felt almost as though she was listening to someone else plead for their livelihood. She certainly never had before. Not once in her life had she been reduced to such a helpless and dependent state. "I will endeavor to hold my tongue and curb my impertinence. Please allow me a chance to prove I can. Please, sir."

"You believe I intend to dismiss you?"

"Yes, sir." She kept her gaze fixed on her feet.

"And you acknowledge I would be justified in doing so?"

"Absolutely, sir."

"So long as we understand one another."

Marion nodded her defeat. She had next to no money and absolutely nowhere to turn, and she'd just been discharged after a mere three days of employment.

"Only promise me you will not teach Caroline such dignified exclamations as *double dungers*," Mr. Jonquil said. "I would have a difficult time explaining that to my mother."

The hint of laughter she heard in his voice brought her gaze back to him. For the slightest of seconds, she thought she saw amusement in his eyes. The look disappeared so quickly she wondered if she hadn't imagined it in her distress.

"You aren't dismissing me, sir?" Her shock did not allow for a more subtle approach.

Mr. Jonquil seemed to ponder the question for a moment, his eyes narrowing. Then, with a look akin to resignation, he shook his head.

She still had her position, although her employer seemed to offer the respite begrudgingly. Once again, she had some degree of security, even if temporarily. Relief like she hadn't known in some time seeped through her. She felt her lips turn up as her heart lightened. "Oh, thank you, sir! Thank you!"

He shrugged, looking a little uncomfortable with her exuberance.

"I'll not disappoint you, sir. I promise!"

Mr. Jonquil rose from his seat behind the desk and walked to the fireplace, turning his back to the flames as if to warm himself. "We had little luck with the nursemaids before you," he said, his face unreadable. "I will expect you to be an improvement."

"Yes, sir." She kept herself to the simple answer, though she longed to ask a hundred questions. Why hadn't he dismissed her? What had the others done wrong? In what way did he expect her to be an improvement? When was the last time he'd had his hair trimmed? She knew for a fact she'd never ask the last question.

"You absolutely must learn your place, Miss Wood." His tone was firm yet not unkind, as though he were offering her sage advice, trying to help her out of a predicament.

But, she reminded herself, wasn't he doing just that? If she didn't learn her place, she'd find herself without a position.

"I will not tolerate chaos in the household," Mr. Jonquil added.

"No, sir." Marion felt remarkably impressed by the appropriate subservient tone with which she'd spoken.

Mr. Jonquil made no note of her improvement. "Mrs. Sanders informed me of the terms of your employment," he said. "Which brings us to another difficulty."

Marion had a sudden vision of the housekeeper with eyes pulled so tight by her severe hairstyle that they were hardly opened. She had to bite on her lip to keep from laughing out loud.

"What difficulty is that, sir?"

"My housekeeper insists she hired a nursemaid as I requested." He gave her a look that absolutely demanded a reply.

"I am not a nursemaid, sir." She had sunk but not *that* low.

"Obviously." Something like a chuckle shook his words.

"There has been a disagreement between Mrs. Sanders and me." She might as well confess. "She insists she thought she was hiring a nurse, but I was hired to be a governess."

Mr. Jonquil didn't reply. He just watched her, as if trying to decide whom to believe. "She told me you are to have Sunday mornings off in addition to one full day off each month and one week of holiday for the year."

Marion nodded, feeling more composed.

"And you are to receive twenty pounds per annum."

"Thirty, sir," Marion corrected before she even realized she'd spoken. That eyebrow arched.

For a moment, she wavered. He obviously didn't believe her. Mrs. Sanders *had* stated her wages at thirty pounds no matter what she insisted now. "I was promised thirty per," Marion insisted.

"You are accusing my housekeeper of cheating you as well as misstating your employment?"

"No, sir," Marion replied cautiously. "Perhaps she is simply mistaken."

Mr. Jonquil watched her for a moment. Marion tried to look more confident than she felt. Then he said, "Her word carries greater authority than yours does." Did he sound apologetic? A little, at least?

Marion shrugged. "Probably because she doesn't say things like *double dungers*."

A ghost of a smile crossed her employer's face, lightening it and making him look years younger. "That might have something to do with it."

Marion smiled back. If Mr. Jonquil knew half the homespun grumblings she'd invented over the years, she'd lose every ounce of credibility she had.

"Thirty pounds per is a generous wage for a nursemaid," Mr. Jonquil said, almost as if in warning. He probably didn't believe her. He had no reason to.

"But not for a governess."

"True."

"I *was* promised thirty."

"By whom?"

"Mrs. Sanders." Marion's wariness grew. "She said as much in the letter she sent offering me the position of *governess.*"

"Do you still have the letter?" He looked doubtful.

"I do, sir." Marion had realized within her first twenty-four hours at Farland Meadows that Mrs. Sanders was unnervingly inconsistent. She'd come to think of the housekeeper as the ogre guarding the castle tower in which Marion was being held prisoner. Picturing her with green skin and chin hair made Mrs. Sanders easier to endure.

"I would like to see the letter, if you please." Mr. Jonquil held out his hand—his large, masculine hand. Hers would be positively dwarfed by it were he to hold her hand. *Now* that *was a rather inappropriate thought to have about one's employer.*

Mr. Jonquil cleared his throat, and Marion realized, to her chagrin, that she was staring at his hand.

"I don't have the letter on my person," she finally said, feeling more and more like a damsel in distress.

A look of disapproval crossed his features. Obviously, he thought he'd caught her in a lie.

"It is in my room, sir." She held her chin up. *She* had been treated unfairly, denied salary, and made to look dishonest in front of her employer. *She* was the one locked in the castle dungeon. Mr. Jonquil was proving a very inadequate knight on a white charger.

"Retrieve it," he instructed. "I would like this misunderstanding cleared up."

Oh, how tempting it was to salute, to call him "guv'nuh" when he gave her that haughty look. She'd been in his company only twice in her life, and yet she'd already come to dislike when he got high in the instep.

Marion shook her head at herself. She, the governess, thought the master of the house arrogant because he had given her orders? She was one of his servants. *Time to come down from the tower and back to real life.*

"You don't care to show me the letter?" he interrupted her silent self-castigation.

Realizing she'd been standing on the spot, shaking her head, Marion nearly laughed at her own stupidity.

"I will just be a moment, sir." She kept her arms firmly at her side, lest they creep to her forehead and she find herself being saucy again. Being an ideal servant was harder than she'd imagined.

CHAPTER SIX

MARY WOOD WAS GOING TO be a handful.

Layton ran his fingers through his hair. He could understand Caroline's fondness for her new governess. Miss Wood was energetic and full of life and . . . strangely enjoyable. How hard it had been to keep a straight face as countless emotions had flickered through her eyes. It had obviously taken tremendous effort for her to keep to the "yes, sirs" and "no, sirs" to which she'd apparently decided to limit herself. That was taking her pledge to rein in her tongue a little far. But Layton had no plans to tell her so.

He pulled the bell tug, and a footman instantly appeared at the door. "Have Mrs. Sanders come here."

While the message was being delivered, Layton stoked the fire. He'd probably be better off letting Miss Wood go. Accusing the housekeeper of lying would certainly be grounds for dismissal. He had to find a way around that problem because he'd promised Caroline that her Mary could stay.

Layton sighed and leaned against the mantel. If only she weren't so attached to Miss Wood. The poor child had been through so many nurse-maids. If one had only stayed for more than a few weeks, she might not be clinging so desperately to her governess.

Governess! For a four-year-old! It just wasn't done. Someone so young should have a nursemaid. Then again, they hadn't had much luck with nurses. Layton couldn't for the life of him understand what drove them away so quickly. Caroline had always been a little shy, but that certainly couldn't account for six defections in the past year and six more in the three years before that.

"You wished to see me, sir?"

He recognized his housekeeper's voice.

"Yes, Mrs. Sanders." Layton walked back to his desk. "I would like to know what you think of our new Miss Wood?"

Mrs. Sanders looked understandably confused—they'd discussed Miss Wood only a half hour earlier, though not in detail. "She is . . . very cheerful." Mrs. Sanders didn't seem to approve of cheerful.

"I have noticed," Layton said. "Is she competent?"

"I couldn't really say." Mrs. Sanders's brows knit. "She is, perhaps, a little free with her speaking. Tends to ramble, she does. I believe she lets her mind wander a bit too often."

"She's young," Layton offered as a reason.

"Twenty next month, I believe."

She somehow seemed younger than that. Naiveté, maybe. The seven years' difference between their ages felt more like decades.

Miss Wood returned, a little out of breath, her cheeks pink as though she'd run from the nursery wing, two stories above the library. Her eyes found Mrs. Sanders, and beneath the flush of exercise, she paled.

So she'd been fabricating. Why did that disappoint him?

Time to play the diplomat.

Layton held his hand out to Miss Wood. Her hand shook as she placed a piece of folded parchment in his hand. He was tempted not to open the blasted thing. Six nursemaids and now the governess. Why on earth couldn't he find someone who met even the basic requirements?

Mary had seemed so promising. Caroline adored her. She was educated. When she wasn't talking like a street urchin, she had the accent of the upper class. She'd already affected a positive change on Caroline—the girl had chattered that afternoon as though she hadn't a shy bone in her body. But lying about the terms of her employment was inarguable grounds for dismissal. With Mrs. Sanders as witness, Layton had no idea how to avoid discharging her in spite of his promise to Caroline.

Managing to hold back a sigh of disappointment, Layton slowly unfolded the letter.

Miss Mary Wood,

I am pleased to offer you the position at Farland Meadows in Nottinghamshire. The position includes Sunday mornings free as well as one day off per month and one week per year. I am prepared to offer you a salary of thirty pounds per annum.

Layton stopped. "Thirty pounds per annum." In his housekeeper's handwriting. He felt his jaw clench, even as his stomach unknotted. Miss Wood had been telling the truth. But how, he wondered, would Mrs. Sanders explain her insistence that the salary was twenty per?

He hazarded a glance at the governess. She wrung her hands in front of her, still pale and unwilling to meet anyone's gaze. It seemed she still expected to be found at fault, despite the evidence she'd produced.

And what servant wouldn't? He himself had pointed out that her position did not hold the weight the housekeeper could claim.

He read on.

> We are in immediate need of your services. If you reach
> Farland Meadows by Christmas Day, you will receive a full
> quarter's salary upon arrival.
>
> Yrs., etc.,
> Mrs. Sanders
> Housekeeper, Farland Meadows

"What day did you arrive at Farland Meadows, Miss Wood?" Layton kept his eyes on the letter in his hands.

"Christmas Eve, sir."

"Good for you," he replied, frantically thinking his way through the muddle around him. He didn't want dissension among the staff, so he needed to tread lightly. He would not, however, tolerate a servant being cheated. "Seven pounds, ten. Worth the effort, I am sure."

There was a heavy pause. Layton looked up at Miss Wood. She fidgeted, shifting on the spot as if reluctant to reply. Her eyes darted to Mrs. Sanders, and an unpleasant suspicion began sneaking through Layton's mind.

He turned his eyes to Mrs. Sanders, who, though she maintained her unruffled exterior, seemed a touch uneasy.

"Miss Wood praised your generosity, Mrs. Sanders," he finally said. "Bonus pay and thirty pounds per annum." He held the letter up so the housekeeper would know she couldn't deny it. "It would seem I have a most capable housekeeper. Considering the rate at which we went through nursemaids, I applaud your efforts."

"Thank you, sir," Mrs. Sanders replied, looking all boosted confidence. Something about that rubbed Layton wrong.

"And intuitive to hire a governess this time," Layton added. He watched indecision flit across Mrs. Sanders's face. He hadn't failed to notice the vagueness of her offer of employment in Miss Wood's letter. "Perhaps that will make the difference we have been looking for."

"Yes, sir." Mrs. Sanders apparently decided to take credit for a decision Miss Wood claimed she had denied previously.

"I have kept you overlong, Mrs. Sanders," Layton said.

She nodded and left, her dignity intact, though Layton's opinion of her had lowered. He sincerely hoped she'd simply remembered wrong during their earlier conversation and that Miss Wood had misunderstood Mrs. Sanders's explanation. But then, there was the matter of the bonus offered. He hadn't yet determined how to reconcile that.

"Thank you, sir," Miss Wood said, her voice uncharacteristically subdued. "I wasn't sure to whom I should apply to acquire my wages. Mrs. Sanders is the one withholding them, and the butler is—"

"Her husband." Layton understood the dilemma immediately. Blast, his head was starting to hurt. He'd not been back home more than a couple of hours and already found himself faced with a household crisis. Philip had never indicated such difficulties at Lampton Park, not that they discussed much anymore.

"Now I am particularly embarrassed over my behavior earlier," Miss Wood said.

He looked up to find her smiling amusedly.

"I must be a complete nodcock to have been so disrespectful to the one person in this house who stood between me and a fortune." She sounded on the verge of laughter.

"Seven pounds, ten." Layton nodded. That was a significant amount for a servant.

"At the moment, that is a fortune," Miss Wood said. "Thank you again, sir."

He nodded his reply.

She watched him closely for a moment, an evaluation he found deucedly uncomfortable. She seemed to grow more amused. "I think Miss Caroline was correct."

"Correct?" he asked a little warily.

"She told me you were only scary because you're a giant," Miss Wood said.

"*A giant?*" he repeated after Miss Wood had left. Is that how Caroline saw him? Not only a giant but something frightening?

He dropped his head into his hands and sighed.

CHAPTER SEVEN

"I FOUND ONE, MARY! I found one!"

Layton stopped at the sound of Caroline's voice.

"Let me get it, dear." Miss Wood's voice joined his daughter's.

Layton stepped toward them. He found Caroline kneeling on a wool blanket on the banks of the Trent along the east end of the Meadows. Layton made a habit of walking along the river—had come there nearly every day since Bridget had left him. He'd never once come across Caroline during his walks, nor anyone else, for that matter.

Caroline sat watching Miss Wood, who was kneeling on the riverbank, scooping at the river with a long twig and laughing as she did so. She always seemed to be laughing.

"Ooh! Ooh!" Caroline bounced up and down, clapping her mittened hands. "You nearly have it, Mary. Just a little farther!"

"A little farther, and I shall fall feet over face into the water, and that, I assure you, would not please anyone. Least of all myself!" Despite her declaration, Miss Wood's tone remained lighthearted. "Perhaps if we wish hard enough, my arms will grow another few inches in the next ten seconds or so before the current pulls it entirely out of my reach."

"You cannot let it get away, Mary!" An uncomfortable amount of emotion entered Caroline's voice. Layton's heart wrenched to hear it. "It's the first leaf we've seen all morning!"

Layton watched Miss Wood turn her face back from the river to look at Caroline. A look of such affectionate concern lit the governess's eyes. Layton caught his breath. He realized with a great deal of regret that none of Caroline's nurses had shown even a fraction of such genuine attachment to her.

"Please don't let it get away!" Caroline cried, now jumping to her feet.

Miss Wood turned back to her task, leaning dangerously far over the water. Another inch and she'd tumble off the bank. The Trent, as Layton well knew, was unpleasantly frigid by the end of December. "I simply cannot reach," Miss Wood said.

"But I am wishing ever so hard. Are your arms longer yet?"

"Perhaps we should wish for something else."

"My arms are far longer than Miss Wood's." Layton's words surprised even himself.

"Papa!" Caroline cried out as Miss Wood let out a yelp of surprise and flailed her arms for a moment to keep her balance.

Layton stood close enough to their blanket to drop down beside them both. He quickly wrapped his arm around Miss Wood's waist and pulled her back from the water's edge. A tingle ran up his arm and through his entire body, and he found himself strangely reluctant to let her go.

Layton realized, to his chagrin, that she was laughing again. He snatched his arm away, though she didn't seem to notice or care. "Save the leaf, sir!" she implored as she gasped out another full-lunged laugh. She put her twig in his hand. "Right there, tangled in the roots of that tree."

He saw it—a sad, soggy leaf—spinning in the water caught between the exposed roots of the bank-bound oak. *This* was the prize she and Caroline were so desperately seeking?

"Please, Papa!"

Layton was no match for Caroline. He slipped his tan kid glove from his left hand, set his left palm against the cold, muddy bank for balance, and reached out with the ridiculous twig, all the while shaking his head at the picture he must be making, fishing a pathetic leaf from a river. But when he dropped it, dripping water, onto the blanket beside Caroline, she smiled brightly and threw her arms around his neck, exclaiming, "Thank you!" at least a half dozen times. Layton couldn't help smiling himself.

"You are the hero of the hour, sir." Miss Wood smiled at him, and he felt himself blush, something he hadn't done since his Cambridge days.

"Now what"—he tried to produce an unaffected tone and succeeded to a vast degree—"did you two ladies want with this arboreal offering?"

"Abormeal?" Caroline asked.

"Arboreal," Miss Wood corrected in the gentlest of tones. "It means something that comes from or is related in some way to a tree."

"Spoken like a governess," Layton said dryly.

"I certainly hope it wasn't spoken like a scullery maid." Just a hint of sauciness touched Miss Wood's voice.

"If you'd used *double dungers* or *guv'nuh*, you would have sounded precisely like a scullery maid." He then had the immense satisfaction of seeing Miss Wood blush every bit as much as he had only moments earlier. Redheads, it had been his experience, tended to turn blotchy when they blushed, clashing with their fiery hair. Miss Wood, however, turned a very even, rather adorable shade of pink.

"Do you think this is one of the Drops of Gold?" Caroline eyed the brown lump of leaf with an almost reverent look.

"Undoubtedly," Miss Wood replied, looking at it in much the same way.

"Drops of Gold?" Layton had no idea what they were talking about.

Miss Wood looked up at him, smiling. "A story I told Miss Caroline last night."

"It was a positively *true* story, Papa!" Caroline's eyes grew wide, and she began bouncing again. "A story about a tree whose leaves turn to gold at the end of every summer and then drop one by one into the river all winter long. And they float all the way down the river and into the sea unless someone finds one and keeps it for their very own."

"And this is a 'positively true story'?" Layton had his doubts.

"Yes it is, sir." Miss Wood lifted her chin defiantly in the air as if daring him to contradict her.

"A tree on which the leaves turn to gold?" Layton was not remotely taken in by the highly fantasized tale. "Where is this remarkable tree?"

"Derbyshire, sir. Upstream of here."

Layton shook his head. "I sincerely doubt any leaves from that far upstream would survive a trip to the North Sea." The leaf on the blanket before them had all but disintegrated already. "They likely would not even escape Derbyshire intact."

"Then this isn't a Drop of Gold?" Caroline sounded heartbroken.

"It most certainly is a Drop of Gold." Miss Wood seemed unconcerned about contradicting him.

"And I can keep it forever and ever?" Caroline looked past Layton to Miss Wood.

"If we dry it sufficiently, it should last for some time." Miss Wood rose to her feet.

Caroline cradled the leaf in her hands and stood as well. "Don't you think it's a Drop of Gold, Papa?" She turned those enormous blue eyes on him.

"Caroline," he said, reluctantly, "leaves do not turn to gold."

"They most certainly do." Miss Wood put an arm around Caroline's shoulders as if protecting her. Protecting Caroline from *him*? Ridiculous!

"I have seen the tree, and unless you can say the same, you have absolutely no right to—"

"I have no right?" Layton threw back. "*My* daughter, Miss Wood. And *my* home. And you are *my* servant. It is, in fact, *you* who have no right to contradict *me*."

Miss Wood's lips pressed into a tiny, tense line, her slender hand clasped in a white-knuckle fist at her side. She didn't say anything, just glared, hundreds of daggers in her look.

"Can we dry off my leaf now?" Caroline's tiny childish voice broke through the tension. Layton had forgotten about her entirely. Again. But Miss Wood, he noticed, hadn't removed her arm from Caroline's shoulders.

She looked down at the wide-eyed child and spoke sweetly. "Of course, dearest. And we will set it on the windowsill of the schoolroom."

"By your father's comb?" Caroline asked.

The governess nodded. A tiny smile tugged at Caroline's mouth. She rarely smiled, not remotely enough for Layton's peace of mind.

Miss Wood turned Caroline toward the house and marched her away, keeping her arm around her charge's shoulder. Neither seemed concerned about leaving him behind. Caroline hadn't even bidden him farewell.

"Miss Wood." He called after her in as stern a voice as he could produce. She turned back, a look of sheer defiance in her eyes.

"Ask one of the chambermaids to sit with Miss Caroline when you return," he instructed. "I would have a word with you in my library."

She bent the tiniest of curtsies in his direction before turning back and continuing to lead Caroline away.

"Papa sounds cross," Layton heard Caroline say in a voice so heavy with nervous emotion it tugged at his heart.

"He is probably just cold, dearest."

"He didn't like that I took the leaf. Maybe I should put it back."

"Your father will not begrudge you your leaf," Miss Wood said. Layton thought he saw her squeeze Caroline's shoulder. "A child must have some pleasures in life."

Those words echoed in his mind as Layton walked slowly to the house, bringing with him the blanket Miss Wood had left behind. He settled before the fire in his library. "A child must have some pleasures in life." Caroline had plenty, he told himself. The reassurance, however, sounded hollow.

In the few days since his return to Farland Meadows, he'd grown accustomed to the Caroline he'd found upon his arrival: the bright-eyed girl who smiled and giggled and talked. Caroline had blossomed.

Someone rapped lightly on the door of the library.

"Come in," Layton called out, not rising from his seat near the fire.

Miss Wood walked in, her eyes still snapping and a tenseness emanating from every inch of her. She, who had never seemed anything but cheerful, entered the room noticeably angry. At the sight, Layton grew angry himself. He'd known she would be trouble. She didn't know her place as a servant in his household.

"You wished to see me, sir." A certain edge to her voice belied the humble demeanor she obviously attempted to adopt.

"Did Caroline's leaf survive its journey to the house?" Layton watched her haughtily, giving her a chance to stew.

"I am pleased to say it did." His scrutiny did not appear to shake her in the least. "Drops of Gold are notoriously hardy."

"Tell me, Miss Wood"—Layton leaned back in his chair and formed his features into a look of mocking civility—"does my daughter truly believe that soggy mess is a gold leaf?"

"A Drop of Gold, sir," Miss Wood answered without a hint of unease in her voice or stature. "There is a significant difference."

"Perhaps you should explain this remarkable fable to me, Miss Wood. So I can decide what is to be done about it."

"Done about it?" Now she looked uneasy.

"I have no argument with Caroline developing her imagination," Layton said. "But to believe such a ridiculous tale as entirely as she obviously does concerns me greatly."

Miss Wood looked as though she were barely biting back some retort. Layton found himself strangely wishing she'd spill her thoughts. Why he enjoyed brangling with her, he couldn't say. He'd never argued with Bridget.

"Do you really wish to hear the story, sir?"

"If you please." Though he hadn't intended to, he sounded mocking.

Miss Wood certainly caught the tone. She looked immediately affronted. Her chin raised a fraction.

"Once upon a time"—She gave him an equally mocking smile, and Layton had to bite back a laugh—"a handsome young man met a kindhearted young lady. They fell quite exceptionally in love with one another, wishing never to be parted for the remainder of their days. They were married on the fairest of spring days, sweet flowers blooming in the air. The young man planted a tree for his new bride: an extraordinary tree, whose broad leaves would turn gold as summer turned to autumn. The tree grew larger and taller, its branches spreading over the banks of a wide river."

Miss Wood spoke as though the words were committed to memory, not extemporized. Her tone had changed as well, growing soft and nostalgic.

"The loving couple was blessed in time with a strapping son and a loving daughter. They spent their summers—the small family—beneath the shading branches of the growing tree, listening to the river. As each summer ebbed away, they watched the leaves slowly turn to gold. One by one these Drops of Gold fell from their branches, swaying in the chilled air as they drifted to the waters below. Away the current would carry them, past fields and flowers, houses and fences. Some would continue their journey down the river until dropping into the North Sea. Still others were collected by people downstream of the tree. All who found one of these Drops of Gold were blessed with joy in life and reason to be hopeful, just like the handsome young man and his kindhearted bride."

Miss Wood finished her story and stood silently, looking out the window of the library, out across the back fields toward the River Trent. Layton found himself entirely unable to speak or reply. Though the story was a happy one, he felt himself unaccountably saddened by Miss Wood's telling of it.

"Surely you can have no objections to such a tale," Miss Wood eventually said. "I can see nothing harmful in it." But she looked quite thoroughly unhappy.

"Who told you the story?"

"My mother," she answered quietly.

"You said you'd seen the tree?"

Miss Wood nodded, still looking out the window.

"Did your mother ever tell you what happened to the loving family? I imagine they lived happily ever after; that always seems to be the case in fairy tales."

"As opposed to real life?" Miss Wood looked at him once more.

"Happy endings are not terribly realistic."

"Is that what you wish me to teach Miss Caroline, sir?" Miss Wood asked. "You wish me to tell her not to expect joy in her life or happy endings. If you wish to ply your daughter with such potent poison, you will need to find another governess. I will not do it."

Their eyes met. For a moment, he held her gaze, daring her to convince him life was all sunshine and flowers. But the fight in him died. He felt too weary to argue further. "I do not want her to be disappointed when life doesn't turn out the way she expects it to."

"If she is taught to expect only sadness and drudgery, she certainly will not be disappointed," Miss Wood said. "Those who look for sadness inevitably find it."

"Even those who expect happiness find the opposite, Miss Wood." He certainly knew that.

"But they find happiness as well," Miss Wood said. "Those moments of joy make the times of sadness and disappointment bearable."

"I believe you are attempting to tell me I ought to encourage Caroline to embrace these honeyed stories you tell her." Layton tried to sound like the puffed-up master of the manor but managed to sound only wistful.

"I am attempting to tell you that you ought to allow her some hope."

"How many of these stories do you have, Miss Wood?"

"An endless supply." A hint of a smile returned to her face, and Layton found himself smiling back. When was the last time a smile had come so easily to his face? Or anyone else's in the house, for that matter?

Unaccountably, he relented. "Try to avoid any that involve the heroine leaping from trees or into rivers or anything of that sort." Layton looked back at the fire to conceal the growing grin on his face. He had no idea why he was smiling and didn't care to try to explain it. "She might be inclined to give such adventures a try."

"Of course, sir."

Layton heard the sound of her footsteps retreating to the door. Some inexplicable impulse led him to stop her. "Miss Wood?"

"Yes, sir?"

"You didn't tell me what happened to the family? In the story?"

She sighed. "That, sir, is another tale entirely."

Miss Wood turned and walked through the door. Layton watched her go, wondering about her story, about the family. It seemed more than a simple bedtime fairy tale. He wanted, almost *needed*, to know how it ended.

CHAPTER EIGHT

"Papa does not go to church, Mary," Caroline had whispered as Marion tucked the carriage blanket around her swinging legs that morning.

"Ever?" Marion had asked, doing her best to mask her surprise. Mr. Throckmorten, the vicar, was not the sort to inspire heavenly devotion in his parishioners, being gratingly top-lofty and a great deal too severe in his sermons. Just that morning he'd called a list of individuals, by name, to detailed repentance. As near as Marion had been able to tell, the majority of those in the area attended services despite him. Or, perhaps they attended to appease the man and reduce their chances of having their misdeeds, small or great, delineated for their neighbors.

"He told Flip that God doesn't like hypnowits." She'd spoken with an extremely decisive nod of her head, a gesture she'd obviously copied from some unsuspecting adult. Marion had nearly laughed out loud.

"Who is Flip, Caroline?"

"One of Papa's boys."

"He has others, I believe you said. But what is their connection to him? Are they friends of his? Or neighbors?"

"They're his brovers."

Brothers! Marion chuckled to herself, remembering the conversation. She'd been trying to identify the boys Mr. Jonquil was supposed to have tucked away in such strange places: with the horses, the blue, the books, all over, and she was certain Caroline had said something about pain and beatings.

She had the morning off, it being Sunday. She sat on the riverbank, watching the water flow and looking for leaves. There wouldn't be many leaves left on that magnificent oak so far upstream in Derbyshire. She wasn't at all sure any of those leaves would reach this far downstream, but she always looked every time she was at the river's edge.

She sighed. "Oh, Mama." Marion missed her mother even more than usual. Mama would have known what to do for Caroline. The poor girl was far too pensive for her four years and, bless her little heart, seemed to expect abandonment at any moment.

Marion closed her eyes and clasped her hands on her lap. She sent a plea heavenward for strength and wisdom beyond what she knew she possessed. She'd seldom felt the absence of her mother more acutely than she had in the short time she'd been at Farland Meadows.

"Was there not sufficient time for prayer at church this morning?"

She knew that deep, rumbling voice in an instant: Mr. Jonquil.

Marion looked up at him and smiled. "It has been my experience that there is seldom enough time for all the petty concerns with which I am constantly bombarding heaven."

Mr. Jonquil looked away from her, out over the river. "What petty concerns have brought you to your knees recently, Miss Wood?"

"Only the other day I prayed rather fervently for a miraculous change in hair color."

That brought Mr. Jonquil's gaze back to her, and he seemed surprised and almost amused. "Hair color?"

"I was told in not so many words that I would do better with a headful of something more subdued," Marion said through her grin. "But, obviously, the Almighty disagreed."

"He didn't grant your petition, then?"

"Hardly." Marion tugged at a loose lock of hair near her right temple. "Still as bright and obnoxious as ever."

"No. It's handsome. The color suits you." Mr. Jonquil turned back toward the river. It was an offhand comment, but Marion felt certain he'd meant it, and she felt herself blush. Thank heaven he wasn't looking at her.

"What have *you* petitioned the heavens for lately, sir?" Marion asked in an attempt to turn the subject away from herself.

Mr. Jonquil picked a stray branch off the ground. "I choose not to waste the Almighty's time, Miss Wood."

"No prayer is ever wasted, sir."

"Give me one reason why God would want to hear from me." A world of bitterness, pain, and disillusionment filled those few words.

Marion realized with shock that he meant it. Mr. Jonquil was convinced his prayers would not only be unheard but also resented.

He told Flip that God doesn't like hypnowits. Marion thought over Caroline's revelation.

"Forgive me," Mr. Jonquil said after a moment of silence between them, though he didn't sound very repentant. He swung the branch in his hand at the trunk of a nearby tree. "That was very un-Anglican of me."

"It was, however, extremely *human* of you, Mr. Jonquil. In my experience, being human is a very good thing."

"Except it can be deucedly unpleasant at times." The twig broke against the tree trunk. "And now I need to apologize again." Mr. Jonquil shrugged. "I really ought to watch my language."

"That is precisely why I use words like *double dungers*. It can mean whatever I wish, and there is no need for apologies."

She thought she heard a quiet chuckle and smiled at the sound. There was something so oppressively unhappy about Mr. Jonquil, an aura of tension that, at times, made him seem ready to explode. It didn't fit him, like he wasn't meant to be burdened so heavily.

"Do you truly believe God does not want to hear from you, sir?" she asked cautiously.

"Tell me this, Miss Wood." Mr. Jonquil turned back toward her, a look of patient indulgence on his face as though he were explaining something quite simple to someone even simpler. "Think of the person who has done you the greatest disservice in your life—lied to you or cheated you out of something that was rightfully yours or something of that nature. How eager are you, Miss Wood, to hear from that person? I daresay you would rather resent the clod's presumption."

Hypnowit. "Hypocrite," Marion whispered, suddenly understanding what Caroline had been trying to say.

"Precisely." Mr. Jonquil turned back to the river, thwacking the branch in his hand repeatedly against the top of his boot. "No one likes a hypocrite."

That, then, was the reason Mr. Jonquil never attended church and chose not to pray. It wasn't a matter of not believing or being unreligious; for if that had been the case, he wouldn't be so obviously bothered by his estrangement from the Almighty, and it did seem to bother him quite a bit. Mr. Jonquil believed in God and prayer but felt he'd disqualified himself from any association with the heavens.

Intellectually, Marion understood, but she'd been taught a very different view of her Maker.

"I told you a few days ago that I have an endless supply of stories," Marion said cautiously.

Mr. Jonquil turned toward her, wariness written all over his face. "Why do I get the feeling you are about to regale me with one?"

Marion smiled as guiltily as she could, hoping the light tone would put him more at ease.

"Do you plan to preach to me, Miss Wood?"

"No preaching, sir."

"Very well." He sighed. "Get it over with."

"It is a good story, sir!" Marion protested with a laugh.

Mr. Jonquil tossed the broken end of his twig aside and dropped onto the blanket across from her. Somehow, he still looked dignified sitting on the ground. Marion was certain she looked as ramshackle as ever. He nodded to her as if giving her permission to begin.

"Once upon a time," she said as though he were a toddler in the nursery. She smiled and lifted her eyebrow.

Then he laughed, spontaneous and genuine. "I suppose I deserved that."

Marion grinned back. "Once upon a time there was a handsome young man and a kindhearted young woman—"

"Same two as before?"

Marion nodded. "—who fell in love and married and in time were blessed with a strapping son and a loving daughter."

"Ah, yes. I remember the strapping, loving children."

"I will never finish if you keep interrupting."

"It is one of my faults, you know, Miss Wood." The corner of his mouth twitched upward. "Flip was forever berating me for interrupting Nurse's fairy tales. 'Layton, you're ruining the story.' Some habits are difficult to break, apparently."

"Apparently."

"So the stalwart children," Mr. Jonquil hinted.

Oh, how she liked this side of her employer so much more than his grumpy side. Or his high-in-the-instep side. Or his glaring, silent side. Heavens, the man had a lot of sides!

"Yes, the children." Marion forced her thoughts back to the task at hand, though she wasn't entirely sure what had inspired her sudden fit of storytelling. "When the strapping son was still quite young, he learned, with the aid of a young boy in the neighborhood, the art of the slingshot. For weeks, no outbuildings or fences were safe against the demonstration of his newfound skills."

Mr. Jonquil smiled as if remembering a few childhood escapades of his own.

"His father—"

"The handsome young man?"

Marion gave him her best governess face and used her most governess-like voice. "Layton, you're ruining the story."

He chuckled. She loved the sound. He ought to laugh more often.

"His father sat him down one day to explain the responsibilities tied to his new-found skills. The father insisted that shooting rocks at fences and ancient barns was one thing, but shooting those same rocks at people or animals or buildings of significance, such as their home or the vicarage, was another matter entirely. Were he to hear of his son using such things for target practice, he would be sorely displeased. The son—"

"The *strapping* son." Mr. Jonquil looked instantly repentant. "Sorry. Please continue."

"The strapping son faithfully obeyed his father's edict and limited himself to targets specifically approved by his sire. But one day, while wielding his faithful slingshot in hopes of knocking a block of wood off the top of a stone wall, the son misfired. His aim failed, and the rock soared far from where he'd intended it to fly.

"It happened that whenever the boy went on romps around his home, he was followed by a spaniel puppy he'd named Tag Along. While he often pretended to find the dog's presence a nuisance, he was, in fact, quite fond of it. Tag Along was, of course, with the son at the time his shot went wide of its target, although the puppy was not precisely at the boy's side. He was sitting along the wall, watching the boy in canine adoration."

"Miss Wood," Mr. Jonquil protested, "I don't like where this story is going."

But she didn't stop. "The shot, as I am sure you have concluded, struck the dog between the eyes. The son ran to his companion, who had grown unaccountably still of a sudden. He attempted to rouse the animal, but it didn't respond to any of the boy's pleas. The dog was—"

"Dead," Mr. Jonquil mumbled. "Miss Wood, I do not want you telling this story to Caroline."

"I am not telling it to Miss Caroline, sir. I am telling it to *you*."

"*I* don't particularly want to hear it either."

"Please let me finish."

He nodded his consent but turned his eyes away.

"At about the time the young son realized his beloved pet would not awaken, he heard his father's voice calling to him. For a moment, he froze, uncertain of what he ought to do. You see, he was terribly overset at the events that had transpired, grieved at the loss of his pet, overwrought with feelings of guilt and confusion. But he was also afraid. His father had told him not to shoot his rocks at animals. He had made his disapproval of such actions quite plain.

"So in fear of his father's condemnation, the son ran away. He ran from his father's continued calls and hid in the woods not far from the tree whose leaves dropped into the river every year. The son did not reply when his father called his name. He did not reveal his hiding spot, so entirely convinced was he that his father would want nothing to do with him if he knew what he'd done. On some level, the boy believed his father already knew and despised him for it."

Mr. Jonquil had grown very quiet and still, but Marion was certain he yet listened. She felt compelled to continue.

"The boy's sobs eventually led his father to him. 'I've killed him, Papa,' the boy said through his tears. 'I've killed him.' But his father didn't rail against him or punish or berate him. He pulled the boy into his arms and held him, letting the lad's tears fall. Together they buried the dog. Together they spoke at length of regrets and mistakes and forgiveness.

"'No matter what you may do, my son,' the father said, 'I will love you always.' And he did. He loved him through all of his mistakes and regrets."

Mr. Jonquil didn't reply or look at her. Only the sound of wind and flowing water broke the silence between them. She wondered if she'd gone too far, if she'd said more than she ought. Marion hoped she'd helped, at least given him something to think about.

"Please do not share that particular story with Caroline," Mr. Jonquil eventually repeated quietly. "I fear she would be quite shaken by it."

"I have plenty of others, sir."

"And where, Miss Wood, do you get your stories?" Mr. Jonquil slowly rose to his feet.

"My mother told me that one."

"And the other also, I seem to remember."

Marion nodded.

"Did she know any happy stories?" He stepped a little farther away from her.

"The Drops of Gold story was happy, sir."

He didn't reply. "Good day, Miss Wood," he said and slowly walked away.

CHAPTER NINE

THEY'D REACHED TWELFTH NIGHT, CAROLINE'S favorite holiday of the year, preferred even to Christmas. She'd mentioned last January's festivities at least a dozen times over the year.

Layton, however, didn't particularly feel like making merry. As much as he'd tried to dismiss it, Miss Wood's story haunted him. *I've killed him, Papa.* Layton could almost hear the little boy's voice, feel the pain there. He knew what Miss Wood had been trying to do, to say. She was attempting to convince him through her little tale that the Almighty forgave mistakes. The boy with the slingshot hadn't intended to do what he'd done.

That was the real difference. Of course the boy's father had been forgiving and understanding. The boy's misdeed had been an accident. What Miss Wood didn't understand, what she'd missed in her story, was that Layton's guilt stemmed as much from what he'd done as from the fact that he'd committed his crime on purpose. And given the option, would do it again.

God, of course, knew that. What was the point in traipsing off to church on Sundays and kneeling in a pose of humble obedience when both he and the Almighty knew he was nothing of the sort? Or petitioning the heavens with his concerns, perhaps promising to be a dutiful Christian if only he were granted some request or another, when he'd given up any claim to being dutiful four years earlier?

No. God didn't like hypocrites.

"Oh, Papa!"

Caroline's cry of sheer glee startled Layton out of his contemplation. He turned away from the window he'd been blindly staring out of. Caroline stood in the doorway of the drawing room, her face framed by perfect golden curls, her tiny hand tightly clasping Miss Wood's. A smile spread across

Layton's face, and he held out his arms to his daughter. She ran directly to him, hugging him tightly around the neck.

"It's tonight, Papa! It's tonight!"

"Yes, my dear. I know." Layton chuckled, checking himself lest he squeeze her too tightly.

"Should I wait up for Miss Caroline, or would you prefer to put her to bed yourself?" Miss Wood asked from the doorway.

Layton looked away from Caroline toward her governess, who was looking on with a cheerful smile. He'd spent four years in a perpetual state of despondency, but in the two weeks since Miss Wood had arrived, her smile had succeeded in providing moments of uncharacteristic lightness.

"I can take Caroline to her room, Miss Wood. I am certain you will wish to join the celebration below stairs."

Her smile slipped almost imperceptibly, and she mutely nodded.

"Please can she stay, Papa?" Caroline asked—pleaded. She continued before he had a chance to reply. "Maggie said that Mary, er, Miss Wood, was a fishy chicken, and I don't think that is very nice and Mar—Miss Wood—won't want to eat cake with someone who says that."

"Fishy chicken?" Layton could not make heads or tails of Caroline's words. He noticed, however, that Miss Wood's smile had returned.

"'Neither fish nor fowl,' sir. Maggie, the chambermaid, commented on the fact that I do not particularly belong anywhere." A hint of embarrassment pinked her cheeks. "I am a servant, but I am afraid my welcome below stairs has been lukewarm at best."

"Have they treated you poorly?" Why the thought disconcerted him, Layton couldn't immediately say.

"No, sir." But she had hesitated. "A new person in the household." She shrugged. "I suppose I haven't found my place yet."

"Can't she stay here with us, Papa?" Caroline looked up at him this time, her bright blue eyes tugging at his heart.

"Servants do not take their meals with the family, Miss Caroline," Miss Wood told her gently, her blush deepening. Obviously, the statement had cost her some of her pride. Governesses generally came from the gentry, families who would have had servants of their own but had endured financial setbacks requiring even their female members to seek employment.

Caroline wiggled out of Layton's arms and crossed the room to where Miss Wood hovered one step inside the doorway. Caroline looked up at her governess, arms akimbo. When she spoke, she sounded decidedly petulant. "But you *aren't* my servant."

Miss Wood knelt in front of the frustrated four-year-old. "But I am your *father's* servant, dearest." Miss Wood ran her hand lightly along Caroline's curls.

"You're my *friend*." Caroline's voice broke on the last word, and she sniffed.

Layton instinctively moved to pull the child into his arms, but Miss Wood was there before him, holding and rocking Caroline. "A fishy bird, indeed," she said quietly, as if to herself.

He suddenly couldn't bear the thought of Miss Wood spending Twelfth Night alone in the nursery, unwelcome both above and below stairs.

"Caroline certainly has the right to invite her friends to celebrate with her," he said.

Miss Wood looked up at him, her smile turned to one of gratitude tinged with resignation. "Oh, sir, can you not see that would only make it worse?"

He furrowed his brow. Worse?

"I will never be accepted below stairs if the other servants are made to wait upon me." She gave Caroline another squeeze before rising. "My sitting to dinner with the family, even once, would only widen the gulf I am attempting to span, sir."

Layton could not argue with the wisdom of her observation. Then Caroline turned her teary-eyed face up toward him. He wished he could do something. Caroline had no friends, and she considered this redheaded, fiery-eyed governess to be one. How could he allow her to be disillusioned?

"Perhaps, Miss Wood," Layton said, extemporizing a proposition, "you would not object if Caroline and I were to bring our cake up to the nursery wing. If she is chosen queen for the night, she would certainly appreciate reigning over the part of the house where she spends her days."

"Oh, please, Mary! Please!" Caroline clasped Miss Wood's skirts in her tiny fingers.

Miss Wood smiled once more. "I think it an excellent suggestion."

An hour later, Layton and Caroline joined Miss Wood in the nursery wing. His knees didn't begin to fit under the miniature table in the schoolroom, and Miss Wood seemed to find his attempts to force his legs into cooperation particularly funny. She barely bit back repeated peals of laughter.

"You couldn't possibly have chosen the taller table, I suppose," Layton grumbled but without any real irritation as he shifted in his undersized chair.

He and Caroline had entered the schoolroom to find that Miss Wood had anticipated them. She'd spread a slightly yellowed tablecloth on the child-sized table and created a makeshift table decoration of pine boughs and slightly damp holly berries.

"Snow," she'd explained with a shrug.

Apparently, the indomitable Miss Wood had spent her dinner hour decorating. Her cheeks were still pink from the cold or perhaps embarrassment. Layton couldn't shake the feeling that she was uncomfortable. With him? And why was that frustrating?

"Miss Caroline, would you please help me with the cake?" Miss Wood spoke as if addressing another grown woman.

Caroline smiled quite proudly and nodded. Miss Wood sliced the small Twelfth Night cake into three pieces and laid each one on a nursery-sized plate.

"Give the first to your father, dearest."

Caroline walked carefully, slowly, around the table and laid the tiny plate in front of Layton. "Did I do good, Papa?" she whispered.

"'Twas perfect, love," Layton answered in a matching whisper and kissed her on the forehead. She giggled and returned to the cake, pulling one plate in front of her own chair before sitting down, the picture of feminine demureness. Miss Wood had, apparently, been instructing Caroline in her mealtime manners.

"Can we look for the coin now?" Caroline asked Miss Wood, her eagerness belying her patient demeanor.

"That would be up to your father, Miss Caroline," Miss Wood answered gently.

Miss Wood turned to look at Layton, expectation brightening her eyes. Something akin to mischief showed in the pair of chocolate-brown eyes. Brown. Why had he never noticed that before? It was an unusual combination: red hair and brown eyes. Yet it fit her somehow, surprisingly and unexpectedly.

"I think we'd better begin our search, Caroline. I'm anxious enough I just might eat the coin and not realize it."

"Oh, Papa!" Caroline giggled. "You are funny tonight!"

"Someone must have put funny pepper in the soup," Miss Wood said, smiling at Caroline.

"Funny pepper?" Layton and Caroline said in unison.

"Don't tell me you haven't heard of funny pepper." Miss Wood looked like she knew they hadn't and found it amusing.

"I have a feeling we are about to hear another story." Layton smiled in spite of himself.

"Not if you are in danger of breaking a tooth on the coin hidden in your slice of cake," Miss Wood answered.

"And how do you know the coin is in *my* slice?"

She shrugged. "I suppose I don't, really. You just seemed so convinced you were about to swallow a small fortune in hidden change."

"I want to hear about the funny pepper." Caroline jumped into the conversation.

"Don't you think we should eat our cake first?" Miss Wood asked.

Caroline appeared to think it over for a minute, obviously torn between the two choices. Finally, she nodded. Miss Wood opened her eyes wide as if overwhelmed by excitement. She held her fork ready and watched Caroline like she would a rival in a race, but with a laugh in her eyes. Caroline held her fork precisely the same way and looked at Miss Wood with the same mock rivalry.

Miss Wood nodded almost imperceptibly. In perfect synchrony, the two females tore into their cakes with their forks.

"I am going to find it, Caroline! I am going to find it!" Miss Wood called out as she dug with remarkable enthusiasm.

Caroline laughed so hard she could hardly search for the coin. Tears trickled from her crinkled eyes, and she gulped for breath. Miss Wood had reduced her slice of cake to a pathetic pile of crumbs and had begun picking apart Caroline's. Squeals and giggles echoed off the walls of the nursery, a sound Layton had never heard, not once in the four and a half years since Caroline's birth.

"It's—It's not—there," Caroline gasped out between giggles.

"Where could it have gone?" Miss Wood asked as though she were completely baffled.

"Papa has it, Mary!"

"He's hiding it from us, is he?"

Then they both turned to look at him, eyes running over with laughter. Layton felt his smile widen. He'd been certain when Miss Wood had arrived that she would be trouble. But watching Caroline, listening to her easy laughter, Layton was never more grateful for another person. Caroline had saved him four years earlier. And now Miss Wood was saving Caroline.

CHAPTER TEN

"That means he's king," Caroline said.

"Not if we get the coin before he does." Marion laughed, an idea popping into her head.

Amusement flashed in Caroline's eyes, and Marion was instantly glad she'd encouraged the girl in a little devilment. She needed to laugh and smile more. She needed to play more. If only Mr. Jonquil could shed a little of his composure so his daughter would feel lighthearted and playful with him.

Marion slipped an arm around Caroline's middle and whispered in her ear. "Tickle take, Caroline. I think it is just the thing."

Caroline giggled. "Like the daughter in your stories," she whispered with childlike glee.

"Precisely."

"What are you two plotting?" Mr. Jonquil asked warily. One look at his face, and Marion knew he was playing along. Marion's heart soared. She would make a family of these two if it was the last thing she did.

Caroline clasped her hand over her mouth and giggled. Marion wiggled her fingers at Caroline. In the next moment, Caroline launched herself at Mr. Jonquil, her tiny fingers wriggling against his waistcoat, attempting to tickle him. He laughed heartily, though Marion was certain Caroline's little fingers weren't nearly strong enough to have any affect through several layers of clothing. Caroline's giggles grew to full-lunged laughs.

Mr. Jonquil held his cake plate aloft and grabbed for Caroline, who managed to skirt away, all the while continuing her attempts to tickle him into submission. Marion swooped in and took the plate from her employer's hand. The game *would* last if she had anything to say about it! They needed this. *She* needed this.

"We have it, Caroline!" Marion called out, dancing around with the cake plate, hoping she wasn't making too much of a spectacle of herself.

"Huzzah!" Caroline shouted then turned back to her father and said with a great deal of pride, "Stanby taught me that word."

Mr. Jonquil's smile widened. Marion froze on the spot. His smile was magical, transforming his face, his entire countenance. She'd always thought her employer handsome, but when he smiled like that, the man was devastating.

Marion felt Caroline tug on her skirts and forced herself back into their little game. She dropped the plate onto the table and knelt in front of it. She and Caroline tore into the slice of cake with all the dignity of a pair of London street sweeps. Crumbs of cake flew in all directions. Caroline laughed so hard she could hardly catch her breath. Marion couldn't help laughing herself. Somewhere beyond the veil of flying cake, she thought she heard deep-voiced laughter joining in.

"I found it!" Caroline giggled, holding a chocolate-smeared gold coin high above her head.

Mr. Jonquil laughed and swung Caroline into the air. Marion grinned. That was how a father and daughter ought to look, ought to behave. She thought of her own father swinging her through the air when she was a mere wisp of a thing like Caroline.

Considering Caroline's initial reticence when Marion had arrived and the complete lack of playfulness on Mr. Jonquil's part, Marion felt she had witnessed the start of a miracle. For a split second, she pictured herself posing for a painting, hands clasped reverently, eyes cast heavenward, perhaps a halo glowing behind her head. The thought made her laugh even harder.

"That coin is mine, you little absconder," Mr. Jonquil said as he kissed Caroline loudly on the cheek.

"Upsmonder?" Caroline asked. "Is that like a *deuced bother*?"

Marion sputtered. Where in heaven's name had Caroline heard that? That phrase was not one uttered by gently bred young ladies, most especially in the company of others. "I did *not* teach her that!" She held her hands out in a show of innocence, praying Mr. Jonquil would believe her. She said *furuncle* and *double dungers* on occasion but nothing stronger.

"Where did you hear that, Caroline?" Mr. Jonquil asked.

Marion winced at his tone. It wasn't particularly harsh but was still such a stark contrast to the playful, loving tone he'd employed only moments before. Caroline, at times, had an overabundance of sensibility. The change would upset her.

Caroline's lip began to quiver then jutted out. *Furuncle!* She was going to cry. So much progress only to end like this.

"That's what Flip said!" Caroline wailed then buried her face in Mr. Jonquil's neckcloth.

"Your Uncle Flip sometimes says things he shouldn't," Mr. Jonquil said after smothering a quick grin. Marion had a feeling Mr. Jonquil was fighting the urge to laugh, and suddenly Marion wanted to meet Flip. Anyone who could make this usually long-faced man laugh spontaneously would be a good ally in her ongoing efforts to bring joy to Farland Meadows.

"Are you angry, Papa?" Caroline's muffled voice quivered.

"Of course not, poppet," Mr. Jonquil said gently. While Mr. Jonquil was not playful, he was always tender toward his daughter. "You certainly didn't know it wasn't something a young lady should say."

Marion moved closer, laying her hand on Caroline's back just above Mr. Jonquil's hand. Caroline needed to come out of this unscathed. "And perhaps you could tell your Uncle Flip to watch his language," she said.

"That is a conversation I would enjoy overhearing," Mr. Jonquil said under his breath to Marion.

For the first time in the short two weeks she'd been at Farland Meadows, Marion saw a side of Mr. Jonquil she'd never imagined. His eyes sparkled with mischief, like a joke was lurking in the background, a joke he was sharing with her. Marion felt her heart skip a beat but told herself the reaction stemmed only from her relief at seeing that Mr. Jonquil was happier, and therefore Caroline would be happier, and thus her job would be that much easier. She almost believed her reasoning.

"Now, dearest." Marion pulled her eyes from Mr. Jonquil and addressed Caroline. "You are our queen for the night. We await your command."

"I have been dethroned," Mr. Jonquil said with a sigh. "This must be how Charles I felt." A smile tugged at his lips.

"Except Charles was beheaded," Marion pointed out. "We only stole your cake."

"I want to hear about the pepper," Caroline said, still leaning against her father and sniffling.

"The pepper?" Mr. Jonquil asked.

"Funny pepper." Caroline wiped her nose with the back of her hand. "Mary's story."

How she adored the child! Candid moments like this one, when Caroline acted like a four-year-old instead of a tiny, reticent adult, tugged at Marion's heart. She wished Caroline to always be so unaffected.

"Sit with your papa," Marion said, reaching out to wipe a tear from Caroline's face. "Let him clean you up a bit, and I will tell you the story."

Mr. Jonquil hesitated for only a fraction of a moment, his eyes focused on Marion's face. She wondered if she'd done something wrong, offended him somehow. But then he sat, holding Caroline on his lap in a chair near the fireplace. He pulled a linen handkerchief from his pocket and dabbed at Caroline's eyes.

Marion watched the girl's transformation. Caroline's smile slowly, tentatively returned.

"Blow your nose, dear," Mr. Jonquil instructed, handing her the linen.

She did and made to give it back, like a miniature version of a gentleman giving his square of linen to a dewy-eyed debutante.

"No, dearest." Marion stopped her, unable to squelch the thought of the girl trying to give back an unlaundered handkerchief to some well-meaning gentleman in fourteen years or so. "You keep the linen but tell him you will have it laundered and will return it to him."

Caroline giggled. "Is that what very grown-up girls do?" she asked her papa.

"Oh, yes. And sometimes, if a gentleman is particularly enamored of a very grown-up girl to whom he has lent his handkerchief, he will wish her to keep it."

"Will some gentleman give me his handkerchief when I am grown-up?" Caroline looked intently into Mr. Jonquil's eyes.

"Probably, and then I will call him out."

Marion felt her breath catch in her throat. Her own father had said that so many times, threatening with a chuckle to call out any young man who showed any preference for his "darling girl."

Caroline grinned and threw her arms around Mr. Jonquil's neck. "Oh, Papa! You are *funny* tonight."

"Funny? I am perfectly serious. The only gentleman's handkerchiefs you will be permitted to accept will be mine."

Oh heavens, how Marion missed her father right then. She could vividly recall sitting on his lap as a child and laughing at his antics and telling him how very silly he was. Those were among her most cherished memories.

Mr. Jonquil looked up at her in that moment, and Marion grew flustered. She blinked a few times, hoping to disguise the fact that tears sat unshed on her lashes. She felt her lips tremble as she attempted to force them into a smile she felt certain looked more like a grimace. Not knowing what else to do, Marion turned slightly away, forcing herself to breathe deeply and rid her mind of these sudden blue-devils.

"Tell me the story, Mary," she heard Caroline say.

One more deep breath, and Marion turned back toward Caroline, who was snuggled against her father. "Once upon a time—" Her voice shook only once. Caroline did not seem to notice, but Mr. Jonquil was watching her with more interest than her story warranted.

"—a handsome young man fell in love with a kindhearted young lady," Caroline finished for her.

Marion smiled. All her stories *did* begin the same way. "They were married and were soon blessed with a—"

"—strapping son and a loving daughter," Mr. Jonquil filled in, his smile full of uncharacteristic mischief, which somehow fit him far more than his usual look of disconnection.

Marion's heart warmed. He might not have been a knight on a white charger, but he'd come to her rescue just the same, helping dispel her sudden sadness. He held his daughter so protectively, so lovingly, that Caroline had survived a scolding without retreating into herself once more.

Marion's smile remained as she continued her story. "While their children were always quite impressively well behaved at the table, one evening meal did not turn out to be a crowning example of their manners." She sat in the chair directly across from the one Mr. Jonquil shared with Caroline, who appeared to be leaning more heavily against him as she listened. "The daughter was still quite young. And the son, you see, found everything about that meal remarkably funny. He laughed and laughed, almost unable to take a breath. Soon the daughter was pealing with laughter as well but only because her brother was in such an unmerciful state of amusement. Their mother began to laugh next. Soon their father's chuckles erupted into full-bellied laughter.

"'I would like to know why I am laughing so uproariously,' the father informed his family between chortles.

"'I haven't the slightest idea,' their mother admitted.

"The daughter couldn't stop laughing long enough to admit her own ignorance. The family turned to the son, who had started the entire difficulty. He only shrugged and continued to laugh as tears ran down his cheeks.

"'I suppose there must be funny pepper in our meal tonight,' the mother said.

"From that evening on, whenever the family found themselves lost in a hopeless case of giggles and guffaws, they were quick to declare that someone had slipped funny pepper into their food."

"But why were they laughing?" Caroline asked without lifting her head from her father's chest. "What was funny?"

"I think, dearest, they were happy," Marion said. "Sometimes people laugh simply because they are so happy."

"Is that true, Papa?" Caroline pulled herself into an even smaller ball.

"It certainly is." Mr. Jonquil's arms wrapped around her, nearly hiding her from view. "My papa always said it was tickle bugs, that they would crawl all over one's skin and make one laugh from all of the tickling. In truth, the laughter came simply because one was happy."

"Did your papa laugh because he was happy?" Caroline's voice grew quieter.

"All the time, poppet."

"Why don't you, Papa?"

A look of discomfort crossed Mr. Jonquil's face at her question. Marion watched him and thought back on the many times that evening that he had laughed, and she wondered as well. Why didn't he ever laugh spontaneously, simply from joy in life? He was haunted, dragged down by something.

"I . . . er . . ." Mr. Jonquil couldn't seem to answer Caroline's innocent question.

"What are we to do next, my queen?" Marion jumped in, the raw pain she saw in Mr. Jonquil's eyes too much for her. "You get to choose, Caroline."

She didn't look up or uncurl herself but remained snuggled up to her father. "Can I go to bed, Papa?" Caroline spoke so quietly Marion could hardly hear her.

"Bed, Caroline?"

Marion felt as surprised as Mr. Jonquil sounded. Caroline had spoken of nothing but the Twelfth Night festivities for a week or more.

"But it is Twelfth Night, dearest," Mr. Jonquil said. "You are queen. You can instruct us to play snap-dragon or ninepins or jackstraws."

"But I am tired, Papa!"

It was a wail if Marion had ever heard one.

Mr. Jonquil looked up, obviously confused.

"No doubt she slept fitfully from anticipation," Marion guessed. "Perhaps we could allow her to be queen on a night when she is more rested."

Mr. Jonquil nodded. "Come on, dear." He stood with Caroline in his arms. "Off to bed."

CHAPTER ELEVEN

Layton had fought sleep as long as he possibly could, but there he was again, standing beside a bed with light blue curtains pulled closed all around. He reached out even though he didn't want to and felt the familiar dread building.

A loud rat-tat woke him with a start. Layton sat straight up in his bed, still in his shirt and pantaloons. The rat-tat repeated, and somewhere in the back of Layton's mind, he realized someone was knocking on the door of his bedchamber. He dropped his bare feet onto the chilly floor and examined himself momentarily in the looking glass above his shaving stand as he passed.

Layton shrugged at his missing cravat and coat, not to mention his lack of footwear. Anyone seeking his company in the middle of the night couldn't possibly expect him to be presentable.

He opened the door then froze from shock. Miss Wood stood in the doorway, a single candle in her hand, a thick blue dressing grown open over a serviceable white night rail, brilliant red hair tumbling around her shoulders. "Miss Wood," he managed to say.

"I am so sorry to wake you, sir." She looked and sounded distressed.

"What is it?" He felt a touch alarmed.

"Caroline." That one word made his heart drop into his stomach. "She's ill. Feverish and . . . she's asking for you."

They took the stairs two at a time. Not until later did Layton stop to wonder how she, being shorter than himself, had managed to keep up with him. Candles burned in Caroline's room, illuminating her flushed face, pale beneath the spots of color on her overheated cheeks. The moment they reached the bedside, Miss Wood began dabbing at Caroline's forehead, face, and neck with a damp cloth.

Layton took Caroline's hand. Even it felt warm. "Darling?" He brushed a damp curl from her face when Miss Wood stopped dabbing in order to rewet her cloth.

Caroline's eyes fluttered open. Layton's heart beat harder. Her eyes were dim from the fever, almost unseeing.

"Papa?" she asked tentatively, her voice gruff and quiet.

"I'm here, dearest." Layton squeezed her hand.

Caroline's eyes drifted closed again. Layton looked up at Miss Wood. She watched the tiny child, looking near tears.

"Should I have sent for the doctor, sir?" Miss Wood did not take her eyes off Caroline. "I wasn't sure."

Layton looked back at Caroline. She was definitely feverish but not restless. She seemed to be resting relatively well. "Children get fevers, Layton," Mater had said once when he'd fretted over a brief illness of Caroline's. "Rest and water. That's what she needs."

He leaned closer to his daughter. "Caroline?" he whispered. Her eyes opened perhaps a quarter of an inch. "Have some water, dear. It will help you feel better."

Miss Wood pressed a glass of water into Layton's hand in the very next moment, as if anticipating the request he had been about to make. He managed to get two mouthfuls of water past Caroline's lips before she drifted to sleep again.

Miss Wood pressed the cool, wet cloth to Caroline's forehead, and they both watched her sleep for several long minutes without a word between them. Layton had grown so accustomed to a chipper, chatty Miss Wood that her pensive silence unnerved him.

"If she does not seem better by morning, I will send for the doctor," Layton said, attempting to reassure her.

Miss Wood looked across the bed at him, and to Layton's surprise, tears coursed down her cheeks. "I didn't know what to do." She sobbed and buried her face in the damp cloth she held in her hands.

Layton kissed Caroline's hand, slipped it under her blanket, and walked around to where Miss Wood sat crying on the edge of his daughter's bed. Her concern for his daughter seemed to surpass even his own. He couldn't imagine a mother being more distraught over an illness afflicting her own child. Caroline's own mother hadn't shown so much concern for her.

"Miss Wood." He laid his hand softly on her shoulder. That same tingle he'd felt when he'd touched her down at the river coursed through him again. "Caroline will be fine, I assure you. The fever will most certainly pass."

"I could never forgive myself if anything were to happen to her." She pulled just far enough away from the cloth for her words to be distinguishable. "To be so useless again."

Her voice broke on the last word. Her anguish was almost palpable. Layton closed his eyes for a moment, trying to block it out, being too strongly reminded of another time when the house had been filled with heart-wrenching sobs. He'd been such a failure then. The memory froze him to his core.

Miss Wood continued to cry. He couldn't bear it. Layton shifted his hand from her shoulder to her chin, tilting her face so he could see her. She tried to smile through her tears. With a jolt, he realized he was well on his way to falling helplessly in love with her, this ball of energy and chaos that ran rampant through his house and encouraged his daughter to steal cake and laugh. His heart wrenched to see her crying.

"What did you mean?" he asked. "'Useless again'?"

And her smile slipped away completely. "My mother . . ." She took a deep, shuddering breath. "She had a f-f-fever . . ."

A surge of sympathy swept through him.

"I tried so hard to help her, but I didn't know what to do!"

Layton wasn't sure how it happened, but the next moment, he was holding Miss Wood in his arms, rubbing her back and whispering what he hoped were soothing words. He expected her to pull away—Bridget always had when he'd tried to comfort her; she'd rejected even her husband's support. But Miss Wood remained, leaning her head against him, her tears soaking through the fine linen of his shirt.

So he held her more tightly, listening to her breathing slowly steady as his heart began to thud more erratically. He couldn't bear to hear her cry any longer. No woman should cry that way.

"I was ten years old," she said from against his chest. "I was so frightened."

"You were only a child. What could you possibly have done?"

"Oh, I know, I know." She pulled back and out of his arms, dabbing at her eyes with the cuff of her dressing robe.

Layton instinctively reached for a handkerchief in the pocket of the jacket he was not wearing. She smiled. "Sorry." He smiled back. "I gave my last square of linen to a precocious young lady who hasn't yet returned it to me."

"The little scamp." Miss Wood managed the slightest laugh, wiping another tear with her cuff. She took a deep breath and seemed to compose herself. "I realize now, looking back, that I couldn't have done anything for my mother, but . . ." Her words trailed off.

He wanted to reach out, to wipe that last tear from her face. He didn't, of course. That would be decidedly improper and, more likely than not, unwanted on her part.

Caroline moaned in the bed beside them. Miss Wood moved as quickly as he, lightly touching the back of her hand to Caroline's forehead.

"Still warm, sir, but not worse."

"'Watchful waiting.' That's what Mater would say," Layton said.

"Mater?"

"My mother," Layton explained. "We've always called her that."

Miss Wood smiled up at him, but the smile looked a little forced. He pulled the chair he'd occupied a few minutes earlier around to her side of the bed, beside the one already situated there. "Please sit, Miss Wood."

After tucking the blankets more closely around Caroline's shoulders, she did.

"Will you allow me to tell you a story?" He could hardly believe himself.

"Do you know stories, sir?" Some of her characteristic playfulness returned to her voice.

"Oh, I have a few." He tried to match her tone and succeeded to a degree.

"I love stories." A look of encouragement entered her chocolate-brown eyes.

"Once upon a time," Layton said with a self-deprecating smile. "Isn't that how I'm supposed to begin?"

She smiled back. "It's your story. Tell it however you choose."

"It's not that kind of story, anyway."

"You mean it is a 'positively true' story?" Miss Wood asked with an ironic raise of her auburn eyebrows. "Even that kind can be told with a 'once upon a time' beginning, you know."

"Are all of yours true, then?" He had wondered about that. The family in her stories seemed quite real.

"I have always said they were" was all the explanation Miss Wood offered.

"Hmm." He watched her for a moment, half expecting her to elaborate further, but she didn't. "I was away at school when my father died." It was an abrupt beginning, he knew. Layton had never considered himself a storyteller. "I was eighteen, which is, I grant you, older than ten but still far too young to lose a parent."

Miss Wood offered an empathetic smile, her eyes never leaving his face. Gads, had he ever talked to anyone about those days after Father died? He didn't think he had.

"All the way home, I kept asking myself over and over, what could have been done, what might I have done differently to prevent his death." The weight of that misplaced guilt sat heavily on him again.

"But you weren't even there when your father died."

"And *you* were only ten years old when *your* mother died, but that didn't keep you from taking the responsibility of it on your shoulders," Layton pointed out.

She winced ever so slightly, his words obviously hitting home. "That is true enough."

"Seeing the whole family in blacks and Mater teary eyed made it that much worse," Layton continued. Miss Wood nodded, obviously remembering a similar experience after her mother's passing. "I spent weeks, months, to a lesser degree years, going over every encounter I'd had with my father before he died, wondering if I could have—should have—seen symptoms or some indication that he was ill."

"Did you find any?" Miss Wood asked quietly.

"Of course. The signs were there, and after the fact, the puzzle was not difficult to piece together."

"Just like looking back now, I can see how very ill my mother truly was." Miss Wood nodded as she spoke. "At the time, it was not so obvious."

Layton instinctively took her hand. "Perhaps the grave nature of her illness escaped you because you were little more than a child. You were so very young, Miss Wood."

She sighed, her eyes focused off in the distance. "I didn't think so at the time."

"How many of us do?" Layton could remember feeling quite grown-up and invincible at ten. "Tell me, Miss Wood, was your mother's care left entirely in your hands? Was there no one else to tend her?"

She nodded wearily. "Until that last night. My father left to fetch my brother home." A look of contemplation crossed her features. "In retrospect, that should have been another clue, I suppose. Father thought her condition serious enough to warrant bringing Robert home from Harrow."

Harrow? Layton wondered momentarily. A family of some means, then.

"He told me to care for Mother. That he'd be back soon."

"Did he return in time?" A familiar dread clung to his heart.

Miss Wood shook her head, the slightest tremble in her lips. Layton squeezed her hand, only then realizing he still held it. Somehow, her hand fit so snugly in his, it felt natural there. "And so you felt you'd let down your father and brother?" She didn't answer his rhetorical question. He hadn't expected her to. "Believe me, Miss Wood, I know how that feels, many times over."

She sat silently. Layton didn't release her hand but told himself he would if she seemed to want him to. He desperately hoped she didn't.

"How did your father die?" Miss Wood asked quietly.

"His heart," Layton answered simply. "It was quite sudden, I understand, though he'd been more tired and pale than usual the last time I'd seen him. He had even joked about his children giving him heart spasms."

"You couldn't have known."

"Precisely, Mary," he cut across her words. "I couldn't have known. I couldn't have helped or prevented what happened. No more than you could have with your mother."

Miss Wood's slender fingers closed tighter around his own, and he felt the clasp clear to his heart.

Caroline shifted again. Miss Wood moved to the bedside to dab a soothingly cool rag along the girl's forehead. Layton watched her, already missing the feel of her hand in his and wondering what it was about the woman that had captured his attention when nothing else, *no one* else, had in years.

He wasn't overly worried about Caroline. She was feverish, yes, but slept soundly with hardly a stir.

He did, however, feel uneasy about his own emotions. This was his child's governess. Everything, her position in his household, his code as a gentleman, the distinction of class, forbade any pursuit. Yet he yearned to do just that, to further their acquaintance, to try to discover what had so captured him. But he owed Caroline a life without further scandals and whispers among the gossipmongers.

Layton kept his eyes on Caroline's sleeping face as Miss Wood returned to the seat beside him. He reminded himself that Miss Wood was out of his bounds. Any connection between her and himself would be scandalous for her as well—far more than she probably realized.

CHAPTER TWELVE

CAROLINE ISSUED THE OCCASIONAL COUGH but little else. Three weeks had passed since her fever broke, and Doctor Habbersham assured Marion that Caroline would recover completely. Even so, January had been exhausting. Marion slept on a pallet on the floor in Caroline's room, afraid that if she left, the girl would take a turn for the worse and no one would be there to tend her.

She found that being close enough to hear the girl's every movement made sleeping difficult. By some miracle, Mrs. Sanders had granted her a half day, saying she looked too tired to be performing her duties properly what with all the coming events and that she should take her morning off to rest.

So Marion sat on a blanket on the banks of the Trent, a second blanket, heavy and woolen, pulled around her shoulders. Winter necessitated the extra layer.

Mr. Jonquil had received a letter from his brother "Flip," whom Marion had discovered was actually "Philip, Earl of Lampton." It seemed Lord Lampton was to be married on the seventeenth of March, and the entire Jonquil family, which she was given to understand was quite vast, was to descend upon the neighborhood shortly, Lampton Park being the estate directly northeast of Farland Meadows along the river Trent. Thus, "the coming events" had the household in something of a frenzy.

Caroline had been promised a new dress specifically for the occasion, something Marion was sure sped her recovery along. Marion had decided to buy herself a dress length of muslin in town in honor of the occasion. She did have an extra quarter's wages waiting to be squandered. Furthermore, for some unaccountable reason, she found herself wishing again and again since the night she and Mr. Jonquil had held vigil at Caroline's sickbed that she looked more presentable.

A week ago, she'd walked into Collingham on the pretense of obtaining a few medicinal herbs for Caroline, which she *had* obtained, and chosen a length of deep blue muslin. It was dark enough to not be entirely inappropriate for a governess, but it wasn't black or gray, which she thoroughly appreciated. She looked to be in a perpetual state of mourning in her current attire. She had no ill-founded expectations of being invited to the wedding, but she wanted to look nice just the same. She would be the most fabulously dressed female in the nursery, which was, she admitted, a rather pathetic accomplishment—but still an accomplishment.

"Do I dare ask what has you so obviously amused?"

Mr. Jonquil! Why did his sudden appearance make her heart flutter? She thought of Mr. Jonquil's story about his father's heart spasms but quickly squelched the panic that thought pricked.

"I was thinking of your brother's wedding," she said.

He looked at her with obvious curiosity. "Philip's wedding?" He leaned against a nearby tree, folding his arms casually across his chest. "Whatever for?"

"It will be very festive." For some unaccountable reason, she couldn't bring herself to admit to her delight in her new dress. "Caroline is already beside herself with anticipation."

Mr. Jonquil smiled ever so slightly. "Let us hope she doesn't work herself into another fever."

"Nothing of the kind," Marion answered with a little chuckle. "It has been the greatest tool in getting her to remain in bed at nap time and retire a little early at night. I simply tell her that if she is sick for the wedding, she'll miss it entirely."

"Devious, Miss Wood." Mr. Jonquil's smile grew, his eyes never straying from her.

Under his scrutiny, Marion felt rather plain and shabby. If only she had her new blue dress on.

"You must be happy for the earl." She hoped Mr. Jonquil didn't notice her flaming cheeks.

"I am." Mr. Jonquil answered perhaps a touch too quickly. He looked away from her, out over the river. "I've met Miss Kendrick. She and Philip are very well suited."

"Then they'll be happy?"

"Undoubtedly." The wistfulness in his tone worried her. Why did Mr. Jonquil never seem happy?

"May I ask you a rather prying question?" she blurted before she could stop herself.

He looked back in surprise. Then, smiling as if he found her outburst amusing, he said, "I suppose."

In for a penny, in for a pound, she told herself. "Caroline has mentioned quite a few people to me in the month or so that I have been here, and other than Flip, who turned out to be an earl, no less, I haven't been able to identify them. Would you mind . . . ?"

"Solving the mystery?" His smile grew to almost heart-shattering proportions. "I'll do my best."

He stepped away from the tree and casually sat on the blanket near her. The heart-fluttering began again, more pronounced than before.

"Who are these mysterious individuals?" Mr. Jonquil took his hat off, laying it on the blanket beside him.

Marion required only a moment to get hold of her voice again. "I'm fairly certain the names she gave me are not their actual names."

"Oh, I am *entirely* certain. Caroline is famous for rechristening people. Yours seems to be the only name she regularly says correctly."

Marion winced a little at that. "Mary," after all, was not her correct name. But that was hardly Caroline's doing. Marion had told the child her name was Mary. "Let me see if I can remember them all." Marion bought herself a moment to regain her composure. "There was a Chasin'. A Stanby. Corbo. Someone she apparently finds so bewitching that she calls him Charming. And a Holy Harry."

Mr. Jonquil's bark of laughter was so unexpected, Marion actually jumped a little before sitting back and enjoying the sound of it and the sight of him with eyes crinkled in amusement, a smile so wide it split his face, the look of devastation gone from his eyes for once.

She smiled herself to see Mr. Jonquil's transformation, and she fervently prayed that the racing in her heart, which had replaced the fluttering, wasn't a symptom of her pending demise. It would be a shame to expire just then, when she'd accomplished so much with Caroline and her father.

"Yes, Miss Wood." He reined in his laughter. "Those are my distinguished brothers. Jason. Stanley. Corbin. Charlie, who probably is a little too charming for his own good. And Harold."

Marion laughed to hear their actual names, which were decidedly close to what Caroline had christened them. "And which one, pray, lives with horses?" She felt her grin grow. "Caroline assures me one of them does."

"Corbin," he answered without missing a beat. "He runs a stud farm about fifteen miles north of here."

"And someone else lives with 'all the books.'" Marion remembered well the conversations she'd had with Caroline.

Mr. Jonquil sat quietly for a moment, a look of contemplation on his face. Then he chuckled again. She loved hearing him laugh. "The brother who lives with the books must be Jason—Chasin', according to Caroline. He is a barrister, and his office, which Caroline has visited, is absolutely crammed full of books."

She grinned, enjoying their conversation immensely. "Flip, she told me, lives all over."

Mr. Jonquil nodded. "As earl, he has more properties than he knows what to do with."

"Someone else lives with 'all the blue.' I defy you to make sense of that one."

"Blue?" That same look of concentration, forehead wrinkled, lips pressed together in a shadow of what must have once been a charismatic childhood pout.

Marion suddenly had a wholly uncharacteristic urge to kiss him. Was her mind going as well as her heart? She could feel herself blush, probably great splotches of bright red.

"Stanley," Mr. Jonquil suddenly said, sounding almost surprised. "She must mean Stanley."

"But why blue?" Thank heaven for the distraction. Perhaps Mr. Jonquil hadn't noticed her heightened color.

"Stanley is a captain with the Thirteenth Light Dragoons," Mr. Jonquil said, something like pride in his voice as he told her. "Their uniforms are—"

"Blue." Marion knew the dragoon uniform well. Her brother, Robert, had served with the Fifteenth.

"Caroline and I saw several young officers from Stanley's regiment in London earlier this year. Obviously, she remembered the uniforms."

Marion pulled her thoughts from her brother, knowing such musings would only lead to tears. She had no desire to cry on a sunny, crisp day when she might otherwise enjoy the company of a handsome gentleman who looked happy for the first time in weeks.

"One of your brothers," Marion pressed on, "I am told, is a disciplinarian of the worst sort, while yet another is, apparently, afflicted with some kind of painful condition. I have not yet determined if these two circumstances are related."

Now Mr. Jonquil looked thoroughly confused. "A disciplinarian?" He shook his head. "No. I can't say any of them could be described that way. The painful condition could very well be Stanley—he suffered a very painful injury in the war."

Marion didn't think so. "It would have to be the last two brothers, sir. She counted them off as she said it. All six."

"Only Harold and Stanley are left. Harold is to take holy orders soon."

"Let us hope, then, he does not espouse beatings as Caroline seemed to imply. Such a thing would hardly recommend him to his parishioners. And Charlie?"

"Seventeen and still at school."

"Harrow?"

"I should think not!" Mr. Jonquil blustered theatrically, pulling a deep laugh out of Marion. "We are an Eton family, Miss Wood. Harrow? Hah!"

They sat there on the blanket chuckling and smiling as if it were the most natural thing in the world. Marion wished it really were, that she were a well-appointed lady seated beside this charming gentleman rather than the plain governess she knew herself to be. 'Twas so enjoyable to pass a morning this way, laughing at such things as school rivalry and childish mispronunciations.

"You still have not solved the mystery, sir," Marion said lightly, smiling across at him. "Caroline specifically said that two of your 'big boys' lived in Painage and Beatin' and—Oh no!" The answer suddenly hit her. "The pronunciation is a little odd, but, I believe she means—"

"Cambridge and Eton," they said in unison before dissolving into further whoops of laughter.

"Poor Harry," Mr. Jonquil said. "To be so unjustly accused of mean-spiritedness. He considers himself something of a model of saintliness and clerical kindness. I absolutely *have* to tell Flip about this." He wiped a tear of amusement from his eyes. "He and I christened Harold 'Holy Harry,' you know. He's been bound for the church from birth and has acted the part every day of his life."

"Much to your obvious amusement." Marion smiled.

Mr. Jonquil's only response was a faintly reminiscent laugh. "Well, Miss Wood, I seem to be quite a hand at solving riddles today. Have you any others to which I might apply my expertise?"

Hundreds, she thought, watching him as her heart thudded alarmingly in her chest. He looked so entirely different. Amusement had replaced discontent in his eyes. The lines on his face had softened. His perpetually stern mouth turned up in an easy smile. She knew, in that moment, what she needed to ask, what mystery she wanted him to solve for her, but she felt suddenly shy.

"I am certain I have pried quite enough for one morning." Marion studied her hands as they twisted the corner of the blanket wrapped around her.

"Come now, Miss Wood. Do not suddenly turn missish on me."

"You would probably find it an impertinence," Marion warned.

"Then I will have no one but myself to blame, will I?"

There went her heart again, even as her brain registered how unbelievably handsome this man seated beside her was.

"Caroline has mentioned . . . that is, she told me that . . ." The question proved harder to pose than she'd anticipated. "Three or four times since I have arrived, Caroline has spoken of her mother."

She saw Mr. Jonquil flinch. She'd been afraid it would not be an easy subject. Still, she pressed on. It had weighed on her thoughts for weeks. "All she will say is that her mother is gone. She either doesn't wish to tell me or doesn't know where her mother has gone. I have narrowed down the possibilities to two. Either she has physically left, that the two of you are separated. Or she is no longer alive."

Mr. Jonquil sat silently, his eyes focused far out over the river, his jaw noticeably tense. Had she made a terrible mistake? Or finally stumbled on the reason for the unhappiness so prevalent at Farland Meadows?

"Bridget," Mr. Jonquil said, his voice tense and steel edged, "my *late* wife, died four months after Caroline was born. I assure you, Miss Wood, Caroline knows as much. I am not such a lamentable father that I would not tell her about her own mother."

He picked up his hat, stood, and walked away without a backward glance or a word of good-bye.

"Oh, Mr. Jonquil," Marion whispered, "I believe I *have* found the problem."

CHAPTER THIRTEEN

LAYTON DIDN'T GO FAR, A hundred feet perhaps, before leaning against the trunk of an obliging tree, arm up, head resting on his forearm. What had possessed Miss Wood to ask about Bridget? He'd been quite thoroughly enjoying himself up to that moment. He hadn't spoken so easily with another person since before Bridget had left him.

"Left him." That was how he always referred to her death, finding it easier somehow. But Caroline knew what he meant. Didn't she? Layton felt nearly certain he'd told her quite clearly that her mother was dead, not simply off visiting. But as he reflected on her versions of his various brothers' occupations and places of residence, his confidence began to slip.

Caroline was only four years old. Which, he told himself, was part of the problem. How much had he told her? How much ought he to tell her? Should he be blunt or careful? Detailed or vague?

"Stupid fool," he muttered. "You have no idea what you're doing."

"Mr. Jonquil?" Miss Wood's voice was quiet, uncertain, and only a few feet behind him.

"What is it, Miss Wood?" he asked rather curtly.

"I am sorry, sir. I would never have . . . If I'd known . . ." Layton heard her take a deep breath. "You said I could ask you anything, that you wouldn't mind the impertinence."

"Perhaps I underestimated your presumptuousness." Layton moved away from the tree and closer to the riverbank, slapping the brim of his hat against his thigh.

"Caroline has asked me about her." Miss Wood stood near the tree he'd just abandoned.

"Miss Wood—"

"And I do not know what to say," she continued on. "She wants to know if her mother was beautiful. What color her hair was. If she told Caroline stories or sang to her. She wants to know if her mother loved her. And I don't know what to say."

Layton spun around to face the intrusive woman, more frustrated than he'd been with her yet. "She was lovely. Her hair was light brown. She told Caroline not a single story, nor sang her a single note. And I seriously doubt she loved the child."

He saw her flinch at his angry tone and felt suddenly sorry. "I cannot tell her that, sir." Miss Wood's eyes lowered, her hands clasped in front of her.

"Blast it, don't start acting the well-behaved servant now," he snapped.

Tears started down her face, and he felt like a churl. He sighed and crossed back to her. With that ridiculous blanket wrapped around her shoulders, she almost looked like a child snuggled up in bed. No. Not like a child at all, he corrected himself as he looked into her face. And he'd made her cry.

"My apologies, Miss Wood. I have been unforgivably short with you."

"I hope I haven't offended you, sir." A crease marred her porcelain forehead, and he longed to wipe it away, knowing full well he'd put it there. "I only wish to understand, to know how I can help Caroline." Her cheeks colored slightly. "And you, sir."

"Me?" Layton watched her rising color and felt his pulse quicken involuntarily. "You wish to help me?"

She nodded. "When I first came to Farland Meadows, I envisioned a place of warmth and joy."

"Which you most certainly did not find," Layton muttered, turning away a little.

"But I *have* seen both here. There have been moments when this has felt like a home, sir. I want that for Caroline. For you. There should be happiness here."

Layton sighed. "There used to be."

"Before your wife died?"

He nodded. He felt her hand gently touch his arm, and even through the heavy material of his jacket, he felt the warmth of that contact.

"Please tell me, sir."

"It is not a fairy tale with a happy ending," Layton warned, careful not to pull his arm away from her soft touch.

"Not all stories have happy endings." She sounded as if she knew that all too well.

"Shall we walk while I bare my soul, Miss Wood?" He tried to laugh but didn't quite succeed.

She smiled at him, her eyes empathetic and caring. With the first step, Miss Wood pulled her hand back from his arm and tucked it into her blanket.

"Why a blanket, Miss Wood?" he asked, suddenly wondering. "Is your coat so insufficient?"

"It is not my turn for stories, sir. It is yours."

"Ah, I've been put in my place." He smiled, and the gesture came more easily than he would have thought. He took a series of deep breaths. Miss Wood didn't press or hurry him, for which he was grateful. He was about to talk of things he seldom allowed himself even to think about, and yet it felt natural to do so—difficult but right.

"I married Bridget—Bridget Sarvol, she was then—when I was twenty-one and she twenty." How old was Miss Wood? he wondered. Nineteen, twenty, perhaps. He forced himself back to the task of telling his sordid history. "We'd known each other our entire lives and had grown up together: friends, at times rivals, but never with any romantic attachment between us. When she reached twenty and had no prospects, despite having had three London Seasons, her father decided to take matters into his own hands and began arranging a match for her."

The horror that darted across Miss Wood's face pulled a chuckle from Layton. "That, I assure you, is precisely how Bridget felt about it. She couldn't, of course, be forced to wed the man her father had selected, who was, by the way, fifty if he was a day and about as intelligent as a turnip. Being underage and entirely dependent on her father, Bridget could certainly be coerced. And her father spared no effort in coercing her."

"Horrible," he heard Miss Wood mutter.

"Mr. Sarvol is not the most kindhearted of men." Layton knew that well. He seldom ran across Bridget's father, but their encounters were inevitably tense and confrontational, just as they had been during Bridget's lifetime.

Layton pressed ahead with the retelling. "I was already living here at the Meadows at the time Bridget was facing a forced match. I lived here alone and had begun to think it might be nice to have a companion, someone with whom I might share my days. I knew I would inherit my mother's title after her death, becoming the Baron Farland, and I needed an heir of my own. When Bridget told me of her situation, I thought of the perfect solution. We got along well enough. And, I flattered myself, I was something of an improvement over a portly, bacon-brained man in his sixth decade."

"A vast improvement." Miss Wood agreed with so much conviction Layton felt his ears grow a little warm.

"Bridget was ecstatic. We'd always been friends, she pointed out. We liked and trusted and cared for each other. What more, she asked, could a person hope for in marriage?"

Miss Wood didn't seem entirely convinced.

"Fortunately for our plans, the heir to a barony was quite good enough for her father, seeing as how the older gentleman he'd selected was a mere baronet and not nearly as well connected." He allowed a generous helping of irony to color his words. "I *am* related to an earl, you know."

Miss Wood laughed at his mock pomposity, as he'd intended. The sound did him a world of good. Her tears were gone, replaced by a smile.

"I am surprised he didn't hold out for the earl himself," Miss Wood said.

"By that time, Philip was gone quite a lot, off fulfilling his duties."

Miss Wood nodded. "Better a bird in the bag than one in the bush, I suppose."

"A lowering comparison, Miss Wood. Remind me to consult you if I ever need to be brought down a peg or two."

"Right-o, guv'nuh!" she said with a laugh and a mischievous wink.

"I was sorely tempted to send you off with a flea in your ear the first time you addressed me that way." Layton smiled at the memory of her saucy salute.

"I am so glad you didn't, sir."

"So am I, Miss Wood. So am I." And he meant it fiercely in that moment.

She tucked her arm through his, blanket and all, as they walked along the winding path that followed the river. Layton didn't know what had possessed her to make the gesture, but he gratefully accepted it, pulling her arm a little closer to him.

"So Miss Sarvol's father accepted your offer and sent the tubby old man packing," Miss Wood cued him.

"Ah, yes." When had the telling of this history become so much easier? "Now, ours wasn't a love match, not in the truest sense of the word, but we were happy. Her father seemed satisfied enough. Though he hardly spared me a glance, he and Bridget wrote to one another when he was in Town."

Layton told Miss Wood story after story of that first year of his marriage as they continued to walk. He spoke of the time he and Bridget had raced on horseback and Bridget had beaten him by more than a horse length and could not be convinced he hadn't let her win. He told her of the time the vicar had come for tea and, much to his and Bridget's shock and eventual amusement, spent a full two hours declaring the house, the furnishings, and the color of Bridget's dress too "worldly" and suggested they'd do well to address their obvious struggle with pride. Layton recounted the myriad experiences that had built their connection into an enduring friendship, though never beyond, as well as the little things that had made their marriage comfortable and happy.

Miss Wood listened attentively, laughing when the stories warranted and nodding her understanding at a recounting of some disagreement or another they'd had during those early weeks and months of adjusting. She was an easy person to talk to, a more than adequate listener. He discovered that talking about Bridget was almost medicinal for him, and the heaviness he usually associated with any thought of her seemed to slowly slip away.

"A few months after we married, Bridget realized she was increasing. We were both ecstatic. I believe she conducted the most rigorous interviews any potential nurse has ever been forced to endure, convinced no one was worthy of the post of raising her precious child. She embroidered more infant dresses than any child could possibly wear. I set an entire army of workmen to fixing up the nursery. I'm not sure there have ever been two people more overjoyed at the prospect of becoming parents."

This was where the story became difficult to recount. The memories seemed to rush at him, painful, difficult, and bewildering. Yet the words poured out of him like a volcano exploding under the mounting pressure built up underneath.

"The time came for her confinement, and the delivery was, thankfully, unexceptional. She was understandably worn down that first week: tired, perhaps a little out of sorts, but nothing to raise any suspicions of coming difficulties."

He felt Miss Wood's fingers close more firmly around his arm. He laid his hand on top of hers, where it rested on his sleeve, noticing in the back of his mind that she wore no gloves and her fingers felt cold even through his own gloves. But the words he'd held back for so many years didn't stop long enough for him to react to her state.

"Bridget was never what one would call perpetually cheerful, neither was she prone to moodiness or pessimism." Layton hardly noticed where they walked. "She was different after Caroline's birth. She didn't leave her room, even after Doctor Habbersham declared her fit enough to do so. After those first couple of days, she never wanted to hold Caroline. After a few weeks, she refused to see anyone but her lady's maid and myself. After two months, even I was barred at times. And she cried for hours on end, sobs that filled the house. She began drawing the drapes on all of the windows in her sitting room and bedchamber.

"By the time Caroline was three months old, Bridget wouldn't leave her own bed. She just lay there in her nightclothes. Crying or sleeping, mostly. I would go to her when she allowed it, try to speak to her. Every visit seemed to end in her either weeping or raging at me.

"I tried to tell her about Caroline, but she didn't want to hear. I don't know if she was unhappy with motherhood or disappointed with Caroline or with me. That's when I started walking along the river. The hours of sobbing became too much. The house felt . . . closed in, like I was suffocating in there, like if I stayed one minute longer, I would be forced to sob myself at the sheer frustration of it all.

"I did everything I could. I visited whenever my presence didn't unduly upset her. I tried to rally her spirits with tales of Caroline's adventures: her first smile, first laugh, Nurse's belief that she was going to produce a tooth despite being not quite four months old. I suggested she write to her father, something she had done regularly before Caroline's birth. Though I was never privy to their correspondence, she did seem to enjoy hearing from him. But Bridget either acted as though I weren't speaking at all, or she cried.

"Then one night, the crying stopped."

"Oh, sir." Miss Wood's tiny voice echoed in his ears.

"I ran to her rooms, convinced something had happened, that she'd taken ill." He closed his eyes, the setting so real he might have been experiencing it all over again: running frantically into a room decorated in blue, eerily quiet. "The window drapes were all pulled back, moonlight spilling across the floor, but the bed curtains were pulled shut. The room was so quiet. The clock on her dressing table had been stopped. I . . . I didn't even hear her breathing."

The story flowed from him then, and he felt powerless to stop the words.

"I walked to the bed. I think I was even shaking. I hadn't been so scared in . . . probably my entire life. I grabbed the bed curtains, knowing I needed to check on her. I kept telling myself she was just sleeping, that everything would be fine." Layton felt a warm tear run down his wind-bitten cheek. His breaths shuddered in and out of him. "I was too late. Too late. She was dead."

Suddenly, Miss Wood held his hand in her two smaller ones, looking up at him. Dawning horror touched her usually cheerful face. Little did

Miss Wood realize, he hadn't reached the worst part of the story. But he couldn't stop. He needed to tell someone after all these years. He needed to tell *her.*

"I sent for Dr. Habbersham, of course, not because I thought he could do anything but to determine what had"—somehow he couldn't say *killed her*—"happened. She didn't look peaceful, like she'd passed away in her sleep. She'd obviously been terribly, terribly ill. *Violently* ill, even. I'd never seen anything so horrible." He felt her fingers tighten around his hand as if she knew he needed that, needed to feel the strength of human contact. "I kept the servants out, hoping to spare them the sight of her final moments. It was while I waited for the doctor that I found it." He took a deep breath, remembering too vividly. "A vial. On her bed stand. It was empty. I hadn't seen it there before, and I wondered about it.

"Dr. Habbersham had no trouble identifying what it had once held. One look at Bridget, and he knew. Arsenic. Pure, unadulterated poison."

"Someone poisoned her?" Miss Wood asked in innocence.

"No, Mary. She poisoned *herself.*"

He heard her suck in a shocked breath. "I had no idea," Mary said, emotion thick in her voice.

"No one has any idea. I haven't told anyone. Neither has Habbersham. He listed her cause of death as a wasting illness. She'd been out of the public eye for so long, it was easily accepted."

"Did you tell your family?"

"Of course not."

"But why?" Mary stepped back from him just enough for him to see her face, tears hovering at the corners of her eyes. "Surely they would have been a support to you."

"I couldn't, Mary. I couldn't." He pulled his hand out of hers and began pacing among the copse of trees they'd stopped under.

"I don't understand why not."

"Because they would have—" He ran his hand through his hair. Sometime during their walk, he'd lost his hat. "Do you know what happens to people who kill themselves, Mary? Do you have any idea?"

She shook her head, her chin trembling but her tears remaining firmly in her eyes.

"Suicide is a felony in England and a sin of some significance. There are repercussions. Consequences." Layton rubbed his face, the tension in his body almost unbearable. This was why he never talked about that time, tried not to think about it. "Someone who commits suicide cannot be buried in a churchyard, cannot receive a graveside service or a Christian burial. Their death is not acknowledged by the parish." He was pacing faster, harder. "Bridget would have been buried at the side of a road, Mary! A stake driven through her heart! It is the law: the law of England, the law of the church. I could not, *could not*, do that to her. I would never have permitted her body to be desecrated that way, relegated to an unmarked grave in a place where her family would be ashamed to bring flowers or go to remember her. The few times I have encountered her father since her death have been in the churchyard—we both needed her to be there. Caroline needs her to be there."

"So you lied," Mary said.

Layton felt the accusation that was entirely absent from her tone. "I lied," he said flatly, defying her to condemn him for it. "I lied to the government. I lied to her family. I lied to the church. I even lied to God. I cannot get her into heaven. But she is in that churchyard. And if I have to lie for the rest of my life to keep her there, so be it."

CHAPTER FOURTEEN

MARION HADN'T TALKED TO OR SEEN Mr. Jonquil in a full week, and the weight of what he'd told her in that copse of trees sat heavily on her heart. His unhappiness, the oppressive feeling of the house, finally made sense. He had endured so much suffering and unhappiness in only a few short months. The events of years ago seemed still to drain the very life from the house and its occupants. The late Mrs. Jonquil's sobs may not have echoed through the halls any longer, but joyful voices and laughter had never returned to claim those echoes either.

She stepped inside his library, entirely uncertain of how he would treat her in light of his confessions. Did he resent sharing his past? Would he look on her as a confidant or an unpleasant reminder of the pain he carried?

"Sir?"

"Yes, Miss Wood." Mr. Jonquil didn't look up from the papers he was reading.

His return to formality told Marion volumes about his state of mind. She was no longer "Mary." It was, therefore, a very good thing she'd chided herself for thinking of him once or twice as "Layton." She regretted the change. While "Mary" wasn't precisely her name, it came so close that she could almost imagine he'd added the final syllable. Those few times Mr. Jonquil had slipped into familiarity, she'd felt more at ease than she had since leaving home.

"I would like to speak to you, sir."

He looked up then, wariness in his eyes. Mr. Jonquil quite obviously thought she meant to speak of his late wife and everything he'd revealed about her.

"About Caroline's birthday," Marion quickly explained. He relaxed noticeably. "I know it is short notice, sir, but earlier today, she mentioned something she would particularly like to have. I would so like for her to have it. I know it would mean a great deal to her."

"What is it she wishes for?"

"Well, sir, we have been working on her table etiquette. I told her this morning what a pleasure it was to have my breakfast with her because she has such pleasing manners. She said rather wistfully that she wished she could have a real grown-up dinner in the formal dining room." Marion took a deep breath and plunged on; somehow, she felt more like a servant than ever asking for this favor. "Caroline spoke on and on about wearing her fanciest dress and wearing her locket and curtsying to the guests. Oh, Mr. Jonquil, I wish you could have heard her. I have never heard her say so much at one time. I think she has imagined just such an evening many times. She is very well behaved. Her manners are flawless.

"I know it isn't the done thing for a child so young to dine with adults, but it seems to mean so much to her." Marion hoped she hadn't given him a chance to disagree. Yet. "I heard Mrs. Sanders say that at least one of your brothers and your mother, the countess, have returned to Lampton Park. If they were to make up the party, there wouldn't really be any impropriety. And I trust they would be lenient if Caroline were a little overawed, though I don't believe she would give you a moment's concern."

"So, a dinner with Caroline as hostess, the guests, adults selected from among her circle of acquaintances," Mr. Jonquil summed up, but Marion couldn't read his expression, couldn't say if he approved of her idea or thought her completely out of line. He rose and walked to the windows of his library.

Marion felt almost desperate. It so obviously was a dream of Caroline's, one of many she'd unknowingly shared with Marion. The child wanted so many simple things that no one could possibly give her—she wished to know her deceased mother, wished for a mother of her own, wished for her father to laugh and tease and play with her when he was so often pensive and quiet and sad. This dinner party was at least possible.

"Oh, please, Mr. Jonquil!" Marion followed him with her eyes as he moved around the room. "I so want to give her this. I will write the invitations myself so Mrs. Sanders won't be bothered. Better yet!" She clapped her hands together. "I will help Caroline write them. Her letters are entirely legible, and I can assist her with her spelling and anything else. She would be delighted."

"That is a great deal of work for an almost-five-year-old to accomplish in a few hours. The invitations would need to be sent today, you realize." He looked ready to deny her.

"Then perhaps I could write the invitations, and Caroline could simply write her name on them. She is quite proficient at writing her own name, and it wouldn't be any trouble."

"I—"

"And I will dress her and fix her hair myself. There would be no bother for the servants. They certainly wouldn't be overset at providing dinner for your family."

"Certainly not." He seemed to laugh.

At *her*? Nearly everyone she'd known would laugh to see her now, begging for a small favor, humbled at her inability to grant a small wish for a child. But she pushed forward.

"Please," she asked one more time. "Do this for her. She has lost so much but asks for so little."

She saw him stiffen but did not wish the words unsaid. Mr. Jonquil turned toward her and stepped to where she stood, his eyes softened somehow. A slight smile turned his lips when he spoke. "You seem to be under the impression that I disapprove of your suggestion."

"Do you not?"

Mr. Jonquil shook his head and stepped closer yet. "There are times, my dear Miss Wood, when your thoughtfulness amazes me."

She could do nothing but listen and watch him, fascinated by the look in his eyes but unable to interpret it.

"I think this dinner you propose is inspired." Mr. Jonquil watched her, standing directly in front of her. "I happen to know that Philip, the earl, and Stanley—"

"The soldier." Marion nodded, knowing precisely to which brother he referred.

"—and Mater are all at the Park. I can guarantee they wouldn't miss a dinner here, especially one hosted by Caroline. They like her far better than they like me." He smiled a little self-deprecatingly. Marion wondered if he believed the words despite his joking tone.

"May I write the invitations, then?" she asked.

"If I may add one more name to the list," Mr. Jonquil said.

"Oh, sir, I feel the party really ought to be limited to people whom Caroline knows well and with whom she would be comfortable."

"I assure you this last guest will not make Caroline the least bit uncomfortable." Mr. Jonquil seemed to be hiding a smile. "She and Caroline are quite fond of each other, actually."

She? Marion tried to swallow back a lump that suddenly formed in her throat. Who was this mysterious lady who held such a position of trust in Caroline's life? Was Mr. Jonquil attached to her as well? But she had no right to even speculate on such things.

"Of course, Mr. Jonquil," Marion forced herself to say. "I will invite anyone you see fit to include."

Mr. Jonquil stepped a little closer and looked directly into her eyes. "Anyone?"

Marion nodded, her heart racing at his nearness.

"Do I have your word on that?"

"Yes, sir." Marion fought the urge to reach out and touch him. Where had her recent wayward inclinations come from?

"Must you attach a 'sir' to every sentence you speak to me?" A hint of frustration touched the lightness of his tone.

"I figure 'sir' is better than 'guv'nuh.'"

Mr. Jonquil chuckled. "Infinitely."

"To whom shall I send the extra invitation, s—" She stopped just before adding her usual ending.

Mr. Jonquil seemed to notice. His smile broadened. He turned away, walking back toward his desk. As he sat, he said, "To Miss Mary Wood."

A few noises came out of her mouth but nothing that constituted any actual words.

"You gave your word," Mr. Jonquil reminded her, taking up his quill again. "I expect the invitation to be extended"—He looked up for the briefest of moments—"and accepted."

"Yes, *sir.*" She added the last with emphasis. "And thank you so very much."

He didn't look up or respond, and Marion knew that was her cue to leave. She ran up the stairs, rushing past Maggie, straight into her room, where she closed the door hard before dancing in a victorious circle at the foot of her bed and then dropped onto it with an exclamation of sheer triumph.

The invitations were sent and universally accepted by that evening. Caroline was ecstatic. She spoke for a full ten minutes without pausing once. Marion listened in complete amazement, grateful beyond words to Mr. Jonquil for agreeing to what must have seemed at the time to be a mad scheme.

They spent the next morning and half the afternoon working out the details: choosing a gown for Caroline and a ribbon for her hair and deciding on a menu, which Marion relayed to Mr. Jonquil, for she had her suspicions that Mrs. Sanders would find the extra work a nuisance. Marion, on the other hand, loved seeing the glow in Caroline's eyes as their plans came together.

By the afternoon of Caroline's birthday, the nursery wing was overflowing with excitement. The dinner was to be at six o'clock, early enough to accommodate the schedule of a young child but late enough not to be ridiculous. Caroline hadn't eaten a thing at tea. Indeed, she hadn't even sat still. Marion had loved every minute.

"Will Papa think I am beautiful, Mary?" Caroline asked, smiling at herself in the tiny mirror on the wall in Marion's room.

"He couldn't possibly think otherwise, dearest." Marion beamed back at her. They'd spent a full hour on her hair alone, not because such time had been necessary but because Marion knew that every girl—every woman, for that matter—needed to feel pretty at least once in her life. For Caroline, tonight would be just the first. *Adorable* was probably the best word for the birthday girl. Her blonde ringlets hung in absolute perfection, and an enormous blue bow in her hair perfectly matched the blue silk of her dress, edged in delicate, childlike lace.

"And what about me, Caroline?" Marion twirled around as if to ask Caroline's opinion of her gray gown, the same one she'd worn to church every Sunday, and her usual coiffure: hair in a bun at the nape of her neck and strands falling loose despite all of her efforts to prevent their escape. She knew perfectly well that she appeared plain and dowdy, but Caroline would enjoy feeling herself the fashion critic.

"You need a ribbon too, Mary," Caroline decreed, perfectly serious and ponderous. She took Marion by the hand and led her back into her own room, with its delicate white furniture and wispy lace curtains. From a box on her dressing table, Caroline pulled a length of ribbon very much the shade of salmon that one regularly saw in an autumn sunset. It would look absolutely dreadful against her red hair. She allowed Caroline to tie it around her bun, knowing it would be lopsided.

"Are we ready now?" she asked Caroline. "You are hostess tonight and must not be late."

Caroline barely managed to walk down the stairs. Marion could tell just from watching her that she was sorely tempted to run. But the young girl took the steps at a sedate pace, posture perfectly upright, the very copy of a society debutante—at least until she saw her father.

A squeal of delight barely preceded Caroline's flight across the floor of the drawing room and directly into the outstretched arms of Mr. Jonquil. Marion smiled as she watched them. These were the moments that gave her hope for those two.

"Who is this grown-up young lady, Miss Wood?" Mr. Jonquil held Caroline back far enough to look her over and pretend to wonder at her identity.

"I found her upstairs, Mr. Jonquil. Since you were in need of a proper hostess, I brought her down."

"Excellent notion, Miss Wood."

"Sillies!" Caroline giggled. "I'm Caroline!"

Mr. Jonquil uttered a perfectly astounded gasp. "This grown-up girl is my little Caroline? No! I cannot believe it!"

"I am, Papa! I am!" She laughed. "I just have a grown-up ribbon, see?"

"That must be it." Mr. Jonquil's smile broke through. "Ribbons have been known to add years to a lady's appearance."

"Do not let word of that get around, sir," Marion said. "Not a soul in London would wear a ribbon again."

Mr. Jonquil smiled at her, a breathtaking smile. For just a moment, Marion was quite unaccountably light-headed.

"I gave Mary a ribbon too, Papa!" Caroline ran to grasp Marion's hand and pull her farther into the room. "Do you see it? It is my very prettiest pink ribbon."

"And how old do I look with this prettiest of pink ribbons?" Marion raised an eyebrow jokingly.

The look of scrutiny Mr. Jonquil leveled at her was anything but playful, as if he were memorizing everything about her. Marion felt the color rising in her cheeks. To cover her suddenly fluttering heart and quivering knees, she tried to laugh. "I suppose that was a rather impolitic question." She managed to shrug.

"Extremely impolitic." Mr. Jonquil's eyes locked with hers in a very discomforting way.

Marion's heart fluttered faster. She pressed her hand to it in hopes of stopping the sensation.

"No matter how I reply, I fear my answer would be taken in offense," Mr. Jonquil said. "My answer would unavoidably be either too young or too old."

"Undoubtedly," Marion answered, her voice sounding strangely breathy to her own ears. Why in heaven's name would her heart not resume a more normal pace?

"Yes, dear?" Mr. Jonquil addressed Caroline, who had been tugging at his coattails for several moments.

Caroline spoke in a whisper far too loud for confidentiality, though her tone indicated she intended their exchange to be secret. Marion pretended not to hear. "Mary is twenty whole years old, Papa. Her birthday was only two days ago. So close to mine!" Caroline's eyes grew wide.

"And why, poppet, did you not tell your Papa that it was Miss Wood's birthday?" But Mr. Jonquil was looking at Marion again with something akin to disappointment on his face.

She must have looked confused at his expression. She certainly felt confused. Why would he have wished to know? She was only a servant.

"We could have given her a present," Mr. Jonquil said. His disappointment seemed to dissolve into almost sadness.

"Oh, I wanted to! But I didn't have anything to give her, and I . . ." Caroline sniffled back sudden tears. "I . . . I wish . . ."

Mr. Jonquil engulfed Caroline in his large arms once more as he knelt in front of her. He whispered something into Caroline's tiny ear that Marion couldn't overhear, and a tremulous smile courageously peeked out through her tears. Mr. Jonquil took hold of Caroline's hand then rose to his feet and turned to Marion.

"Miss Wood," he said in that voice she remembered from their first encounter, one filled with aristocratic command. She felt herself stiffen at the sound of it as she looked up into his eyes. But the moment her gaze met his, she relaxed. There was a twinkle there that belied his demeanor. "As master of this house, I am declaring tomorrow your second birthday."

"My *what*?"

"Cake and presents and general merriment." Mr. Jonquil went on as if she'd made no inquiry. "A few days late but a birthday celebration just the same."

Marion and Caroline replied in perfect unison. "Oh, sir, that is hardly—" and "Oh, Papa!"

"Go to the window, poppet," Mr. Jonquil instructed gently. "See if Flip and Grammy and Stanby are here yet."

Caroline obediently ran off with a smile splitting her face.

Mr. Jonquil turned to face Marion, a look in his eyes that made her breath catch in her lungs and her heart flutter once again. She wasn't entirely sure what it meant or why she felt the way she did, but something in her wanted him to continue looking at her just the way he was at that moment.

CHAPTER FIFTEEN

Mary wasted not a moment of their sudden privacy before protesting again. "It would be too much, sir. For a servant—"

"Let us do this for you, Miss Wood," Layton interrupted, stepping ever closer, fighting the urge to brush his fingers along her cheek. He'd avoided her rather obsessively since their hours-long discussion of his past in the woods weeks earlier, thinking he'd regret his decision to unburden himself if he were forced to face her. But it seemed Mary—he'd come to think of her that way, even though the name didn't seem to fit her somehow—was all he thought about lately. He'd wonder where she was and what she was doing. He'd wander to the schoolroom when he knew she and Caroline were on one of their outings and would marvel at the change she'd wrought there. It was lighter and cheerier and full of wilted brown leaves. They, no doubt, were still collecting the legendary Drops of Gold.

Once, he'd even gone to the nursery wing in the middle of the night, telling himself he only meant to check on Caroline, which he did, but then he sat in a chair near the empty fireplace and just listened to the quiet stillness of Mary's domain. He endured no gut-wrenching sobs, no night-long pacing up and down the room he knew was hers. She was peaceful, and he needed peace. He *needed* it.

"You told me when I first came here that I needed to learn my place." Mary shook her head. "I couldn't—"

Layton quit suppressing his natural instinct and reached up to touch her face lightly, hesitantly. Her cheek was every bit as soft as it looked. He cupped her face in his hand and looked directly into her eyes. "Someone reminded me recently how very little Caroline asks of any of us, especially considering how much she has lost in her short lifetime." He allowed his hand to drop from her face, though he immediately missed the contact, the closeness he felt caressing her cheek. He seized her hand with his two, needing to regain some degree of contact. "Caroline was so obviously desolate at not being able to acknowledge your birthday. Please let her. You have done so much for her, for us."

"I really haven't—"

"Do you know she sat on my lap for a full thirty minutes last night and talked—hardly pausing for breath the entire time?"

A smile spread across Mary's face. Layton longed to touch her cheek again, to brush back that lock of fiery red hair that constantly flung itself against her temple. He contented himself with gently squeezing her fingers, though it wasn't nearly as satisfying.

"She can chatter on at times." Mary laughed lightly. "That is just Caroline."

"No, Mary." Layton shook his head. "It is a miracle. A miracle." The last word he whispered, his own astonishment at the change in his daughter nearly undoing him. He lifted her hand to his lips and kissed her fingers almost reverently.

"Sir?"

"No," he objected, voice low, her fingers mere inches from his lips. "Do not 'sir' me to death tonight, Mary. You are a guest this evening." He held her hand still, astoundingly reluctant to let it go.

"Guest or not, I shall have to 'sir' you, as you call it, once your family has arrived. It would be highly improper to do otherwise." A tender smile touched Mary's face.

How he longed to hold her to him in that moment, to plead with her to look at him that way always. Her soft reminder, however, put things back in their places, brought back memories of failure he had no desire to relive.

Layton released her hand. "Forgive me, Miss Wood." He hoped his disappointment was not too obvious. He was, after all, in the wrong, the one encroaching and pushing the bounds of propriety.

She opened her mouth as if to speak. What she meant to say, he would never know. Caroline's shouts of "They're here, Papa!" rang through the room, and the moment was lost.

"Count to five, Caroline," Mary instructed quietly.

Caroline stopped on the spot, her lips moving silently as she transformed before his very eyes from a shouting, jumping child to a calm, demure young girl. He was pleased to see her smile hadn't faded and even more pleased to see Mary's smile had grown as she watched Caroline. Smiles hadn't come so easily at the Meadows since Bridget had left them. Sanders stepped inside the room, his usual look of pomposity firmly fixed on his face. Why Sanders's stuffy posturing should suddenly bother him, Layton couldn't say. The butler cleared his throat and announced, his voice full of self-importance, "The Right Honorable the Earl of Lampton. The Right Honorable the Countess of Lampton. The Honorable Captain Stanley Jonquil."

Layton managed not to roll his eyes. Why must Sanders announce Layton's own family as if they were visiting nobility? They were visiting, and they were nobility, but it was still ridiculous.

The new arrivals all filed in as Sanders completed his overblown announcement. Stanley, as Layton could have predicted, barely hid a smile at the pompousness of their arrival. Layton had to admit his younger brother cut quite a dash in his blue Dragoon's uniform. With his arm almost completely healed and much of the pallor he'd borne the past months gone, he looked like a healthy twenty-two-year-old again.

Mater wore her customary black. Her face, as always, was lit in a broad smile, her eyes twinkling merrily. Her smile broadened when she looked at Caroline and softened when she turned to Layton. She sat on a sofa, looking entirely satisfied with life. She nearly always looked that way.

Philip's appearance made Layton shake his head. Absurd was the best word for it. Philip was considered an out-and-out dandy: bright colors, affected drawl, an excessive number of fobs on his watch chain, quizzing glass ever at hand, and a certain air of careless stupidity. It was truly absurd. Philip was probably the most intelligent person Layton knew and was at times serious to a fault. The charade had begun the year Layton and Bridget had married, and Philip hadn't dropped it yet.

"Welcome to Farland Meadows, Lord and Lady Lampton, Captain Jonquil," Caroline said in a tone of voice that told Layton in an instant she'd spent some time memorizing her little speech. She curtsied quite perfectly.

That golden eyebrow of Philip's arched in surprised amusement. "Miss Jonquil." He executed a flourishing bow, which set Caroline to giggling.

"Oh, Flip!" She laughed. "You bow almost as good as Mary!"

Philip pressed his hand to his heart as if wounded. "Almost as well as Mary? *Almost*? And who, I must ask, is this Mary, whose bows so far outshine my apparently paltry efforts?"

"He's silly like you, Papa!" Caroline flashed an enormous smile at Layton that melted his heart in an instant.

"Yes, dear." Layton smiled back. "Your uncle Flip is excessively silly."

"I should call you out for that, young man." Philip eyed Layton through his quizzing glass. "Silly, *indeed.*"

"No, no, Uncle Flip." Caroline looked up at Philip. She popped her fisted hands onto her hips, elbows jutted out as if ready to read him a deep scold. "Papa is supposed to call *you* out. But only if you give me a handkerchief and tell me to keep it because you think I'm a beautiful, very grown-up girl. But you only say that after I tell you I will clean all my junk off it and give it back to you. You say you don't want it back even with all the junk scraped off."

"Then your Papa calls me out?" Philip's chin quivered, but his voice remained impressively calm.

Caroline nodded with authority. Layton had to bite his lips closed to hold back the laugh ready to burst from him. He looked across the room to where Mary had slid and saw she held a hand over her mouth.

"Why would he do that, Miss Jonquil?" Philip's eyes danced. "Surely he would understand my allowing you to keep the linen, even though you'd . . . ahem . . . *scraped the junk off.*"

"'Cause, Flip," she said as though he were completely stupid, "I'm not supposed to keep linens from anyone but Papa. 'Cept I gave back the last one he gave me."

"Did you scrape off the junk first?" Stanley asked, leaning casually against the mantel and watching Caroline with obvious enjoyment.

"'Course I did. Mary said a very grown-up girl never gives a junky handkerchief back to a gennleman. And she taught me how to be a good hostess." She skipped to the sofa where Mater watched her with something like shock on her face. "You saw me curtsy, didn't you, Grammy? Like this." She bobbed again, grinning from ear to ear. "Mary showed me, and we practiced yesterday until we started laughing. It's hard to curtsy when you laugh. I kept falling down, so Mary said I didn't have to practice anymore. Then she told me how to say, 'Welcome, Lord and Lady Lampton and Captain Jonquil.' Like that. Only when she said it, she made a silly face like she'd ate a sour apple. And then I laughed again, and she said it was useforless. So we practiced making my hair grown-up and that was fun. Am I a good hostess, Grammy?"

"Oh, child." Mater gave a watery smile and hugged Caroline to her, kissing the girl's rosy cheek. She looked up at Layton. "She has so much to say," Mater said in obvious disbelief. Caroline had always been quiet, even with her family.

"So this Mary is not only an excellent bower but a *coiffeuse* and a model of decorum as well?" Philip looked at Layton with a mixture of amusement and curiosity. "I must ask her opinion on my cravat pin. No doubt she has expertise in such matters also."

"Caroline." Layton stepped to the sofa, where Mater was still holding Caroline to her. "You must introduce your uncles and grandmother to our other guest."

"Oh." She popped off the sofa. "I forgot."

Layton nodded his understanding and watched her bounce across the room. But she stopped only feet from Mary and spun back around to face him. "Why didn't Mr. Sanders announce Mary?" she asked. "She's a guest."

"Miss Wood was already here, dear," Layton explained.

"She should get announced too." Caroline's brow furrowed adorably, and she was obviously trying to make sense of the discrepancy. "She could stand outside the door and wait while he said all the 'Honorable' things."

Layton looked at Mary just as she looked at him, her eyes wide with amusement.

"Honorable things?" she mouthed to him silently.

Layton nearly laughed out loud.

"Mr. Sanders is seeing to our dinner, Caroline," Layton reminded her. "We cannot pull him away from his duties."

"You could announce her, Papa!" Caroline said quite decisively. "Just pretend you're the butler."

"Pretend I'm the—" Layton sputtered out the ending.

"I think you would be an excellent butler, Layton." Philip swung his quizzing glass on its long purple ribbon. "I daresay you could look every bit as starched up and self-important as Sanders."

At that, everyone in the room laughed except Caroline, who didn't understand the observation.

"Please, Papa?" Caroline pleaded with him, looking up with those enormous blue eyes that he knew would be the bane of his existence once she was old enough for young men to begin noticing them. "Announce Mary, please."

"All right, poppet." He motioned Mary on with his hand, cupping it behind her elbow once she was close enough. Gads, she smelled good: cinnamon, which fit her perfectly. "Did you put her up to this?" Layton asked under his breath as he walked her toward the door, trying to ignore the all-too-familiar frisson of energy that quaked through him whenever he touched her.

"Caroline invents enough mischief on her own without any help from me," Mary said.

"She didn't used to, you know." Layton bit back a smile as he turned the doorknob and opened the door from the drawing room.

Mary looked back at him as she stepped through the doorway. "Is that a complaint, sir?" she asked with a saucy raise of her eyebrow.

Layton followed her out and leaned a little closer, until he could smell her again. "No," he whispered. Her answering smile made his heart beat harder. "How shall I announce you, Mary?" he asked, still whispering, still a little too close for his own comfort. "With pomposity and arrogance?"

"Any good butler would." Her eyes grew big, filling with mischief. She whispered instructions before standing silently in the corridor to wait for his announcement.

Layton returned to the room, trying hard to control his features. His mouth seemed determined to turn up despite his efforts to look serious and stiff like a true butler. He cleared his throat. Mater and Stanley laughed at his flawless imitation of one of Sanders's more well-known mannerisms. Philip simply raised his quizzing glass.

"Miss Mary Wood," Layton announced to the guests in the room, "The Right Honorable Governess."

Sputtering laughs echoed around the room, Philip's included. Mary stepped inside, chin raised as if she were a duchess. She eyed the room with all the self-importance of the highest-ranking nobility. Anyone watching her would think she was the daughter of a duke or marquess rather than the hired governess in the home of the heir apparent to a minor barony.

Layton watched her make her own flawless curtsies as Caroline introduced her quite properly to his family. He smiled, grateful no one was watching him. Layton knew his heart would show in his eyes and his wholly inappropriate *tendre* would be apparent to anyone watching—that the entire room would know in one glance that he had fallen in love with a woman he could never marry. A gentleman didn't marry his child's governess without repercussions. He hadn't enough standing in society to withstand the scandal *that* would create. He owed it to Caroline not to attach any more unflattering speculation to their already gossip-clogged name.

CHAPTER SIXTEEN

THE EARL OF LAMPTON WAS a dandy but a harmless one. Marion had come to that conclusion before the first course of Caroline's dinner last night. He had a knack for saying vastly conceited things without sounding the least bit arrogant. Marion hadn't laughed so much during a meal since the time Robert had spent an entire dinner hour in a perpetual state of giggles. He had been nine at the time; she'd been six. It remained one of her favorite memories.

Marion sighed quietly to herself, missing her brother. It had been almost a year. How much had happened in those few months.

"Disappointed?"

She looked up at Mr. Jonquil. How long had he been standing there? As always, her heart rate picked up at the sight of him. She knew from hours' worth of self-reflection that she was half in love with him.

And why shouldn't she be? Marion watched him from where she was sitting near the fireplace. He was a little rumpled after putting Caroline to bed, but if anything, he looked *more* handsome. And he was smiling. No one could blame her for melting under the power of that smile.

"I am sorry we had to postpone your birthday celebration," Mr. Jonquil said.

Marion shrugged. "Caroline was all but asleep. I think she's had a few too many excitements these past few days. What with having her family here for her birthday yesterday."

"They can be a bit much," Mr. Jonquil said. "I hope you weren't overwhelmed, Miss Wood."

"Not at all." Marion smiled up at him, setting aside the dress she hoped to complete before the earl's upcoming wedding. "Not even an earl can intimidate a Right Honorable Governess."

Mr. Jonquil let an almighty laugh escape before checking himself with a guilty glance toward Caroline's bedchamber. "I hope I didn't wake her."

"So do I," Marion said dryly. "I'll be up with her if you have."

Mr. Jonquil smiled vaguely but didn't speak. His gaze wandered around the room but inevitably slid back to her. "Why didn't you tell me it was your birthday, Mary?" he asked quietly, his eyes once again avoiding hers. "I would have liked to . . ." He cleared his throat awkwardly. "Did you have a good birthday? All things considered?"

"I did, sir." She wanted to reach out and take his hand but held herself in check.

"No, Mary." He turned back to her in an instant. "Not 'sir.' Not when it's just me here."

"But it wouldn't be—"

"I just . . . I need . . . I need you to be a . . . friend, Mary. Someone I can . . . Someone to talk to." Mr. Jonquil paced in a tight circle, obviously uncomfortable and noticeably in earnest. "Not 'Mr. Jonquil.' Not 'sir.'"

"Should I call you 'guv'nuh,' then?"

Mr. Jonquil smiled again, precisely as she'd hoped he would. "'Layton' would be fine, would be *splendid*, actually."

"Oh, I couldn't—"

"Just for now," he quickly explained. "I . . . I'll . . . I'll understand if you can't . . . I mean, if you don't want to . . . or don't think . . ."

Marion rose from her chair and crossed to where he stood running his fingers through his hair. She laid a hand on his arm and smiled up at him. They stood there, eyes locked for a moment, and the lines on his face softened.

"Layton does fit you much better than 'guv'nuh.'"

"I should hope so. Though—and I know I'll probably regret this— 'Mary' somehow doesn't suit you."

He looked so suddenly apprehensive that Marion had to laugh. She pressed a hand to her mouth to stifle the sound.

"I take it, then, I haven't offended you." His smile was almost boyish.

"My given name is Marion," she explained.

"Marion," he repeated on a whisper. He brushed his fingers along her cheek, which, of course, made her heart race even more and her cheeks heat. Half in love? Marion wasn't entirely sure she wasn't all the way there. "Marion." He smiled gently. "Yes. That suits you much better."

"I was named for my grandparents: Mary and Ian. And why I just told you that, I have no idea." Marion felt her flush deepen.

"Probably because I told you all the minute details of my life." Layton shrugged, his hand dropping back to his side again. "Paying me back in kind, I suppose."

"You want all the sordid details of my past, then?" Marion retraced her steps, retaking her seat and her sewing. She was not particularly anxious to sew, but her heart had begun throbbing almost painfully at Layton's closeness, and she needed a moment's reprieve.

"Yes." Layton sat with an air of authority. "I believe I do want all the sordid details."

Double dungers! This could get sticky. Marion thought of the forged references she had given to Mrs. Sanders, of the various white lies she'd uttered since her arrival, a handful of facts she'd conveniently left out the few times she'd been compelled to speak of her history.

"There is not much to tell, I'm afraid."

"Which county did you call home as a child?" Layton—she liked having leave to think of him that way—obviously didn't mean to let her off so easily.

"Derbyshire." Marion wondered if he heard her longing. She missed home. "I've left that county only once in all my life. Before now, that is."

"I have been to Derbyshire many times. Whereabouts in that county?"

"Near Swarkestone," Marion replied. That was true enough. She prayed he didn't ask for any details.

"You've lived there all your life?" He watched her with obvious curiosity. Could he sense her reluctance to continue this line of conversation? Would he wonder why?

Marion nodded. "My father took me to London once when I was very young, younger than Caroline, in fact. That was the last time I left the area I still think of as home, until I was grown and needed employment."

"Why did you need employment, Marion?" Then, almost under his breath, Layton added, "That name is so much better."

Marion had to smile. She agreed with him on *that* point. "Why does anyone need employment?" Marion philosophized. "My financial situation quite suddenly reversed. It was either work or starve. I felt working the preferable course of action."

"Your family is genteel, then?"

"Quite." She had no intention of divulging more than that. "I once had dreams of putting servants in their places rather than being the humble recipient of such censure myself." She smiled, probably a little wistfully. She had had so many dreams once upon a time.

"Haven't you any siblings who might have looked after you?" Layton looked concerned, watching her with a level of scrutiny that made her nervous. There was only so much she could tell him without risking everything she'd worked for. "Surely your father must object to your seeking employment."

Lud, wouldn't he! "My father's objections have been rendered quite moot," Marion said.

"Ignoring his wishes—"

"My father is dead." She quickly got to her feet, suddenly very tired of the interrogation. "I do not wear gray because I am fond of it, nor because of my lowly station, which I assure you I do not need to be reminded of."

"Forgive me, Marion." The next moment, he stood beside her, taking the half-finished dress from her clenched hands and laying it carefully along an arm of the nearest chair. He looked at her, his embarrassment obvious. "I didn't realize . . . I hadn't intended to be unfeeling."

Now what had brought on the tears? Marion turned away from him, blinking furiously in an attempt to keep her emotions hidden.

"This is a recent loss, then?" Layton asked gently.

Marion nodded and brushed a fingertip across her cheek. She hadn't actually cried over her father's death in several months. What wretched timing!

"Did he leave you nothing, my dear?" She felt his light touch on her arms, just below the shoulder, as he spoke behind her. "Nothing for you to live on? Some kind of dowry?"

"He was a good man." Marion fought the urge to lean back against him, to share the burden of all she'd lost in the past twelvemonth. He seemed to care about her, seemed genuinely concerned for her. Would he object if she sought support? If she laid her head on his shoulder and sobbed out all the pain she'd buried inside herself during those, the worst three months of her life and the nearly nine that had followed since? She sighed at the uncertainty of it all and felt his fingers close a little more tightly around her arms. "My father was not one for planning ahead, I am afraid. He most likely assumed there would be ample time to provide for my future."

"I can be a procrastinator, Marion." Layton's breath ruffled the hair on the back of her head. "But I have already seen to Caroline's affairs, should something happen to me. It was arranged before she was born, signed the day of her birth. As her father, I could do no less. It would have been inexcusable."

Marion turned to face him, careful to step back a little to put some much-needed distance between them. Her heart hadn't stopped pounding since he'd interrupted her sewing some several minutes earlier. "Tell me, Layton. If you'd been faced with adjusting your will and arranging for future guardians and trustees for Caroline shortly after your late wife had died, could you have done it?"

She saw his face pale significantly and wondered if she'd erred in bringing up such a difficult subject. He seemed to struggle with an answer but finally managed.

"I would like to say I could have, would have done so somehow. Perhaps after a little time had passed." He shifted awkwardly. "I suppose I'm not entirely certain I would have been up to it. Her passing . . . *weighed* on me. Everything was hard after that, overwhelming."

"Exactly," Marion answered knowingly, her own thoughts filled with an "overwhelming" period in her own family's life. "After my mother died"—a break in her voice gave away her uncharacteristically raw emotions—"my father felt that same way. His melancholy grew over the months and years. He began neglecting things no gentleman would—even his children. It was as if his entire world had collapsed when Mother died, and he hadn't had the will to repair it. I believe he had always intended to make provisions for me when I was a little older, not wanting to think about death any sooner than he must. He hadn't anticipated—"

She couldn't finish. What a watering pot she had turned into! She offered a wet smile and a shrug of her shoulders at her own tumultuous emotions. He smiled a little shakily at her as well.

"What of your siblings?"

"A brother, three years older than myself. Robert. His future was written into Father's will when he left for Harrow. Mother died only a few months after he began there."

"Yes, you told me your father had gone to fetch him back when . . ." He didn't finish the sentence. He seemed to recover himself. "Robert couldn't take you in? Provide for you from his inheritance?"

Marion shook her head.

"He would be only twenty-three," Layton said. "Certainly he cannot have a large family to support already. Was his inheritance so paltry?"

She took a breath before forcing her answer. "Robert was buried the same day as Father." She simply let the tears flow. "They were buried beside Mother. My entire family lies in the frozen ground in Derbyshire now. And I am here."

She took a breath that came out as a sob.

"Oh, Marion." There was no pity in his tone, only heartfelt understanding. This man who had lost so much as well. That made the tears fall faster.

Layton remained beside her, brushing back a strand of hair as he handed her a handkerchief.

"I hope Caroline really did scrape all her junk off," Marion said with a tear-stained laugh.

Layton's chuckle joined hers. "You are refreshing, Marion." He smiled as she dabbed her eyes. "Bridget could never have laughed in the midst of her tears. At the end, there, the tears never stopped."

"My mother always said, if given the choice between crying and laughing, she'd much rather laugh."

"A philosophy I believe you embrace as well."

"Religiously," Marion admitted, her smile still watery but a little easier to conjure.

Layton's face grew quite serious. "Teach me, Marion," he said, hand cupping her jaw. "I need to laugh again."

"I have heard you laugh," she said, heart suddenly fluttering in her throat.

"That has been your doing." His thumb lightly brushed her cheek. "You are changing us all, performing your miracles."

His eyes fastened on hers, and his hand remained gently against her face. Not another word escaped him as he watched her, though she heard his breathing pick up pace. Hers followed suit. His gaze dropped for a moment to her lips before his jaw seemed to set and his eyes closed.

"I should go," he said with something like a frustrated sigh.

"It is getting late," Marion conceded, torn between wishing he would stay and feeling grateful that the tension he seemed to bring into the room would leave with him.

Layton nodded and stepped back. He took a long, deep breath. Marion did the same, but it didn't help. Her heart still fluttered, her mind felt muddled.

"I will scrape my junk off your linen and return it to you," she offered with a smile.

"Keep the handkerchief, Marion," he said, his look still intense.

"Keep it?" Snippets of a conversation with Caroline about gentlemen and handkerchiefs echoed in her mind, and her heart began pounding harder. He wanted her to keep it? As a token of some sort?

A sort of strangled moan resonated from Layton's throat. He crossed to her in two long strides, pulled her to him in a single fluid motion and kissed her, lips to lips, gentle, anxious, and far too short-lived.

"Keep it, Marion," he whispered as he pulled away then spun on his heels and left.

The spicy scent of him lingered after he'd gone. Marion lightly brushed her fingers along her lips. He'd kissed her! Kissed her on the mouth! And had given her his handkerchief.

Marion wrapped her arms around her waist, letting the tiniest of squeals escape as she spun in a circle. As improbable as she might have thought it an hour earlier, it seemed Layton felt the same as she did. Maybe, just maybe, he loved her too!

CHAPTER SEVENTEEN

LAYTON KNEW HE WAS SCOWLING. He hadn't slept a single minute of the previous night, his mind too full of Marion. *Marion.* Though he'd tried to convince himself otherwise, Layton was in love with her. She made him smile and laugh, somehow managed to free him now and then from his usual despondency. And what had he done? He'd kissed her! Therefore, Layton was scowling.

He, who had always prided himself on being a gentleman, had kissed a gently bred young lady who resided under his roof and hadn't a relative to her name to protect her. "If I ever hear you've mistreated a lady, young or otherwise, I'll box your ears until you cry like a little girl," Father had told each of his sons in turn before they'd left home for school at the start of each term. He'd always smiled as he said it, but they knew he meant it.

The only time Father had ever taken a switch to Layton had been after just such an occurrence. With Bridget, actually. When Layton was eight, Bridget had bested him quite soundly in a rock-skipping competition and had boasted of it for an overlong time, it had seemed to him. So he'd pushed her in the river. Father had tanned his hide after making him apologize to Bridget and Mr. and Mrs. Sarvol. It was one of the more humiliating encounters of his young life. But, to Father's credit, Layton had never misused a female since. That is, until Marion and that kiss.

Ah, that kiss. It had been utterly earth-shattering. Any doubts he'd harbored about his feelings for Marion had disappeared in that moment, not simply because he'd enjoyed kissing her, which he certainly had, but because the impossibility of their story having a happy ending had hit him so forcefully, and the realization hurt more than he could have imagined. It still hurt. If he'd felt less for her than he did, the pain wouldn't have been so intense.

She came from a genteel family, that much had been established. But genteel was hardly sufficient to overcome the unavoidable scandal that would arise from a marriage, for that was what he truly wished for with Marion. He had been out of society for so long that his own standing wasn't enough. They'd be ostracized. Bridget's untimely and somewhat suspicious passing would be brought up again. He'd gone to London briefly the autumn after she'd died to see to some business matters, and he'd more than once stumbled on a conversation speculating on what had led to Bridget's death.

Even Mr. Throckmorten, during his obligatory visit to Farland Meadows after Bridget's death, had wondered aloud at the oddity of one so young passing so suddenly. Layton had already endured months of pointed scoldings over Bridget's absence at church. If he were a capable husband and a decent Christian, the vicar had told Layton, his wife would have been present at services. Further, he would not have come to church himself looking burdened and depressed if he didn't have reason to feel guilty. If Bridget did not wish to go about with her family or have visitors in her home, she clearly was unhappy in her marriage. Layton had endured lecture upon lecture from the vicar but had mostly dismissed the criticism.

Until Bridget had died. Until he had lied about it. Until he had sold his soul for the sake of his dead wife and the child he would have to raise without her.

A misalliance, no matter how deeply he cared for Marion, would be fodder for those who chose to wonder about Bridget's passing and his own descent into near hermit-hood afterward. The harshest of gossips would cut Marion and likely him as well. Caroline's future would be jeopardized despite her being the heir to the title Layton would inherit when Mater passed from this life.

No. He couldn't do that to Caroline. She'd already been robbed of a loving mother, something for which Layton couldn't hold himself entirely blameless. Certainly he could have done more to help his wife, latched onto some indication of the direness of Bridget's situation that he ought to have seen.

And it wasn't only Caroline he worried for. Marion would hardly escape unscathed. There were names society associated with governesses who married above their stations: adventuress, jade, no-better-than-she-should-be. She would be made to endure cuts, disapproving glances, general unkindness. He could not put her through that, could not be the reason she would face such things.

She would simply have to be Miss Wood again. He would be the stiff, apathetic employer once more and put a careful distance between them.

Perhaps he ought to think about looking elsewhere for a wife. The very thought made him groan and no doubt deepened his scowl.

"Good morning." He knew that cheerful voice, but hearing it did little to lift his spirits.

"I thought you'd be at church this morning." Layton looked out over the river rather than at her.

"I returned nearly an hour ago," Marion said. "I have the remainder of the morning to myself so I came here."

"As always." Layton nodded. He knew she sat by the river every Sunday morning, no matter the weather. Though he would have denied it if asked, it was part of the reason he'd walked in circles around that part of the bank instead of his usual route toward Lampton Park. He wanted to see her again. To torture himself, he admitted inwardly.

Layton turned toward her, slowly, apprehensively. She wasn't sitting on the ground on a blanket, probably due to the fresh dusting of snow they'd received overnight. Instead, Marion stood near a tree, blanket wrapped around her shoulders, the wind blowing her amazingly red hair in all directions. And she smiled just as she always did, perhaps a little more brightly than usual—something he wouldn't have thought possible. She looked so obviously happy. He liked that about her—even in moments of sadness, an underlying joy followed her.

"Caroline enjoyed sitting with your family at church today." Marion's eyes twinkled happily as she spoke. "Lord Lampton escorted her from the family pew with all the deference he would show a duchess. It was all she could do not to giggle out loud, though I am certain Mr. Throckmorten would have disapproved quite vocally."

The vicar disapproved of most everyone and everything. Haughty superiority and blanket judgments were the man's specialty. Layton pushed his opinion of the vicar to the back of his mind.

"Flip always could pull a smile from her," he said. "The rest of us were happy if we managed to get her to speak."

"You have made her giggle more times than I can recall of late." Marion seemed almost to scold him for forgetting. "Hearing her speak of her 'silly' father, one would think you were a traveling performer."

Layton nearly smiled. Caroline *had* laughed several times and smiled at him whenever they were together. Here were more of Marion's miracles.

"You seem troubled." Marion stepped away from the clump of trees she'd been standing among and moved toward him.

The crisp, cold air suddenly smelled of cinnamon. Layton turned his eyes back to the river, barely holding back a tense, frustrated groan. Coming where she was, stopping to talk, hadn't been a good idea.

"I suppose I am a little tired," Layton answered stiffly.

"Or cold, more likely."

He felt those eyes on him, searching, studying. "Unless you are sporting a heavy coat beneath that blanket, you are probably colder than I am." Layton stepped a little closer to the riverbank and a little farther away from her. Distance was key.

"I am a little chilled," she admitted with a hint of a laugh. "I knew my excursion would be short today, but I had to come."

"Why is that, Marion?" Her Christian name slipped out before he had time to check it.

"Tradition, I suppose." Her offhand tone held a wistfulness that piqued Layton's curiosity.

"Another story?" he pressed.

"Of course."

"Well, then, I am eager to hear it." Layton turned back toward her and smiled, a mistake he recognized in an instant. She returned his smile, and it was all he could do not to kiss her again. Instead, he walked a little past her and leaned against a tree, hoping he looked suitably casual and unaffected.

"Once upon a time." She smiled a touch saucily, and Layton looked away as subtly as he could manage. "A handsome young man and a kindhearted young lady met and fell in love. They were married and soon had two children, a strapping son and a loving daughter."

Layton smiled in spite of himself at the familiar opening. He hadn't been expecting one of her storybook stories. Something in her tone when she'd told him her trips were tradition had led him to think this story would be a chapter from her own history.

"The kindhearted young lady was a very attentive mother and a lover of nature. Every Sunday, after church, she walked with her daughter along the banks of a mighty river, watching the birds in the sky, admiring the flowers during the spring, noting the changing leaves in autumn, searching for Drops of Gold in the winter when they stopped to sit beneath their amazing tree.

"Every week, they walked along the river, stopping in the same spot to watch and admire and share their thoughts and dreams. When the daughter was but a babe, her mother wrapped her in a blanket to keep her warm. As the daughter grew, she continued to wrap a blanket around her shoulders during their walks. Her father often joked that there was no need for clocks on Sundays with his two ladies keeping so rigorously to their schedule.

"They walked every Sunday without fail. Until one day when the young girl was all of ten. Sunday came and went without a single person walking that particular stretch of bank or sitting beneath the magnificent tree." Marion's expression grew strangely distant. Her tone lost most of its cheer. "The girl's mother was ill. Very, very ill. She told her daughter she wished they could walk again one more time. But by the next Sunday, she was dead.

"Her daughter never missed another Sunday walk nor the chance to sit along the river and watch. It was a balm for her grief and a tonic for the loneliness that would come afterward."

The story ended there, abrupt and unresolved. And Layton knew, suddenly understood, the truth about all of the stories: the handsome young man, the kindhearted young lady, their strapping son, and their loving daughter. This was Marion's family, her memories, her history. The Drops of Gold he'd so inconsiderately dismissed the first time she'd shared the idea with him were her connections to her past, to a much-mourned mother. The boy who'd accidentally shot his dog was her brother, the same brother who'd caused such ruckus at the dinner table. The father who'd laughed along, who'd searched out his son in the tragedy, was her father. The mother, who was so obviously the sunshine of the tiny family, was Marion's mother, the mother she still seemed to mourn heavily and for whose death she carried in her heart a feeling of responsibility.

"Oh, Marion," he whispered. How had this woman managed to brighten his life, his and Caroline's, so much when her own was so rife with tragedy?

She turned her face up to him. The shimmer of an unshed tear stood in stark contrast to the smile she offered. "I love to sit here—or stand, as it were—and think of her, to remember all of the things we spoke of. I have fished out more Drops of Gold in my twenty years than is probably advisable. I'm bound to expect something spectacular out of life after collecting so many harbingers of good fortune."

"Then the stories are true." He hadn't meant to sound so disbelieving, but the realization came as something of a shock.

"I always said they were." A chuckle softened the scold.

"Does Caroline realize you are telling her of yourself, of your family?"

"No." Marion shook her head. "There is a certain degree of anonymity to telling these things the way I have. I can warn Caroline against a few of my own childhood entanglements without being required to admit my folly." She laughed lightly, but a serious look crossed her face. She moved absently toward him. Layton welcomed the nearness, wishing pointlessly that she could always be at his side. "Eventually she will want to know how the story ends, what becomes of the family she now knows nearly as well as I do."

"And the story doesn't end well." Layton finished the thought for her. He barely resisted the urge to reach out and touch her hair as a breeze fluttered through it.

He heard her sigh before she said, "I think Caroline has endured quite enough tragic endings." Their eyes met, and Marion smiled a little tremulous smile. Layton's heart flipped in his chest. "I think we all have," she added.

"And yet you smile." Layton shook his head in amazement.

"Life has a way of repaying the prices it exacts along the way, making up for our losses. Knowing that, I have reason to hope, to believe things will get better."

"Optimism." Layton smiled. "You *have* been collecting those Drops of Gold." When had he taken hold of her hand? He didn't let go, just wondered how it had come to be there.

"Have I made you a believer, then?" She looked up at him with twinkling brown eyes and a playful smile on her lips. "You were rather unconvinced when I told you the story the first time. I wondered if you even believed there was such a thing as hope."

"Perhaps I just needed a few Drops of my own," he said, squeezing her fingers.

She didn't reply but continued to watch him, her eyes and smile soft and tender.

No, he didn't need a Drop of Gold. He needed Marion. How was he ever going to get on without her?

"Something *is* bothering you."

Gads, did he just whimper? He must have done something, made some kind of sound. Marion slipped her hand from his. He wanted to object, to plead with her to stay, if only for a moment, knowing in the end he'd lose her. He couldn't bear the thought and closed his eyes as if to shut out the world around him, the world that would keep them at a distance.

"Marion."

"I haven't left you, Layton."

He felt her hand press softly to his cheek. Layton pulled back, hating that he had to. He turned away, toward the river. Why did God hate him so much? To let him find Marion only after he could no longer have her, when his own past prevented any future between them? It was cruel, the kind of thing a vengeful Deity saw fit to inflict on an undutiful subject. Fitting.

"Layton?" The uncertainty in Marion's voice cut him to the quick.

"Your free time is probably nearly at an end." He kept his eyes firmly fixed on the Trent.

"I have nearly an hour remaining." A question hovered in her tone.

Stiff, apathetic employer, Layton reminded himself. Setting his features, he turned back. Marion watched him, a smile still on her lips. He knew his facade slipped a little. "It is growing increasingly chilly, Miss Wood."

She stared a little harder at his return to formality, brows drawing together in confusion, her smile slipping almost imperceptibly.

He pushed on. "You should probably return to the house before you catch cold."

"I am quite warm, I assure you."

"Miss Wood," he said in his most autocratic voice, "you can hardly perform your duties as Caroline's governess if you contract an inflammation of the lungs. I am asking you as your employer to return to the house."

"As my *employer*?" she asked, forehead wrinkling further.

He kept himself aloof, needing her to go, to give him room and time to adjust to the situation, to ready himself to see her every day and yet keep a proper distance, to reconcile himself to the fact that she was beyond his reach.

"But you said when it was just the two of us—"

"I should never have asked to be permitted such familiarity, nor should I have allowed it." His jaw tensed almost painfully. With a supreme effort, he kept his fists unclenched.

"Familiarity?"

"An overly friendly—"

"I know what it means, Lay—sir." She spoke over him, though she didn't speak loudly. Her smile had entirely disappeared, and her brow was drawn in consternation. "You said last night, you wanted to be . . . my friend."

"I do not believe that is a good idea." He reminded himself to remain firm. He needed distance.

Her somewhat blank expression dimmed visibly, a slight frown marring her usually cheerful face. Marion's fingers floated to her lips as if she were unaware she'd even made the gesture. "But I thought . . ." She little more than whispered. "You . . ." Her brow creased further. "We . . ." Her fingers remained pressed to her lips.

That kiss. He knew that was what she was thinking of. How could he apologize or say he regretted it? On some level, he did. But on every other level, he didn't regret it in the least. His only regret was that he could never do it again.

"I assure you, Miss Wood"—How it rankled to call her that when he still thought of her as Marion—"*that* will not happen again."

She mouthed a silent "Oh." Marion's hand dropped to her heart. All the color drained from her face, and for a fraction of a moment, she seemed to sway. Before Layton could so much as reach out for her, she steadied herself. She looked into his eyes once more, hers filled with confusion and pain.

Layton shoved his hands in the pockets of his greatcoat, the temptation to hold her to him, to kiss away her suffering, almost too great to resist.

"I believe it is growing cold, sir." Marion's eyes dropped to her feet, her voice nearly too quiet to hear. "I'll return to the house. And . . . warm up . . ." She didn't move for a moment or look up.

"A good idea." Layton forced himself to turn back toward the river. He couldn't bear to see Marion so downcast.

He stepped closer to the water, holding his breath as he waited to see what she would do. After a moment of thick silence, he heard her steps slowly crunching in the snow. As he watched the flowing waters of the Trent, a single yellow-tinged leaf floated closer to him.

"I've found a Drop of Gold, Mar—Miss Wood," Layton said and heard her footsteps stop.

He looked over his shoulder at Marion and saw her do the same.

"Would you like me to fish it out?"

She shook her head, a completely unfamiliar bleakness in her eyes. "No, Mr. Jonquil."

"But—"

"It's only a dead leaf, sir," she said quietly. "What good would it do?" Then, silently, shoulders slumping, she walked away.

CHAPTER EIGHTEEN

"Yes, Miss Wood?"

Marion froze on the spot and felt the blood drain from her face. "I'm sorry, sir," she answered shakily. "I didn't realize . . . I hadn't thought . . . I hadn't expected you to be in here. I apologize for interrupting you."

She managed the entire halting speech without once looking up at him. There was no need, really. She knew precisely what she would have seen. He'd be seated at his desk, reading papers or entering items in an account book, a pensive, brooding look on his face, golden hair a little mussed. Her heart would break if she had to look at him.

"Was there something you wanted?"

It didn't do to want things, she thought to herself. She had learned that lesson rather abruptly, rather painfully only two mornings before. She'd allowed her hopes to soar to new heights the night Layton had kissed her. She had thought he felt as much during that kiss as she had and that what he was communicating was truly the message he meant to send. The very next morning, she'd come crashing back to reality.

I assure you that will not happen again, he'd said as though he'd found kissing her utterly repulsive. Then he'd rebuffed her for the closeness that seemed to have grown between them. She hadn't realized until that morning along the banks of her beloved river that words could inflict physically painful wounds. Her heart still ached. Physically. Painfully.

"I . . ." She took a fortifying breath, suddenly nervous to so much as speak in front of him. Marion knew she'd have no trouble being an appropriately humble servant from then on. Nothing crumbled a young lady's pride like complete and utter rejection. It had most certainly put her firmly in her place. "I was returning *this*, sir." She hastily placed a precisely folded square of linen on the desk she knew Layton sat at then retreated a few steps almost frantically.

Every inch of her wanted to flee, run before he could hurt her more. But she was a servant, an employee, something he'd quite pointedly reminded her of. She couldn't leave until he dismissed her. So she stood still and aching, spine stiff and straight, eyes focused on the floor.

He didn't reply immediately, and she didn't dare look at him for a reaction. Knowing he sat there, completely indifferent to her—or, worse, thoroughly repulsed by her—made her ache. The pain that radiated through her when she thought of all that had occurred was at times almost overwhelming.

"Caroline and I have been invited to the Park this evening." Layton used precisely the tone the master of the house would use when addressing a servant. Marion's heart broke further at the sound, but she didn't flinch. She prayed her pain wasn't written all over her face. "As Mater is expecting it to be a late night, she has wisely suggested Caroline retire in the nursery there. There is no governess at Lampton Park, so you will be accompanying her."

"Yes, sir."

"Did you and Caroline ever have your birthday cake?"

The question was so unexpected and so quiet that Marion looked up at him. He wasn't watching her; his eyes were instead fixed on the glowing coals in the fireplace. He looked bothered by something.

"No, sir." She'd managed to convince Caroline that she'd had too much cake of late, what with Caroline's birthday, and that they ought to postpone the treat. She didn't happen to tell Caroline she intended to postpone it indefinitely.

"You should." Layton's eyes turned toward her. "It would certainly be an acceptable indulgence."

An acceptable indulgence? This after his speech about the unacceptable friendship that had arisen between them? He watched her, his expression unreadable. Was it possible he was laughing at her? That he knew what she'd come to imagine about his feelings for her and found it amusing? Amusing that the governess of all people fancied him in love with her?

Marion lifted her chin a fraction, forced her lips to not quiver, and summoned the tiny shred of dignity she felt she still possessed. She focused her eyes somewhere over his left shoulder as was proper for a servant. "I know my place, sir. I have been quite firmly put back there, and I assure you I have no intention of wandering from it again."

"M—"

"If I may be excused, sir. I will need to pack a few things for Caroline if she is to be away from her room tonight."

There was a long, heavy pause. Marion didn't allow her gaze to shift or her posture to slip. The increasingly familiar sting of tears behind her eyes grew tenfold, but she didn't allow a single drop to fall. She tensed her jaw to keep it from quivering and managed to keep her head held high.

She thought she heard Layton sigh. Then, in a somewhat strangled voice, he said, "Of course, Miss Wood. I am certain you have many things to do."

How she managed to reach the nursery wing without running or crying, Marion never knew. But when she saw her thrice-daily tray sitting beside the door bearing her usual cold midday offering, the tears began flowing anew. She would take another meal alone at the school table. She'd been received coldly by the staff before, but after her questionable inclusion in the family dinner on Caroline's birthday, she'd been positively unwelcome below stairs.

So much for her goal of gaining entry into that world, knowing she'd also lost claim to the one above stairs. Layton's attentiveness in the two months she'd been at Farland Meadows had lulled her into thinking she hadn't entirely lost her grip on the Polite World. Oh, how she'd been shown the folly of that assumption. As penance, she would now be entirely alone.

Caroline was five, so Marion could plan on spending the next eleven or twelve years closeted in the nursery with absolutely no one but the child for company. No wonder so many nurses had come and gone at Farland Meadows. It was a lonely, miserable existence, made vastly worse by her own poor decisions.

For a fraction of a moment, she was tempted to seek out another position in a household with less animosity amongst the servants and with anyone but Layton as her employer. But then Caroline's innocent, pleading face filled her thoughts, along with the heartwrenching question she'd asked the day they'd met: "Are you going to leave me too?" Marion knew she could never leave. She'd simply endure the isolation and love the child and hope it was enough.

Marion brought Caroline to the drawing room of Lampton Park shortly after dinner that evening. Only two ladies were present: Lady Lampton and a new arrival, Lady Cavratt. All but the youngest two Jonquil brothers were in residence, along with Lord Cavratt, who was considered an honorary member of the family. It was assumed, Marion overheard Lady Lampton say to the pretty young lady sitting beside her, that the gentlemen would linger over their port just as though they hadn't seen one another in years rather than the handful of weeks it had actually been.

The countess, however, was mistaken. Within seconds of Marion and Caroline's arrival, the gentlemen—a whole covey of them—stepped into the richly and tastefully appointed room.

"Papa!" Caroline cried out upon spying her father among the men whom no one with eyes could fail to identify as his brothers.

The Jonquils were all tall, golden haired, blue eyed, and, except for Layton, sleekly built. Where his brothers were trim, Layton was broad. The contrast made him stand out but not, in Marion's admittedly biased opinion, unflatteringly so.

The one darker-haired gentleman in the group crossed almost immediately to the woman seated at the countess's side, their mutual smiles of affection quickly identifying them as the married couple whom Lord Lampton had described at Caroline's birthday dinner as "nauseatingly in love with one another," though Marion was certain she'd detected a smile at the back of the earl's eyes as he'd said it. Captain Jonquil had remarked that he'd been ill more than once when forced into the combined company of Lord Lampton and his betrothed.

Marion, after noting that her charge was quite satisfactorily settled between her father and grandmother on a sofa not too far from the fireplace, slipped into a darkened corner, as was appropriate for a governess. She would have brought her dress to work on if she hadn't given up the entire enterprise two days earlier. Being the loveliest dressed person in the nursery, especially considering she was likely to be the *only* person in the nursery during the wedding, no longer held any appeal for her. Instead, she sat on a straight-backed chair near a planted fern and watched the stars twinkling outside a tall, diamond-paned window.

Nearly three quarters of an hour passed this way. Marion lost herself enough in memories of earlier days and happier years to render herself almost deaf to the merriment around her, almost oblivious enough to keep her own discouragement at bay.

Marion closed her eyes, quite tired of gazing at the stars as if they would offer balm to her wounded heart and shattered pride. *I assure you* that *won't happen again.* She'd been entirely unable to rid her mind of Layton's words or his tone when he'd said them. She still couldn't manage to think of him as Mr. Jonquil, though she would never address him as anything but. There had been a time when she might have reasonably hoped to be given that right without being labeled presumptuous. Her situation had not always been so lowly.

She heard footsteps approaching from behind, coming to a stop not far distant. A governess was not part of such gatherings, so she kept herself still and hidden in the shadows. She would be overlooked, as she was supposed to be, and the guests would hold their conversations without realizing she was even there.

"Your description of Layton's transformation led me to believe I'd find him back to his old self," one of the nearby guests said to another, as if trying to prevent his being overheard. Apparently, Marion had played her role well—she was entirely unnoticed and forgotten.

"I shouldn't have worn the lemon-yellow waistcoat," Lord Lampton replied in his instantly recognizable drawl. "Most likely, he's brooding in a fit of jealousy."

"Really, Philip," the first voice chided. "Can't you be serious for one moment?"

Marion opened her eyes again and looked in the direction of the voices. Lord Lampton and Lord Cavratt stood facing one another, Lady Cavratt on her husband's arm. Marion didn't move, didn't make a sound, but listened.

"Aside from the elegance of your waistcoat," Lady Cavratt intervened, "what do you suppose is weighing so heavily on your brother?"

"The exquisite cut of my jacket?" Lord Lampton suggested, preening himself a bit.

Marion watched Lord Cavratt's lips twitch in spite of himself.

"Let us overlook the splendor of your wardrobe," Lady Cavratt suggested.

"Impossible, m'dear." Lord Lampton waved his quizzing glass as if to swat away the inconceivable suggestion.

"How soon does Sorrel arrive?" Lord Cavratt asked as if she couldn't appear too soon.

"Friday." A slow, besotted smile spread across Lord Lampton's usually mocking face.

"Good," Lord Cavratt answered shortly. "By this time next week, she will have conveniently shoved that ridiculous quizzing glass—"

"Crispin!" Lady Cavratt cut him off.

Lord Lampton spluttered back a laugh. Lord Cavratt smiled as if he would very much like to laugh along. An interesting pair, those two: one who apparently *affected* to be a frippery sort and the other who went to great lengths to appear dour.

"I believe we are supposed to be plotting against your brother Philip," Lady Cavratt reminded the earl with a smile.

"'Plotting against?' You know, Catherine, there was a time when I thought you timid and impressionable," Lord Lampton replied with a chuckle and a little less of his usual idiotic overtones.

"And there was a time, Philip, when I thought you vain, careless, and not terribly intelligent," she quickly countered.

For this speech, Lord Cavratt kissed his wife gently on her blushing cheek, earning a smile from Lord Lampton. Lord Cavratt's arm settled around his wife's waist, but his eyes focused on Lord Lampton. "So what happened, do you think? With Layton, I mean?"

"I'm honestly not sure. Though I am told I am not terribly intelligent." He bowed slightly to Lady Cavratt, who blushed deeper and leaned her head against her husband's shoulder. "I assure you, he was in rare form Friday last. He smiled regularly. Laughed. Seemed much more the Layton we knew growing up. I thought he'd finally turned a corner, was getting past whatever has weighed him down all these years. Perhaps it was just my new dancing slippers—I was wearing them that evening, I should confess."

Lord Cavratt rolled his eyes, but his lady wife pressed on. "But *what* precisely has been weighing on him? Crispin has said many times how very much Layton has changed but has never indicated a reason for the transformation."

"If I knew precisely what the cause was, I would have addressed it years ago." Lord Lampton's tone turned perfectly serious and perceptive. The shift caught Marion's attention further. She found herself leaning ever so slightly forward to listen closer. "I first noticed a change after Caroline was born, though I am certain *she* is not the cause of his difficulties."

"Indeed. Caroline is the only person from whom he hasn't cut himself off," Lord Cavratt acknowledged.

"But then, Bridget, his wife," Lord Lampton added with a look at Lady Cavratt, who nodded her understanding, "was ill for several months after the birth. A mysterious illness at that. She didn't see anyone or go out. She died after only a handful of months had passed."

"Perhaps he is mourning for his late wife," Lady Cavratt suggested, though the others didn't look convinced.

Marion felt like shouting. *He feels responsible! He feels weighed down by lies and guilt!* If only they knew.

"Their marriage wasn't like that," Lord Lampton said. "They were fond of each other. Friends. But theirs wasn't a connection deep enough to account for his dropping out of life for losing her. He would certainly miss her, mourn her loss. It wouldn't have destroyed him like this though. There must be something more."

There is! Marion silently answered. They needed to know; they might be able to help him. And despite all of the pain she'd felt over the dratted man, she wanted to help Layton. She wanted someone to lift this burden for him.

"It seems to me you need to find out what that something more is," Lady Cavratt said.

"Believe me, Catherine," Lord Lampton answered, sounding almost fierce, "I have been trying for five years. I'd give anything to know."

CHAPTER NINETEEN

"Perhaps your uncle Flip would like to see the watercolors we created last week," Marion whispered in Caroline's ear two mornings later.

With an enthusiastic nod of her head, Caroline scampered from the schoolroom into her bedchamber. Soon the sounds of rummaging floated through the air. It would take Caroline several minutes to locate them, something Marion was counting on.

"That was well maneuvered of you, Miss Wood." Lord Lampton spoke with obvious curiosity. Marion watched him tug at his cobalt-blue waistcoat and flick an invisible speck of lint from the sleeve of his claret-colored jacket. "I assume you have some business with me."

He wandered to the schoolroom window, swaggering as always but quite obviously on his guard, every inch the aristocrat. He reminded her rather forcibly of Layton in that moment, of the facade he affected when he meant to squelch someone's—*hers*, usually—pretensions. Marion swallowed with some difficulty, telling herself she had to do this. *Had* to.

"Yes, my lord." Her voice quivered. *No need to feel unequal to the task*, she admonished herself. He was only an earl. She'd conversed with dukes and a marquess on a regular basis. Of course, she hadn't been a servant at the time.

Lord Lampton turned to face her, one golden eyebrow raised in almost haughty inquiry. He spun his quizzing glass on its ribbon as he waited.

"I know I am being terribly presumptuous in even addressing you, but, I—" She took a deep breath to steady her nerves. A slight hint of a smile pulled at Lord Lampton's lips, and she relaxed a fraction. Layton looked terribly like that when he was holding back a smile. Maybe she wasn't about to be eaten after all. "I . . . I have this . . . um, friend—No," she quickly corrected. "Acquaintance, let's say, who has this . . . problem . . ."

"Perhaps you ought to ask your employer for advice." Lord Lampton watched her a little more closely.

"That would not be a good idea, my lord. Believe me."

He chuckled lightly. "I believe you." His eyes grew a little less cold. "So what is the problem this acquaintance of yours needs so desperately to have addressed?"

"This person is more an acquaintance of yours than mine," Marion said, though she found the admission painful.

The smile disappeared from Lord Lampton's face, and Marion saw, for the first time, a man she would be ill-advised to cross. Her heart suddenly began racing. *You* must *do this*, she reminded herself.

"This person has a problem, Lord Lampton." She pushed the words out so quickly, she struggled to take in the air she needed. "I am not in a position to offer any help, but I know more of it than those who might be able to help him—*this person*, that is." She looked up nervously. No longer the empty-headed dandy, Lord Lampton was all earl at the moment. Had she made a terrible mistake? Marion thought of Layton's face, the agony she'd seen there when he'd related his difficult history. No. She *had* to help him.

"This person lost a loved one under less than ideal circumstances. She had been unwell, not in body so much as in mind. Melancholy to the point of . . . I'm not sure how to describe it." Marion felt flustered, trying to explain without bending confidences too far, needing Lord Lampton to understand something she didn't understand herself. "Without speaking ill of the dead, my lord, this particular lady seemed, by her own husband's description, though I think he hardly realizes the implication, almost . . . almost mad. Not in a violent or dangerous way. But unnaturally sad and despondent.

"I am told she refused to so much as hold her infant daughter, whose arrival she had apparently been quite eagerly awaiting. She spurned all efforts by her husband to comfort her."

Marion began talking faster, feeling guilty and afraid they'd be interrupted at any moment. She hadn't told Lord Lampton the identity of the person whose history she was spilling, but he listened, slowly nodding his understanding. She was as good as breaking her word to Layton. *For his own good*, she assured herself without much success.

"He didn't know what to make of it, what could possibly have caused such all-encompassing sadness. He kept it a secret, even from his family, hoping, I imagine, that she would improve somehow."

Lord Lampton pushed away from the window, his look one of pained concern as he began pacing. Marion kept herself glued to the spot as she rushed on through the recitation she'd practiced for hours the past two nights.

"She didn't die a natural death, Lord Lampton."

He looked at her then, eyes nearly as bleak as Layton's had been when he'd told her what she was telling his brother.

"He didn't want . . . He wanted to spare her and their daughter the disgrace of . . . of a . . ."

"Suicide's burial," Lord Lampton whispered, mercifully finishing the phrase for her.

Marion nodded as she pushed on. "So he kept it secret. The doctor ruled her death the result of a wasting illness, no doubt a favor to . . . this person. It was put about that she had died that way. He never told a soul otherwise. By then, I think, he was too beaten down and overwhelmed to know that they would have supported him rather than condemned him."

"Condemned him?" Lord Lampton asked, her words obviously causing him pain.

"He passed her death off as something it wasn't," Marion tried to explain. "Knowing what she'd done would have implications with the law and the church, he . . ."

"He lied." Lord Lampton nodded his weary understanding. "He lied to—"

"The government. The church. God."

Lord Lampton rubbed his face with his hands.

"That bothers him," Marion pushed the final confession out. "That he is perpetrating a fraud, especially against the Almighty."

"Of course it would." Lord Lampton sighed. Then he mumbled as if talking to himself. "He always was the most faithful of all of us. Even more so than Harry, just not as obnoxious about it. Lying to God would bother him a great deal."

"He told me he doesn't think God cares one bit about him," Marion said.

"So all these years, it wasn't grief."

Marion shook her head. "Guilt," she said.

Lord Lampton crossed the floor to her and grasped her hands for a moment. "Thank you, Miss Wood." He spoke with an intensity that, until that morning, she would have thought entirely foreign to him. "You are indeed a Most Honorable Governess."

Marion smiled at the reference to the last truly enjoyable evening she'd had. But the smile, she knew, didn't quite reach her eyes. She wasn't entirely sure about what she'd just done. "I was told all of this, no doubt, in a temporary fit of thoughtlessness," she hastened to tell him. "I was made to understand that it was quite a closely guarded secret."

"Do not worry, Miss Wood." Lord Lampton smiled reassuringly. "I have no intention of telling this 'close acquaintance' of ours that I am in possession of these new bits of knowledge. But they will prove more helpful than I think you know."

"It would mean my job and my integrity."

Lord Lampton raised his hand as if to swear an oath. "May my cravats wilt," he swore, "if I reveal the source of my information."

Marion smiled in spite of herself.

Lord Lampton's expression grew mischievous. "That is my betrothed's favorite of all my oaths."

"It can be trusted?" she asked, not entirely joking.

"Miss Wood." Lord Lampton's tone became serious once more. "I love my brother. Seeing him so nearly himself again only last week was among the happiest moments of my life. I have attempted for half a decade to accomplish what you have now put within my grasp."

"And, please, Lord Lampton, don't tell the vicar."

The request clearly surprised him. "Mr. Throckmorten is the absolute last person I would tell something of this nature. He would likely turn it into a sermon and denounce Layton to the entire neighborhood."

She'd had that thought herself. Indeed, the more Sundays she spent at Farland Meadows, the more convinced she was that Mr. Throckmorten had added to Layton's feelings of guilt.

"Thank you, my lord. And thank you for not telling Mr. Jonquil about this conversation. I don't want him to hate me any more than he already does."

"If he hates you so much, why are you doing this for him?"

She could feel the color rising in her cheeks. Regardless of his feelings for her, Marion loved Layton. She figured she always would. But it was more than that. In little more than a whisper, she said, "I want him to be happy."

"Then it seems, Miss Wood, you and I are allies and not enemies. So you needn't look so petrified the next time you find it necessary to speak with me."

"I am only the governess, my lord." Marion felt her low status more by the minute.

"In the Jonquil family, you are poised to be a heroine. Unfortunately, it seems I am the only one likely to know as much."

"I would appreciate that, my lord."

"Now, if I am not much mistaken, I am about to be accosted by mounds of watercolors." Lord Lampton quite suddenly appeared the very picture of a mindless dandy. How did he affect such an all-encompassing transformation so quickly? "Tell me, Most Honorable Governess, shall I clash?" He smoothed out his waistcoat.

"Not at all, Lord Lampton."

"Ah, the *mademoiselle d'art.*" He bowed rather theatrically, and Caroline giggled as she hurriedly crossed the room to where her Uncle Flip awaited her, paintings clutched in her tiny fingers.

Marion wandered to the window, watching the light flurries, wondering if she'd done the right thing.

CHAPTER TWENTY

LAYTON STOOD AT THE DOOR of the Lampton Park library and watched two of his brothers with confused interest. Philip and Jason, who historically tended to grate on each other, sat at a table, books and papers spread out in front of them, obviously in the midst of an involved and serious discussion.

"What is this, a council of war?" he asked, still leaning against the door-frame.

Philip looked up, the dandified, feather-headed expression he usu-ally wore absent. That, combined with Jason's uncharacteristically patient look—he was seldom indulgent, especially when faced with Philip, whose posturing seemed to irritate Jason more than any of the other brothers—made Layton wary. What *was* going on? Philip shrugged a little self-depre-catingly, a mannerism he once used quite regularly but which Layton hadn't seen in many years, since before Philip began acting like a fop. Now Layton really was worried.

"You see before you your usually resourceful elder brother with a rather sticky legal situation on his hands," Philip answered before turning his head back toward Jason and the papers they were perusing.

Layton's heart dropped into the pit of his stomach. "Are you in some kind of trouble, Philip?" He heard the panic in his voice. He crossed the room and took a seat beside his two brothers. Philip looked back at him and smiled, though a little uncomfortably. "The legal question isn't actually mine." He scratched the back of his neck. Gads, it was good to see him acting more like himself, at least somewhat serious, his actual smile and not the half smirk he usually wore. "A friend, actually. Good *ton* but not a lot of connections, you know. Not sure where to turn. Seems her—"

Layton raised his eyebrow at the "her." Knowing how ridiculously enam-ored Philip was of his betrothed, Layton couldn't resist a little good-humored jesting. Philip made an identical raise of his own eyebrow, and Layton chuck-led lightly.

"Her husband has fallen into a remarkably persistent state of blue-devilment, beyond what might be overlooked or explained away. I've flipped through a few of Father's books of medical terminology. This particular friend seems to be suffering from something termed 'chronic melancholia.'"

Layton's ears had pricked at the words "persistent state of blue-devilment." Philip might just as easily have been describing Bridget in those last few months. And "chronic melancholia"? Could there actually have been a name for it?

"Can anything be done for this man? This friend of yours?" Layton tried to sound casual. Had he missed something? Some treatment along the way that might have helped Bridget? "Cupping or some medicinal concoction?"

"It's nothing like that, Layton." Philip shook his head. "It's a condition of the brain, a form of madness, it seems."

"Madness?" The thought hadn't occurred to Layton during the time he'd watched Bridget deteriorate, nor over the years that had passed since. "Bedlam, then?"

Philip shook his head again. "It isn't a violent madness. He's hardly a danger to others."

"Only himself," Layton muttered, but Philip apparently heard him.

"That, of course, is the problem." Philip leaned back in his chair. "Every-thing possible is being done to ensure the man is watched and cared for, but there is no guarantee he won't do himself a harm. He has apparently hinted at such."

Layton nodded numbly, knowing all too well what this anonymous friend of Philip's was enduring.

"And should this gentleman follow through on his apparent intentions, his wife would be left in an unenviable state, to say the least."

Indeed, thought Layton.

"Aside from the emotional ramifications, which I am not in a position to address, I am seeking out her legal options," Philip said. "Which, as you know, is Jason's forte."

Layton looked at Jason, hoping his curiosity didn't strike either man as overabundant.

"*Felo de se*," Jason said in what Layton and Philip had always labeled his "barrister's voice": remarkably authoritative, considering he'd first affected it at the ripe old age of seven. "Suicide is a felony. And as such, any person guilty of said crime is punished, *post mortem*, with the forfeiture of all properties to the crown. This lady, being young and female, both of which are a liability, legally speaking, would be left penniless, without even her widow's jointure, on top of the burden of losing her husband."

"She could lie about his death," Layton suggested in what he hoped was a casual tone of voice.

"Depending on the circumstances of his death," Jason interjected. "Which I feel we must state is purely theoretical."

"This isn't a deposition, Jason." Philip rolled his eyes. "Don't be stuffy."

Jason's lips pursed, the look he assumed with alarming frequency when around Philip. Layton had never really understood the animosity. "As to lying," Jason went on as if there'd been no interruption, "that wouldn't be at all necessary."

"But you just said—"

"There are extenuating circumstances." Jason spoke with that tone of indulgence he used whenever someone showed what he considered to be a significant lack of understanding.

"Such as?" Philip looked over at Layton for a fraction of a moment, just long enough to roll his eyes, and Layton found himself smiling despite the topic. They had enjoyed baiting their younger brothers as boys.

"Suicide is only a crime if committed by someone capable of understanding their actions," Jason said, still using his barrister's voice. "Thus, a suicide committed by a child or by one who is mentally incompetent would not be considered a crime. There are no ramifications, legally speaking."

"And this 'chronic melancholia' is considered a form of madness?" Layton asked, his head spinning.

Jason nodded. "There is apparently sufficient evidence to establish that the man is, indeed, mad and, therefore, mentally incompetent. The difficulty will be in balancing the need to declare him such should an unfortunate event take place with the necessity of keeping that diagnosis secret for the interim. She could lose control of all of her affairs should her husband be declared mad during life, her being—"

"—young and female," Philip finished for him. "Therein lies the issue."

Layton nodded absently. *Mentally incompetent. No legal ramifications.* The words swirled and collided in his mind. He'd never considered that Bridget might be excused, at least on a legal level, for what she'd done. She really hadn't been herself those last few months, especially at the very end. "Mentally incompetent" seemed the perfect phrase.

Chronic melancholia.

Madness.

Hundreds of tiny memories, seemingly insignificant moments, flashed through Layton's mind. The time Bridget had asked him if he was home from Cambridge for a visit and seemed genuinely confused when he explained that he'd been out of Cambridge for several years. Or when he'd come into her sitting room to find her having tea with someone who wasn't there at all, deep in conversation. She'd become absolutely infuriated when he'd asked to whom she was speaking.

So many things like that.

Philip and Jason continued discussing the case. Layton rose slowly, thinking.

"Layton?" Philip asked.

Layton waved him off and wandered to the door. He debated with himself all the way down the corridor, out the front doors, and onto the front lawn of the Park.

Had Bridget really been mad? No one in her family had ever suffered with madness. Not that Layton knew of, at least. If she had truly lost her faculties, what had brought it on? Certainly not old age or poor health.

He couldn't entirely convince himself. It seemed so drastic a diagnosis. And yet, it fit almost perfectly.

"Papa!"

The sound snapped Layton from his thoughts, and he realized, with a great deal of surprise, that he'd wandered all the way to the edge of the Meadows property. Caroline was running toward him, braids bouncing behind her, cheeks pink from the chill.

How would he explain any of this to Caroline? When would he? He didn't completely understand it himself.

Layton bent down mechanically to pick Caroline up, a movement he'd made so many times it didn't require thought. The debate continued in his mind without reaching any real conclusion.

"Are you sad today too, Papa?" Caroline asked as she ran her fingers up and down across his cheek the way she did when checking for stubble.

"'Too,' poppet?" he asked, finally managing to concentrate on his daughter.

"Mary is sad," Caroline said, a little pout on her lips.

"How do you know she's sad, dear?" Layton thought uncomfortably of the unintentional encounter of a few mornings earlier when Marion's unhappiness had been readily apparent. She'd borne it off well but hadn't been able to entirely disguise the telltale quivering of her chin. The pain in her eyes was so raw Layton had nearly thrown away Caroline's entire future and begged Marion to forget everything he'd said and stay with him, to accept social ostracism and be his wife, to trust him enough to put *her* fate in the hands of a man who was such a dismal husband that his first wife actually took her own life.

"She doesn't smile as much," Caroline answered. "And she isn't as silly."

Smile *as much*. Isn't *as silly*. Marion, that wonder of optimism and eternal hope, still smiled and enjoyed Caroline despite her unhappiness. So different from Bridget.

"She isn't going to leave me, is she?" A mountain of worry sat in Caroline's words. "All the others did."

The other nursemaids, she likely meant. They had gone through quite a few. If memory served, they'd all seemed remarkably unhappy before they'd left. He'd never kissed any of *them*, so that could hardly be *his* fault. Could it?

"Have you asked your Mary if she is planning to leave?" Layton's heart constricted painfully at the thought of Marion leaving the Meadows—though, in all honesty, he'd given her very little reason to remain and quite a good reason to go.

Caroline shook her head. "I don't want her to go, Papa." She leaned her head against his shoulder and played with the top button of his waistcoat.

Approaching footsteps saved him from needing to answer, which would have been tricky. Caroline was apt to repeat the things she was told. Layton looked in the direction of the footsteps.

Marion.

The air caught painfully in his lungs at the sight of her. That red hair he'd come to love so well. The pert mouth so often turned up in a smile. A few steps closer, and he'd be able to smell cinnamon. But she stopped, her eyes averted like a proper servant.

She was paler than she had been, and her eyes seemed a little puffy and red rimmed. She'd been crying, though she held herself perfectly calm and still at the moment.

"Miss Wood," he managed to get out while thinking, *Oh, Marion*, quite hopelessly in his mind.

"Mr. Jonquil." She curtsied.

"Your daily exercise?" Layton asked her.

Still, no color returned to her cheeks. "Yes, sir. We were nearly ready to turn back when Caroline spotted you."

"I am glad she did." He felt Caroline wrap her arms more tightly around his neck. "I will walk back with you two."

"No," Marion answered a little too quickly and far too forcefully. She quickly corrected herself and continued more demurely. "Caroline, I am certain, would appreciate your escort back. I will return more quickly. There is a lot to do before the wedding, sir."

"Miss—"

But she had already gone. *Fled* would be a good description.

"Come back," Layton silently pleaded, though he knew he had no right to. "Don't you leave me too."

Philip was a wreck! Layton watched him pace in front of the dark library windows, watching the barely discernible front drive. Miss Sorrel Kendrick, his intended, was supposed to have arrived that morning.

"Staring out the window is not going to bring her here any faster." Layton tried to hold back his amusement.

Philip looked over his shoulder and offered a self-mocking smile. "I know." He laughed at himself, his dandified mannerisms once again entirely absent. Philip's head snapped back in an instant as the sound of carriage wheels broke the silence outside.

"Has she arrived, then?" Layton asked.

Philip's grin was all the answer he needed.

Layton followed his elder brother to the front steps, where the Kendrick women were alighting from their carriage. The youngest member of the family, Mr. Fennel Kendrick, would be arriving in two weeks' time, accompanied by the youngest Jonquil, Charlie, as both boys were currently at Eton. The patriarch of the family was dead these several years, thus the widow Kendrick and her two daughters arrived on their own.

Philip offered the appropriate greetings to Mrs. Kendrick, whom Layton recognized easily from his short stay in Suffolk over Christmas. The girlish ribbons and bows and flounces gave her away rather quickly, so out of place they looked on a matron of indeterminate years. The younger sister, Miss Marjoram, was the next up the steps, all dainty, feminine beauty. But Philip, Layton noticed with a smile, was anxiously watching the carriage.

Miss Sorrel Kendrick finally emerged, awkward on a stiff, uncooperative limb and leaning heavily against her walking stick. Layton never had learned the reason for her near-crippled state.

"You are late, my love." Philip swung his quizzing glass in one hand as he offered her the other.

"I assumed you would need the extra hours for your valet to complete his ministrations," Sorrel replied, eying him with amused mockery.

"He has done admirably, hasn't he?" Philip swaggered a little more as he walked her up the stairs.

"Yes, he's made you almost presentable," came the dry reply.

Those two were well suited, Layton thought to himself. He'd felt it from the moment he'd met his future sister-in-law, though there had been no understanding between the two of them at the time.

Philip was obviously about to make some glib reply when Sorrel's leg seemed to give out beneath her and his smirking expression immediately melted into one of concern. "Are you hurt?" He had quickly wrapped a supporting arm around her waist.

She shrugged, though Layton thought she looked embarrassed. He stepped a little farther from the doorway and, hopefully, out of sight. "I don't travel well," Sorrel explained as though it were a shameful admission.

"I know." Philip's hand gently caressed Sorrel's cheek, a gesture almost poignantly loving.

Layton felt a pang of something—jealousy, regret—watching them. To love so much and be so obviously loved in return. It seemed entirely out of his reach.

"Fortunately for you, your betrothed is quite unbelievably strong." Philip moved to apparently lift Sorrel into his arms.

"Philip," she protested. "I am not an invalid. I am perfectly capable of—"

"Pax, Sorrel!" Philip held his hands up in surrender. "I am not attempting to demean your abilities or capabilities or anything of the sort."

She didn't look entirely mollified.

"I am simply being shamefully selfish."

"Selfish?"

"Seeing the woman he loves in pain without being able to alleviate her suffering is the worst possible experience for any man." Philip grew quite serious and unaffected. "I'd like to avoid that rather acute torture. With your permission, of course."

Sorrel pressed a quick, affectionate kiss on her fiancé's lips and whispered, "I love you, Philip."

"It's the jacket, isn't it? Weston, you know." Philip smiled haughtily. How did Sorrel put up with his constant transformations?

"If you are done extolling the virtues of your tailor, I would appreciate your getting back to the business of alleviating your apparent torture," Sorrel answered in a voice of command.

Philip laughed and lifted her easily into his arms. "What do you say we pass by the drawing room and scandalize my enormous family."

"I seriously doubt they would be scandalized by anything you do, Philip."

His laughter faded as the couple happily disappeared down the corridor.

Scandalized? Hardly. Mostly, Layton felt lonely. He longed to have someone to talk to the way they did, easily, with the familiarity that comes from a deep-seated understanding of one another. Conversations had often been that way with Bridget before Caroline was born. Theirs might not have been a love match, per se, but they'd had a friendship of long standing that easily bred contented companionship.

He'd found that companionship again with Marion. It had come so quickly, so effortlessly, that he couldn't say when the connection had been forged. And as that connection had persisted and grown, he'd come to love her as he'd loved no one else before. He'd found the possibility of happiness . . . and it was pointless. Heaven had arranged that.

He'd failed Bridget so entirely. Despite the idea of her illness being a form of madness, something out of his sphere of understanding, Layton couldn't entirely shake the thought that somehow he'd been responsible. If only he'd been a better husband, if only he'd loved her more, treated her better, then perhaps she would have recovered or even been well to begin with.

Philip was right. Seeing someone you cared for in pain was an awful experience. First, Bridget struggling with whatever it was that had afflicted her, rebuffing his futile efforts to help her. Then Marion, such soul-wrenching pain in her eyes every time he'd encountered her since his ham-fisted explanation of their situation.

Suppose things had been different, that he'd had enough standing in society to weather the scandal a union between them would create? Suppose she hadn't been a governess at all? He still wasn't sure he could have married her. He'd only fail her like he had Bridget. He couldn't see her go through that.

Yes. Philip was right. *Acute torture.*

CHAPTER TWENTY-ONE

THE WEDDING GUESTS HAD BEEN arriving for two days, though nearly a month remained before the ceremony. Marion had overheard Stanley telling a fair-haired beauty, whom she'd come to understand was the younger sister of the bride-to-be, that everyone was so shocked that someone had actually agreed to marry his oldest brother that no one who knew the earl could do anything but engage in a weeks-long celebration.

Thus far Marion had managed to keep to the nursery wing throughout the inundation. She and Caroline were seldom at the Meadows. They would climb into the Farland carriage and make the ten-minute drive to Lampton Park. Layton likely would have forgone the carriage altogether except for Caroline's obvious enjoyment of it all. She said more than once that she felt very grown-up being driven about.

Marion loved watching Caroline, loved her enthusiasm over such small, simple things. Seeing that excitement never failed to bring a smile to Marion's face. Often during their carriage rides, she would look to Layton, wondering if he found his daughter's elation as captivating as she did. Inevitably, their eyes would meet, and Layton would smile at Marion for the briefest of moments before resuming his more somber expression. That fleeting connection between them wrenched her heart anew, and yet, she enjoyed it. She never stepped out of place, always diverted her eyes the very next moment, and didn't speak. Layton didn't speak to her either. Caroline obligingly filled in what would have been an awkward silence.

Twice a day they made the journey. Once to the Park. Once back. Layton took Caroline to the drawing room, where she was oohed and ahhed over. Marion took herself to the nursery wing, where she sat alone and waited. She quietly collected Caroline in time for her luncheon then sat again as the girl slept. It was quiet and peaceful and miserable.

But, she told herself, at least she hadn't seen any of the guests. Until the first morning of new arrivals, Marion hadn't thought through her particular entanglement. Despite Father's having been a veritable recluse during the last ten years of his life and the isolated nature of their existence in the years before that, there was a slight possibility someone among the guests would recognize her. That, she knew all too well, could be disastrous.

"Miss Wood." A male drawl broke Marion from her musings the third morning of what she had come to think of as her exile to the nursery wing of Lampton Park.

"Lord Lampton." She rose and curtsied.

"May I introduce you to my betrothed, Miss Sorrel Kendrick."

Marion exchanged curtsies with the dark-haired beauty, noting as she did that Lord Lampton's future wife significantly favored one leg. She seemed so comfortable with her walking stick that Marion came easily to the conclusion that the condition was not a new one. If Lord Lampton could overlook what most gentlemen would consider an insurmountable flaw in his beloved, why couldn't his brother have loved *her*? She was a servant, true enough, and red haired and outspoken to boot, but were those such horrific shortcomings?

"I have heard a great deal of praise for you, Miss Wood," Miss Kendrick said.

Marion flashed a concerned glance at Lord Lampton. How much had he told his betrothed of their last and only conversation?

"But not too much praise, I assure you." Lord Lampton's look was one of detached amusement. He was in his disguise again, though why he insisted on affecting a cover, she couldn't say. "I would hate to have my dear Sorrel bash you over the head with her infamous walking stick in a fit of jealousy."

Marion saw Miss Kendrick roll her eyes and knew that she was fully aware of her intended's playacting and that she loved him despite it, or perhaps, to a degree, *because* of it. She felt a pang of jealousy, wishing in that moment that the man she loved could love her despite her situation. Could love her *at all*, she corrected herself.

"The countess has sent me to you to address a domestic matter," Miss Kendrick continued on. Marion sensed a certain nervousness in her manner. "It seems my training is to begin early."

Training to be the countess, no doubt. No wonder Miss Kendrick was nervous. Generally speaking, most misses were not raised to be countesses, just as most ladies were not raised to be governesses. Marion understood what it was to feel out of one's place and learning an entirely new role.

"How may I be of service, Miss Kendrick?" Marion hoped to put the future Countess of Lampton at ease.

"A family—guests—due to arrive soon, will be bringing with them both a governess and a nursemaid," Miss Kendrick said, obviously thinking through her words as she said them. Marion softened her servant's demeanor with the slightest empathetic smile. "We thought perhaps you would appreciate the opportunity for some occasional time to yourself. But I had wondered about Miss Caroline. I was told"—she sent an accusatory glance at Lord Lampton—"that Miss Caroline was likely to be easily overwhelmed by groups of people, though I am beginning to think my fiancé's word is not to be trusted."

"His assessment is, I assure you, not so much inaccurate as it is out-of-date." Marion barely kept back a laugh at the teasing tone of Miss Kendrick's words and the almost theatrical look of wounded innocence Lord Lampton assumed. "Miss Caroline is greatly changed over these past two months."

"Since your arrival, Miss Wood?" Lord Lampton asked with a lightness that didn't ring entirely true.

"Those are words waiting to be twisted, Lord Lampton. I think I would do best not to answer."

"My approach as well, Miss Wood." Miss Kendrick smiled at her. "Do you believe Miss Caroline will adjust to having her nursery inundated?"

Miss Kendrick was obviously a no-nonsense, straightforward kind of person, rather different from Marion, but Marion felt entirely at ease with her. Under different circumstances, they might very well have been friends.

"I cannot say how Caroline will react," Marion said, "having never seen her under similar circumstances. I can always take her back to the Meadows should she seem overwrought."

Miss Kendrick smiled in obvious relief. Yes, they would have been friends, indeed. Miss Kendrick smiled up at Lord Lampton, whose expression matched her own. "It seems your mother gave me an easy task. Or perhaps I am better at countess-ing than I thought."

"Both, I imagine," Lord Lampton replied.

"I was also instructed to have a look around while I was up here," Miss Kendrick said, looking around with a little blush.

"That's Mater." Lord Lampton laughed. "She dotes on grandchildren."

The remark sent a furious red blush across Miss Kendrick's face, something Marion would have had a hard time imagining had she not seen it.

Looking very much like she was escaping, Miss Kendrick limped across the large play room and began peeking into the adjoining rooms.

"Well, Miss Wood," Lord Lampton said, his voice low, "I think you should know that you have made a liar of me."

"I . . . what?"

He straightened his bright red waistcoat and continued, as if offhand. "I had to tell my brother a Banbury tale about a nonexistent London acquaintance in order to make use of the information you provided me with."

"What did you learn?" Marion asked then quickly checked her tone. "If I may be permitted to ask."

"A great deal, so far." Lord Lampton's eyes never left Miss Kendrick as she slowly inspected the nursery wing. "The condition your 'friend's' wife suffered from has a name, it seems, and is recognized by many noted physicians as a form of madness."

"Madness?" She whispered the word, knowing somehow that the diagnosis was of utmost significance.

"The law doesn't condemn a person for doing what this individual's wife apparently did if that person is mad," Lord Lampton quickly explained as Miss Kendrick slowly made her approach. "I managed to get that information to him in what I hope was an inconspicuous manner."

"What of the views of the church, Lord Lampton?" Marion pressed. "I think God's condemnation has weighed on him most."

"I am still deciphering that question, Miss Wood."

In the next moment, arm in arm, Lord Lampton and the future Lady Lampton left the nursery wing. Marion allowed a breath of relief. She had helped Layton. It didn't make him love her. But she'd helped.

⁓

"Hartley!" Philip jovially greeted His Grace with the ease of an old friend, one of the growing list of friends Layton and Philip didn't have in common.

"Still posturing, are you, Lampton?" The duke slapped Philip firmly on the shoulder. "Thought you'd give that up now that you're settled."

"*Nearly* settled," the Duchess of Hartley corrected her husband with a teasing smile. "If his *dame de l'amour* does not object to his acting like a babbling fool, why should you?"

"That was not terribly helpful to my cause." Philip raised an eyebrow at Her Grace.

She returned the gesture with a cold, cutting glance down her very fine nose. Philip laughed and raised his arms in surrender.

"She does that well, does she not?" His Grace smiled affectionately at his wife, much as one would expect a very newly married couple to do, though Layton knew they'd wed nearly ten years earlier.

"She is positively terrifying!" Philip even managed a dramatic shudder.

The duchess, however, had already regained her usual gentle expression. She turned her gaze to Layton. *"Monsieur Layton."*

The proper greetings were exchanged, followed by polite inquiries into the health of each other's children.

"Already quite happily settled in the nursery," His Grace said of his own brood.

Layton's mind almost immediately focused on his own ladies in the nursery. Despite his best efforts, Layton's affection for Marion remained unchanged. If anything, his feelings had intensified. He looked forward to their twice-daily rides to and from the Park. It was the only time she smiled at him anymore. He found he needed those smiles.

He worried about her. Marion hadn't regained much of her coloring over the last two weeks. She still looked pale, fragile, hurt. While the idea that Marion might be nursing a broken heart was at least a little gratifying, he hated himself for what he seemed to be putting her through. Surely she understood the impediments, the whys of their necessary separation.

Did she know how much he loved her? Layton wondered. That he depended on her enduring cheerfulness? Admired her honesty? Adored her dedication to Caroline?

A rap on the door snapped Layton back to the present. Philip and the duke and duchess had crossed to a far window at some point while Layton had been woolgathering. Only he watched the door as it opened.

Marion! Almost as if he'd conjured her up just by thinking about her.

"Hello," he quietly greeted, knowing he smiled too largely for propriety.

Her entire face lightened for a moment, an answering smile on her lips. "Might I speak with you about the nursery, sir?"

That "sir" broke his heart, even as he memorized every nuance of her smiling face.

"Of course." He heard the sounds of Philip and the Hartleys moving toward them.

Marion opened her mouth to tell him something, but the duke's voice broke in. "Marion!"

Her head snapped up instinctively. Layton watched her, glanced at the duke, then looked back at Marion again. She smiled broadly, and tears gathered in her eyes.

"Roderick!" she exclaimed and positively ran past Layton to the duke's outstretched arms.

She hugged him enthusiastically then did precisely the same thing to the duchess, who held her far too tightly and far too long to be anything but a dear friend.

Had Marion just called the Duke of Hartley by his Christian name?

"What are you doing here?" His Grace asked, sounding genuinely confused. "We were planning to stop by Tafford after Lampton's wedding."

Then Marion unaccountably began to sob. Layton began crossing to her but checked himself.

"*Ma pauvre amie.*" Her Grace stroked Marion's hair, an arm reassuringly draped around her shoulders, precisely what Layton would have liked to do. "Come now. We will find you a cup of tea and wash your face. You will feel much better, you shall see." She looked up at Philip. "Where is Lady Marion's bedchamber?"

Lady Marion! The look of shock on Philip's face must have mirrored Layton's own.

"Never mind." The duchess waved off the answer she had been awaiting. "She can come to mine."

Without a single word of explanation or even a fleeting look at Layton, Marion left, crying into the lacy handkerchief the duchess lent her. If she hadn't returned the one Layton had asked her to keep, she could have used *his*!

"What is going on?" Philip demanded the moment the door closed.

"I might ask the same thing," His Grace said. "Lady Marion's whereabouts have been unknown for several months. A discreet search has been conducted with no results. Until now."

"*Lady* Marion?" Philip shook his head in obvious disbelief.

"Yes. Lady Marion Linwood."

"Linwood," Layton muttered under his breath. Not Marion Wood, then. He digested that bit of information. Mary was a perfectly unexceptional pet name for Marion. He'd thought nothing of that discrepancy. But to give him the wrong surname was tantamount to hiding her very identity. She'd pretended to be someone she wasn't. She'd lied to him.

"Linwood!" Philip seemed shocked. "As in the Marquess of Grenton's family?"

"Her father, *late* father, I should say, was the Marquess of Grenton, a friend of my late father."

The Marquess of Grenton. Marion had told him her family was genteel. The family of a marquess was far more than that. She hailed from the aristocracy. She was a lady of rank and position and title. She had to have known *genteel* didn't correctly describe her upbringing. She had to have known that word alone was deceptive.

The duke continued his explanation. "My parents and I spent our summers in Derbyshire, near Tafford: Grenton's seat. Marion and I grew up quite as brother and sister. I didn't realize you knew her."

"Obviously we didn't," Layton grumbled as he paced to the window. He hadn't even known her real name.

"She has been employed as Caroline's governess," Philip explained behind him.

"Governess!"

"I didn't realize her rank when she was hired," Layton defended himself. "She presented herself as Miss Mary Wood and never bothered to correct that misrepresentation."

"Why would she invent an identity?" Philip asked to no one in particular. "Hire herself out as a servant? Why the need to dupe all of us?"

She'd said she had no money, that she'd been destitute. Was that even true? All the things she'd told him of her family, of her circumstances, had it all been fabricated?

Layton had opened his very soul to Marion, and she had never even told him who she really was.

CHAPTER TWENTY-TWO

MARION OPTED TO SNEAK UP the stairs to the nursery the next morning. Adèle and Roderick had taken great pains to explain to her that she was, as of that moment, no longer employed by Mr. Jonquil and that she was remaining at the Park as a guest of the Duke of Hartley. Her reputation and social standing quite depended upon it. And, they assured her, neither were entirely in shreds. Being the daughter of a marquess was not without its benefits. Although, growing up, the greatest benefit she'd ever seen in it was sitting beneath a shade tree with her family. They were not particularly hung up on their rank.

Despite now being gowned in splendid clothing, thanks to her being quite close in size and height to Adèle, Marion was unhappy. She missed Caroline. So she slipped into the nursery wing, hoping to go unnoticed.

"Mary!"

Perhaps not entirely unnoticed.

"My darling girl!" Marion exclaimed, clasping the child to her fiercely. "How I missed you last night."

"Papa read me a story and tucked me in," Caroline reassured her. "He said you will not be my governess anymore." She spoke as if completely convinced her father was short a brick or two.

"I am afraid not, dearest," Marion said.

Her lips stuck out in a pout. "He said your name is not really Mary."

"My given name is Marion," she confessed. "Mary is short for Marion."

"Oh." That seemed to settle *that* question. "I like Marion better."

"Do you?" Layton had said the same thing.

Caroline nodded. "Everyone has been calling you *Lady*. Do I need to call you that?"

"Do you remember when I first came to Farland Meadows," Marion asked, "and you said you wanted to be just plain Caroline because that would mean that we were friends?"

Caroline nodded, wide-eyed.

"I would like you to call me Marion or Mary. Because we are friends."

The look of confusion hadn't left Caroline's eyes, and Marion began to worry. Was it all too much for the child to take in? Had she lost the girl's trust?

"Why won't you be my governess anymore?"

Marion sighed and searched for the correct words. "I would like to take Caroline down to the library," Marion informed the reigning governess, using the lady of the manor voice her mother had schooled her in when she was as young as Caroline. The governess seemed to hesitate for a moment then reluctantly agreed. "Come with me, Caroline," Marion instructed. "I will tell you one more story."

The library was empty, just as Marion had hoped. She sat down on a royal-blue brocade window seat and pulled Caroline onto her lap. For a moment, she simply held the girl and looked out over the snow-covered grounds of now-familiar Lampton Park. She liked it nearly as well as Tafford, where she'd grown up, but not as much as she adored Farland Meadows. Despite the staff who disliked her and the initial feeling of suffocating sadness in the house, she had grown to love it and rejoice in the slow transformation she'd seen there.

"Is this story about that family?" Caroline asked, snuggling close to her.

"Mm-hmm." She hugged Caroline tightly for a moment. "That family in all of our stories is *my* family, Caroline. My real family."

"Really?" Caroline sounded amazed.

"The handsome young man is my father. The kindhearted young lady is—"

"Your mother?" Caroline guessed.

"Yes. The strapping son is my brother, Robert. And the loving daughter is—"

"You!" Caroline said in obvious amazement.

"And all the things I told you about the Drops of Gold and the silly pepper and so many other things"—she squeezed Caroline as she said it, and the angel-child giggled—"are all true things that actually happened to my family while I was growing up."

"You told me they were positively true."

Marion realized Caroline had never doubted her claim. Ah, the faith of a child! "Well, I need to tell you some things about my family, dearest, so you will understand why I cannot be your governess anymore." Marion felt Caroline nod her head silently. She could tell the poor girl was nervous. "When I was a young girl, several years older than you are, my mother became very ill. Though we cared for her and did our best to make her well again, she didn't get well."

"Did she die?"

"She did," Marion answered plainly, honestly.

"Were you sad?"

"Yes, I was. I still am sometimes because I miss her." Marion held Caroline and thought of times like this with her own mother, being held when she was confused or tired or sad or happy. It was both a comforting recollection and a painful one.

"But I still had my father and brother, and we were happy together. When my brother was all grown-up, he decided he wanted to be a soldier and help the other soldiers who were fighting in the war." Marion pushed down the burning lump in her throat.

"Like Stanby?"

"Yes, dear," Marion whispered. Tears stung her eyes, and her throat felt like it was closing off. She sat silently for a moment, trying to regain enough composure to continue. Marion was determined that Caroline know she was not being abandoned and that Marion's change of situation in no way meant she had stopped loving her. "My brother Robert was brave. He wanted so badly to keep his family and his country safe."

"Was he a good soldier, Mary?" Caroline asked.

She hesitated as she thought back on his letters. "I *think* he was," she answered frankly.

"I know he was," a voice declared.

Marion looked over her shoulder. Captain Stanley Jonquil stood watching her, a look of pain on his face. Marion wiped at a tear trickling down her cheek but didn't release Caroline. "You knew my brother?"

"Lieutenant Robert Linwood, Viscount Yesley. Fifteenth Light Dragoons," Captain Jonquil confirmed, crossing the room to sit on the wide window seat then turning to look at her and Caroline. "We all called him Bobert."

Marion nodded. "He wrote about his nickname."

"Everyone called him all sorts of a fool for joining up, he being the heir to a marquess and no spare. But none of us would have felt as confident going into combat without him there. I fought with the Thirteenth, but I knew him well."

The tears flowed faster, pictures of a smiling boy pushing her in a swing, teaching her to snatch sweet biscuits from under Cook's nose, running across Tafford with his loyal dog, returning wet-cheeked without it. He still seemed so real to her, as if she would turn a corner and he would be there laughing at her look of surprise.

"He fell at Orthez," Captain Jonquil said.

"Yes," she choked out. Marion felt Caroline's short arms wrap around her neck, an act of childish comforting that kept Marion from being overwhelmed by the grief she'd been too at a loss, too overwhelmed, to fully experience nearly a year earlier.

"He saved the life of his commanding officer," Captain Jonquil said authoritatively. "I don't know if you were told that."

Marion shook her head.

"He was a good soldier. And a good man." Captain Jonquil handed her a handkerchief. Marion dabbed and wiped, trying to get herself under control.

"I'll scrape the junk off it, Stanby," Caroline promised, hugging Marion even tighter.

Marion half sobbed, half laughed, a trembling smile turning up her lips. Captain Jonquil chuckled as well.

"Thank you for telling me, Captain Jonquil."

"If Bobert had known you were working as a servant, he'd have skinned me alive." Captain Jonquil shook his head. "He talked of 'Maid Marion' all the time."

Marion laughed at the old nickname.

"But his consolation seemed to be that your father would take care of you should anything happen."

Marion sighed. "News of Robert's death reached us within days of Orthez." Marion took deep breaths to keep her emotions under control. "Father was struck down by it. A stroke, the doctors said. Within a matter of days, he was dead. He and Robert were buried next to my mother on the same day."

"And why did you then decide to become a governess?"

"I had no choice." Marion tried to put into words the panic that grew over the months that followed the burial. "My father made no provisions for me. None whatsoever. I had no allowance to live on, no dowry to tempt a suitor, though I was hardly in a position to consider matrimony. The estate passed to a distant cousin I have never met, who doesn't even live in England—the West Indies or America or something like that. The solicitors were squabbling over control of the estate, one insisting he acted for the new marquess, the other insisting he would do nothing without the express written instructions of this cousin of mine.

"I couldn't pay the servants' wages, and the solicitors would not do so. Soon the house was unstaffed, the larder empty. I wrote to relatives, seeking help, but those who returned my missives indicated they could not take on a charity case. I did the only thing I could think of."

"You lied."

Marion turned on the seat so quickly she nearly tumbled Caroline to the floor. Layton stood not five feet behind her, watching, obviously listening.

"You made up a name," he continued, sounding almost accusatory. "Hid your background. Probably even forged your references."

"I didn't know what else to do." Marion pleaded with him to understand.

"You could have told me."

"If I had told you when I first arrived that I was the daughter of a marquess and was working at your estate without the permission of my guardian, you would have fired me."

He didn't argue. She hadn't expected him to. Any gentleman with sense would have immediately dismissed a disaster waiting to happen.

"Was there never a point when you trusted me enough to tell me the truth?" Layton asked quietly.

"I couldn't," Marion whispered. *You had enough burdens*, she added silently.

"Of course not."

"Where will you go now, Lady Marion?" Captain Jonquil asked. Marion had forgotten he was even there.

"Rod—er, Hartley—is writing to my cousin, the new Marquess of Grenton. He is my guardian."

"Perhaps he will allow you to remain for the wedding." Captain Jonquil's eyes shifted between Marion and Layton.

Marion shook her head. "I think it would be best if I left."

"No, Mary! No!" Caroline cried, clinging to her to the point of near suffocation. "Don't leave me!"

Marion looked to Layton for support, for some kind of intervention.

"Come on, Caroline" was all he said, and he held his hand out to his daughter. "Lady Marion must do what she feels is best."

He scooped up Caroline and walked out.

CHAPTER TWENTY-THREE

"The daughter of a deuced marquess, Flip!" Layton grumbled. He let out a frustrated breath. "Sorry 'bout the language, Harry."

Harold nodded his forgiveness, which made Layton roll his eyes. Harold was so ridiculously pious that even the least offensive interjections required his forgiveness. Holy Harry at his most devout could be a little much.

"What exactly bothers you about her parentage, Layton?" Philip asked. "Is it that she outranks you?"

That rankled a little, yes. "No. A little, maybe. But not like that . . ." He ran a hand through his hair. "She must think I am a pompous imbecile."

"I always did think she was pretty intelligent," Philip said.

"Shut up, Philip."

"Sorry, brother." Philip didn't sound sorry in the least. "What, in your opinion, has led Lady Marion to this rather unflattering assessment of your character?"

"You should have heard some of the peals I rang over her head," Layton said as he paced. "She was the most impertinently behaved servant: talking back, taunting, jeering, acting like . . . like . . ."

"The daughter of a deuced marquess?" Philip asked innocently.

"Exactly." Layton spun back to look at him. "And I lectured her about proprieties and proper behavior and being conscious of rank and position."

"And it turns out she outranks *you*." Philip laughed out loud, head flung back.

"It's not that funny, Flip," Layton grumbled.

"Look, Layton," Philip said placatingly, "considering the circumstances and what she hadn't told you about herself, your lectures were more than justified; they were necessary. She can't hold that against you."

"Yea, but it's still—"

"Deucedly embarrassing," Philip ended for him. "Sorry 'bout the language, Harry."

Another nod of pardon.

"Except I get the feeling that's not the only thing that is bothering you," Philip said.

Layton dropped into an armchair near the fire and sank down in a posture of defeat. "I just don't understand why she didn't tell me."

"The poor girl figured she'd lose her job," Philip said.

"I wouldn't have fired her."

Philip raised a skeptical eyebrow.

"Maybe at first," Layton conceded. "But . . . later . . . I thought . . ." That kiss flashed through Layton's mind, along with their conversations at the river's edge and the day she'd spent listening to him spill all of his secrets. He had trusted *her*. Why hadn't she trusted him? Philip watched him expectantly and a little too closely. "Never mind." Layton shook his head. "I shouldn't have interrupted you two. Get on with whatever you were talking about."

He turned his attention to the fireplace. *Lady* Marion Linwood. Well, eligibility was no longer an issue. She was the daughter of a marquess, bosom friends with the Duke and Duchess of Hartley. If Philip was to be believed, the Linwoods were extremely close with at least two other leading families. What an idiot he must have seemed when he told her his misgivings.

He had told her his misgivings, hadn't he? Now Layton couldn't remember. Not that it mattered, really. She hadn't told him anything about herself aside from her once-upon-a-time stories of her childhood. She hadn't trusted him enough to let him help her, let him bear some of her burden.

Neither had Bridget. He really was a failure.

"Just to be clear, has this unfortunate gentleman actually taken his life?" Harry asked.

Layton listened more closely. Was Philip still looking into that situation?

"No, I am relieved to say," Philip said. "But she is worried about the possibility."

"Ah."

Layton watched Harold steeple his fingers the way he did when about to relate some aspect of doctrine he found particularly intriguing.

"Well, in cases like this," Harry said, "the law actually has taken its cues from the church. Just as the courts do not condemn a person who is mad for taking his life, neither does the church consider it a sin."

"Meaning, that if a person is mad or suffering from madness, suicide would not, for that person, be a sin?"

"Exactly," Harry answered.

"And this person could have a Christian burial?"

Harry offered a nod so knowing that the Archbishop of Canterbury would have been hard-pressed to re-create it.

"That is clear doctrine," Philip pressed, "not just your opinion?"

"It is the position of the church," Harry answered, unruffled by the skepticism.

"And God wouldn't condemn this person either?"

"God *can* be merciful, Philip," Harry replied.

"I know," Philip answered.

For just a moment, it seemed like Philip's eyes slid to Layton, but it was so fleeting that Layton couldn't be sure. And he didn't think about it much. Far too many thoughts were flying through his overworked brain to leave room for thoughts of Philip.

Was it possible God didn't look on Bridget's final act as a sin? That she wasn't condemned for what she'd done? That *he* wasn't condemned for obtaining a Christian burial for his late wife? He'd entertained for an extremely brief moment in the days after Bridget's burial the thought of asking Mr. Throckmorten about the intricacies of doctrine surrounding suicide. He'd dismissed the idea immediately, however, knowing the vicar would have been quick to condemn, thorough in his public denunciation, and efficient in his effort to see that the neighborhood shunned Layton adequately.

Layton barely registered a comment from Philip as he all but staggered to the door. "I'm heading back to the Meadows," Layton mumbled over his shoulder as he walked out of the library.

He walked almost blindly down the stairs. He'd accepted the fact that Bridget had been mad in her final months. He didn't understand why or what had brought it on. The worry that he had contributed to her condition continued to nag him. But regardless of its source, her state of mind absolved her in the eyes of the law. That had only just begun to sink in.

But forgiveness from God? For himself and Bridget both? His heart raced and pounded at the possibility, but he couldn't bring himself to believe it. He had lied to the heavens, but perhaps it did not matter in the end.

Layton squinted against the unusually bright sunlight as he stepped outside and made his way to the stables. "Saddle Theron," he instructed a groom who had appeared at his arrival.

Layton needed to make a much-overdue journey.

"I have met your cousin, Marion," Roderick tried to reassure her. "You have nothing to fear at his hands."

"But I don't know him at all. I feel like a burden. He probably wishes I'd never been found."

"Nonsense, Marion!" Adèle lightly scolded. "The new Lord Grenton was frantic when he contacted us trying to find you. I can only imagine he was relieved when he received Roderick's letter yesterday."

"He is really coming here?" What would this unknown cousin think of her? Would he be upset by the burden of her care?

"Posthaste, I would think," Roderick said.

Tea was interrupted by a knock at the drawing room door.

"Maybe that is Layton," Lady Lampton said, her brows furrowed with a hint of worry. "I thought for sure he would return for tea."

"Where did he take himself off to?" Miss Sorrel Kendrick asked, the question seemingly directed at Lord Lampton, who just shrugged and watched the door.

The butler stepped inside and announced quite properly, "The Marquess of Grenton."

Marion nearly dropped her teacup. She looked to Roderick, who had already risen. He offered her a reassuring smile. Marion rose as well and turned to face the door as the new arrival entered.

What she saw shocked her more than she could have predicted. This stranger could have been her own brother, not so much for his likeness to Robert but for his close resemblance to herself. He sported a head full of deep red hair, not fiery like hers but red just the same. His eyes were the same shade of dark brown. Something in his face reminded her instantly of her own reflection.

"Lord Grenton." Roderick offered a bow.

"Your Grace." Lord Grenton returned the gesture.

"May I introduce you to Lady Marion Linwood, your cousin." Roderick brought the gentleman to Marion's side. She curtsied as he stared. Perhaps he saw the resemblance himself.

"Lady Marion." He bowed his head.

"Lord Grenton." The name felt odd on her lips. Lord Grenton had always been her father.

As if reading her thoughts, he smiled and said, "I haven't quite grown accustomed to the title, I am afraid. Especially coming from someone who looks strikingly like my sister, Beth."

Marion smiled then. He had a sister.

"Perhaps you might be persuaded to call me Cousin Miles," Grenton suggested. "It would be less awkward for both of us, I am sure."

"Cousin Marion would do for myself as well." She liked him already.

"Well, Hartley," Cousin Miles addressed Roderick once more, "you seem to have worked a miracle. I was beginning to fear I would never locate my mysterious cousin."

Roderick smiled. "I am certain Lady Lampton would excuse us to allow the two of you to become acquainted and satisfy one another's curiosity."

Lady Lampton expressed her desire that they do just that, and Roderick and Adèle accompanied Marion and her newfound cousin to a small sitting room not far from the more formal drawing room. As they all settled in, Marion took a moment to study Cousin Miles. Besides the startling resemblance, he was intriguing. His face was bronzed from obvious hours spent in the sun, and he carried himself more like a laborer than a gentleman.

"Cousin Marion." He addressed her once the door was closed behind them all. "I cannot begin to offer my apologies for what you must have endured these past months. Had I realized the chaos you'd been thrown into, I assure you—"

"Best start at the beginning, Grenton," Roderick suggested.

Cousin Miles nodded. "I have lived in the West Indies for four years, Cousin Marion. I inherited a sugar plantation there from my father and have been overseeing it. It came as something of a shock to hear that I had suddenly become the heir to a cousin I didn't know, one who was a marquess, of all things. I knew nothing of the circumstances of my inheritance beyond the bare facts with which I had been provided.

"I took my time arranging my affairs before returning to England. I was not informed I had a dependent nor that two sets of solicitors were haggling over the management of the entire thing." He took a deep breath, apparently still frustrated by the ordeal. "Everything was a mess by the time I arrived at Tafford. I'd been in residence several days before one of the retainers, a Mrs. Goodbower"—Marion grinned at the reference to her onetime nurse—"mentioned you. A few well-placed questions, and the situation began to lay itself out. My late cousin had a daughter who had been left penniless and helpless to address the disaster those imbeciles had made through their squabbling. I realized she had left, and no one seemed to know where she had gone.

"Afraid I might do damage to your reputation or situation, I began inquiring of what family I could learn of."

"Which is probably when you contacted me," Roderick jumped in.

Cousin Miles nodded. "I had heard in the neighborhood of the connection between your two families. All of my efforts were futile." He looked at Marion again. "I couldn't find you."

"I came here. Well, not *here* exactly. Farland Meadows. They have been good to me."

"I am grateful to hear that." Cousin Miles sounded entirely sincere. "I intend to offer my thanks to Mr. Jonquil personally. You ought not to have been forced to seek out employment. I have every intention of providing you with an appropriate dowry and a roof over your head for as long as you would like. My sister and her husband are at Tafford now. You can return whenever you would like. All the proprieties have been seen to."

"Thank you, Cousin Miles."

"I only hope, in time, that you will see fit to forgive me for all the anguish you have unnecessarily endured."

She shook her head. "It was hardly your doing."

Cousin Miles nodded his gratitude, no doubt feeling she was being gracious. Why did men insist on blaming themselves for things that were not at all their fault?

"When did you leave Tafford?" Cousin Miles asked after a moment.

"The morning of Christmas Eve."

Cousin Miles shook his head. "We missed one another by less than a week, Cousin Marion. Rather ironic, don't you think?"

Ironic? Perhaps. And very, very fortunate. If she hadn't left home and come to Farland Meadows, she'd have never met Caroline or Layton, never have fallen in love. His rejection still stung, but she couldn't regret the past months. Not entirely.

If only she could know she'd made a difference.

CHAPTER TWENTY-FOUR

HE HADN'T BEEN TO THE churchyard in nearly a year, but Layton knew the way. Searching out a headstone covered in snow felt strange—he only ever made this pilgrimage in the summer, on the anniversary of her passing.

He and Mr. Sarvol had come to something of a compromise regarding that yearly pilgrimage. Layton came in the morning, and Mr. Sarvol waited until afternoon. They did not dislike each other necessarily. Running into one another had simply become too uncomfortable. Mr. Sarvol always seemed as though he meant to say something. Layton would brace himself. Then his father-in-law would turn gruff and acerbic, and they inevitably parted more at odds with one another than they'd been before.

Layton saw no sign of Mr. Sarvol as he walked the snow-dusted grounds of the churchyard toward Bridget's marker. He easily found the simple, polished stone.

"Bridget Hannah Jonquil. Wife and Mother. Oct 19, 1788 to Jun 27, 1810." Layton ran his gloved fingers over the engraving like he had each of the five times he'd come, thinking how terribly young she'd been.

Layton stood there, tensed and waiting. The weight of his lies always sat heaviest on him in the churchyard. Those lies were the reason Bridget was there. That always made him feel like the worst of hypocrites: standing in the shadow of a place of worship, in a sanctified graveyard, visiting the burial place of a woman who, in the eyes of God, had no right to be there. And he, the reason she was.

So he'd come back to this place to roll around in his mind the possibility that his lies hadn't been such grievous actions after all. If Philip were to be believed, and Harry, for that matter, Bridget's condition those final weeks changed everything. Her madness had ensured her pardon. This final resting place that he'd fought so hard to give her might rightfully be hers.

He wanted to believe it. Wanted it badly. But he still felt uneasy, uncertain.

Wind whipped through the graveyard, rustling the bare branches of overhanging trees. Layton continued to stand there, chilled to the bone, waiting for some kind of answer.

"Wife and Mother." He read the epitaph aloud. He supposed he ought to have included "beloved" or something of that sort. It was customary. But theirs hadn't been that sort of marriage. He'd loved her like a friend, and he wondered, looking back, if it had been enough.

Footsteps crunched the snow nearby. If it was the vicar approaching, he was prepared to beat a hasty retreat. Mr. Throckmorten would no doubt subject him to a lecture on the importance of coming to services each week, along with yet another scathing assessment of the state of his soul. Those were the only things the aging vicar ever said to Layton since Bridget's death.

Mr. Sarvol would have been nearly as unwelcome as the vicar. Layton didn't know if the man blamed him for his daughter's death or simply wanted nothing to do with the man who had been her husband. He had never shown any interest in Caroline, which had solidified Layton's disinclination to pursue the connection.

Layton warily glanced in the direction of the approaching footsteps. Corbin, the Jonquil just younger than Layton, walked silently up the row of grave markers.

"Good day, Corbin," Layton offered when his brother stopped beside him.

Corbin nodded with an awkward smile. "Throckmorten's mount has been favoring a leg" was Corbin's quiet explanation for his presence at the vicarage.

Layton nodded at that. Corbin had a way with horses, a talent he'd turned into a relatively profitable undertaking. Corbin owned the most successful stud farm in the Midlands.

"Did you leave him a liniment?" Layton asked, his eyes back on Bridget's grave marker.

"Mm-hmm."

They stood in silence, and for the first time since Bridget had begun her sojourn there beneath the ground, Layton felt some degree of comfort within the walls of the churchyard. He silently thanked Corbin for just being there, knowing his brother would be embarrassed if Layton actually told him so. Perhaps all those years Layton had just needed someone to stand with him.

"Caroline looks more like Bridget all the time," Corbin said after several minutes had passed in silence.

"Does she?" Layton tried to see the two of them in his mind. Bridget's image wasn't as clear as it had once been.

Corbin nodded. "Her . . . coloring is . . ." He took a deep breath in the middle of the sentence, something he'd always done. His natural timidity made conversations difficult for him. ". . . more like yours. But . . . something in her face, I think . . . reminds me of . . ."

Leaving off the ends of his sentences was normal for Corbin as well. His family had learned to simply finish the thoughts for him silently. *Bridget*, Layton thought to himself.

He looked back at Corbin after a few minutes had passed in mutual silence. Corbin's lips were moving slightly, no words coming out. He'd done that for years, rolling words around in his mind before speaking, thinking through his words before he let them out. Corbin had been known to mentally sort through his thoughts for days, weeks sometimes, if what he wanted to say was really important. For things that were crucial or hard to speak about, he'd sometimes waited for years. His first horse, Whipster, had been in the stables for two years before he'd managed to tell Father what that gift had meant to him.

The family had learned over the years to listen when Corbin spoke. His words would inevitably be sincere and important to him.

"I always . . ." Corbin cleared his throat awkwardly, eyes focused on the smooth granite headstone at their feet. Layton gave his brother his undivided attention. "You and Bridget were . . . I know it wasn't a love match, but . . . you were good to her, and I . . . Well, Father would have been proud of you for that . . . and I . . . If I ever . . ." He let out a frustrated breath. "I'm not saying this right," he mumbled.

"You're fine, Corbin," Layton reassured him.

After a fortifying breath, Corbin plunged on. "If I ever meet someone, could I . . . Would you mind . . . if I asked you for advice now and then?"

"You want *my* advice?" Layton could only stare.

Corbin nodded, entirely serious.

"Certainly," he managed to say through his shock. "I'll do my best."

Corbin smiled and stood still and silent. For the first time in years, Layton felt almost at peace standing on hallowed ground.

"You made your wife happy," Corbin said with a nod, his eyes focused in the distance. "I want . . . I'd like someone to be able to say that about me someday."

You made your wife happy. Did Corbin really believe that? But Layton knew Corbin—he wouldn't have said it if he didn't believe it.

"Thank you, Corbin." He laid a hand on his brother's shoulder.

Corbin just nodded.

"Did you ride here?" Layton asked.

"Elf." Corbin named his favorite mount.

"Come on." Layton pushed him down the row. "I'll ride back with you."

Corbin didn't put up any resistance.

"So have you actually met a lady, or were you speaking purely hypothetically?" Layton asked as he mounted Theron.

Corbin immediately turned several shades of red.

Layton laughed out loud. "Tell me about her."

"I . . . I haven't actually . . . spoken to her," Corbin admitted, still red and stumbling over his words more than usual.

"But you've seen her at least?"

Corbin nodded.

"Is she pretty?"

Corbin's eyes opened wider, and he nodded rather emphatically. Layton couldn't remember the last time he'd had a real conversation with Corbin. How long had it been since he'd overlooked his own difficulties and just been a member of his own family?

"Find someone to introduce you," Layton suggested.

"But . . . what . . . what if she thinks I'm . . . an idiot or something?" Corbin said uncomfortably.

"You're a Jonquil. Of course she'll think you're an idiot."

Corbin laughed, and so did Layton.

"You just have to convince her you're not." Layton chuckled, nudging Theron on.

"How do I do that?" Corbin looked doubtful, but he was still smiling.

Layton thought of Marion and what she must think of him. "When I figure that out, Corbin, I'll let you know."

꙳

The first person Layton came across upon returning to Lampton Park from the churchyard was Caroline, who was taking enthusiastic marching instructions from Stanley on the back lawns. She smiled and waved at Layton before taking up her practice once more.

He'd never taken her to her mother's graveside. The thought had only entered his mind on a few occasions, and he'd always dismissed it under the weight of a great many arguments. He told himself she was too young, that she hadn't the understanding of death and its finality to grasp what she would see there. He argued that her thoughts of her mother should be of a vibrant young woman, not a cold, inanimate slab of stone.

Had he been wise in that decision? His thoughts flew back to a conversation with Marion very early in her time at Farland Meadows. She hadn't been certain Caroline even knew her mother was dead.

What else did Caroline not know?

Caroline skipped to his side, wearing her angelic, broad smile. "Did you see me marching, Papa?"

"I did. You looked just like a soldier."

Her eyes twinkled. "Little girls aren't soldiers, silly."

He brushed a hand over her sweet, golden curls. "Will you walk with your silly papa?"

Without even a moment's hesitation, Caroline slipped her tiny hand in his. She waved to Stanley, who locked eyes with Layton. Layton recognized the unspoken question. He nodded, assuring his brother that he needn't look after Caroline any longer.

"If you'd been here, Papa, you could have marched with us. Stanby would have taught you how to 'do the thing properly.'" She lowered her voice on the last phrase, obviously doing her utmost to mimic her uncle's description. "Where did you go?"

Here was the opportunity to introduce the topic he'd avoided all of Caroline's life. "I went to the churchyard." He watched her closely, but the mention of the graveyard didn't have any noticeable effect. His next breath came out tense and shaky. "Your—" Another quick breath. "Your mother is buried there."

Tears didn't pool in the small girl's eyes. Shock didn't pull at her features. She simply nodded and continued walking, swinging their arms. "Your papa is buried there too," she said. "And Mama's mama, and Grammy said her parents are there. It sounds very crowded. Is it crowded, Papa?"

Relief and sadness warred for possession of his mind. Caroline knew her mother was buried. She, in fact, had a more extensive understanding of the passing of her family members than he ever would have guessed.

But he could hardly take credit for her ease with the topic. Mater had, it seemed, walked her through that difficult topic.

"Crowded?" He forced his tone to remain light. "Not terribly. There's room for everyone." There had even been room for a woman so broken by illness of the brain that she'd ended her own existence. There had been room for Bridget. The thought was comforting. "Did Grammy tell you anything else about your mama?"

Caroline skipped a little ahead of him, pulling his arm along with her. "She said Mama was pretty. Mary said so too, but she said she didn't know her. Did Mary know Mama?"

"No, dear. No, she didn't." His thoughts hovered on Marion for a moment. He wanted to talk to her but didn't know what he would say.

"Mary said she is sad sometimes because her mama is dead." Caroline looked up at him, her brow puckered in thought. "Sometimes I feel sad because my mama is dead. Mary said I can love Mama even if I don't remember her."

Layton reached down, scooped Caroline into his arms, and held her tight. The miracles Marion had worked in their lives continued to pile up. She had touched a lonely place in Caroline's heart that he, the girl's own father, had been too intent on his own suffering to even see.

"Of course you can love your mama, poppet. I'll tell you all about her as you grow up so you can know her for yourself."

She rubbed her hand against the bristles on his cheek and chin. "Was her hair yellow like mine?"

"It was brown, but it curled like yours does."

"Oh." Her eyes grew wide a moment. "What did you call her? Did you call her Mama?"

He felt a smile tip his mouth. "I called her Bridget. That was her name, like your name is Caroline."

"Did she name me Caroline?"

Layton nodded. They had chosen to name the baby for Bridget's mother if it was a girl and Layton's father if it was a boy. "Caroline was her mama's name."

They continued to talk as they walked slowly around the grounds. She wanted to know the oddest things about her mother. They spoke of which foods she had particularly liked, whether she had enjoyed snow or preferred sunshine. Caroline asked if her mother rode horses and if she could run fast. On and on the questions went, and she never seemed to tire of hearing the answers.

Though he'd avoided even thinking of Bridget more than necessary in the years since her passing, Layton had discussed her with two different people that day alone. The experience was, in many ways, freeing. Yet, a weight remained on his heart.

Layton still felt uneasy thinking back over the year and a half he'd spent as a husband. He didn't feel like he'd done the job very well and didn't want to disappoint someone else. And there yet remained the question of the truth he'd kept hidden. He was beginning to hope that in laying Bridget to rest in the churchyard, he hadn't done anything wrong. But he never intended to tell anyone beyond those who already knew, and someday, he'd tell Caroline the true nature of her mother's illness.

So he'd go on being a liar of sorts. He hadn't yet decided where that put him, whether he ought to feel guilty or justified. That was one of the things he wanted to ask Marion. Her opinion had come to matter to him even if her view of him was rather bleak.

"I won't! I won't!" A petulant child's voice echoed loudly off the walls of Lampton Park a few hours before dinner on Saturday. Layton instantly recognized it as Caroline's, though he'd never heard her sound so uncontrollably angry.

"What is going on?" he asked, stepping into Mater's sitting area and finding Caroline red faced, teary, and stomping her feet. He'd never seen her like that. "Car—"

"Layton." Mater stopped him. "No coddling. She has done something entirely unacceptable, and I have insisted she apologize. She has refused."

"And that is the reason for this . . . ?" How did he describe what he was watching? Pouting, stomping. Gads, Caroline even sounded like she was growling.

"Tantrum," Mater finished for him. "I am perfectly content to wait for her to change her mind."

"But I—"

"You're too soft a touch, my dear," Mater said gently but firmly. "Allow me to address this issue."

Layton knew that look in Mater's eye, the one they learned at an early age never to argue with. "May I at least ask what she did?" He couldn't imagine.

"Caroline? Would you like to tell your papa what you have done?"

"No!" Caroline nearly shouted.

Layton stared. She had never acted like this before.

"Leave us, Layton," Mater said to him under her breath. "She will come around faster if you leave her be."

Bowing to Mater's vast experience—she'd raised seven children, after all—Layton quietly, confusedly, left the room.

What had happened? Caroline was always a well-behaved child, quiet and obedient. Layton passed the open door to the east sitting room and heard a sniffle. Convinced pandemonium had descended on the Park, Layton peeked inside. Marion stood at the window, her back to him.

He hadn't seen Marion in days. She had clearly been avoiding him. Layton wasn't sure how he felt about that. Something in him wanted to see her again and talk to her one more time. He'd heard from Mater that she and her cousin, the new Marquess of Grenton, were leaving the Park on Sunday to return to Derbyshire. Layton couldn't allow things to end the way they were.

He took a single step inside before realizing Marion was crying. He quickly pressed down memories of Bridget's ceaseless weeping. Marion was different. Tears were infrequent. And she'd never pushed him away when he'd offered his support.

"Marion?" he asked uncertainly.

She turned at his voice. A spot of tender red marred her face, low on her left cheek. Had someone hit her?

Layton rushed to her side. He carefully cupped her face in his hand, looking for any signs of significant injury. He felt some relief at not finding blood or a deepening bruise. Still, she'd clearly been hurt.

"What happened?"

"She says she hates me." Marion's voice broke with painful emotion.

"Who—" But then he knew. "Caroline." He sighed. "Did she hit you?" He brushed his thumb lightly over the mark on Marion's face.

She nodded, not pulling away from his touch. "With a book. Because I'm leaving. She said—" Marion drew in a shaky breath. "She said she never wants to see me again. And that . . . that she hates me!"

Her expression crumbled in misery. Layton pulled her into his arms. The aroma of cinnamon that always surrounded her filled his senses again. The feel of her in his embrace settled over him like a comforting blanket. He'd needed her there, needed her close again. He hated that only her injuries gave him that right and only for a fleeting moment.

"Oh, Layton, I don't want her to hate me," Marion whimpered. "I love her. How can I leave with her feeling this way?"

She'd called him "Layton." Not "Mr. Jonquil" or "sir." She even leaned into him, resting her head against his chest. He rubbed her back in slow circles, feeling her breathing even out as her sobs subsided. He knew some satisfaction in having comforted her but wished for so much more. She was leaving and taking his very heart with her.

"Perhaps you should stay awhile longer," Layton suggested, trying to sound casual. "Caroline might come to understand the situation better if given more time."

"That would only postpone the inevitable." Marion pulled back the tiniest bit, enough to wipe at a tear but not so much that he didn't still hold her. "My cousin is here only because I am, and I know he has a great deal to do back at Tafford. He means to leave in the morning, and I can't ask him to wait longer than that."

"No. I suppose not."

She took a deep breath and stepped out of his arms. Layton only just kept himself from reaching for her again. If she was really leaving in the morning, if he was never going to see her again . . .

"Marion, I need to thank you."

She turned to look at him. That made it harder.

He forced himself to continue, however awkwardly. "For all the times you listened when I . . . when I needed someone to talk to."

Marion touched her hand lightly to his face. Anything else he might have said stuck in his throat. Layton closed his eyes, committing the moment to memory. If his past hadn't been so riddled with failures, his own conscience so troubled with doubts, he might have been blessed to know the joy of her touch every day for the rest of their lives.

"I only hope you've found some degree of peace," she whispered.

"I'm beginning to," he whispered back. He was beginning to feel some peace regarding Bridget's burial and the deception he'd enacted after her death. But he could not be certain he was blameless for her unhappiness. If he'd caused that pain, any part of it, he could never trust himself with Marion's well-being.

Her fingers left his face. He nearly reached for her, nearly pulled her back and asked her to stay a moment longer. When he heard her steps move away from him and out the door, he wished he had.

But until he knew he hadn't failed Bridget, knew he wouldn't destroy Marion the same way, he couldn't stop her. He couldn't confess that he loved her more than he'd loved anyone before.

Perhaps, he thought with a twinge of fear, it was time he started praying again.

CHAPTER TWENTY-FIVE

MARION HAD NEVER FELT LESS like going to church. Perhaps if the kind and loving Mr. Martin from back home were offering the sermon rather than the sharp-tongued Mr. Throckmorten, with his constant condemnation of his congregation and dire warnings of the hopeless state of the majority of their souls, she might be more enthusiastic. Although, if she were being entirely honest, Mr. Throckmorten had very little to do with her reluctance.

She was leaving Nottinghamshire immediately after services, leaving Farland Meadows and Caroline and Layton. She had imagined in all her naiveté that during her sojourn as Caroline's governess she would make a difference and Caroline would blossom into a happy, contented young girl. She had hoped to see Layton shed some of the burdens he unnecessarily carried. Even if he never came to love her the way she'd hoped, she wanted him to find peace again.

None of that had happened. The last time she'd seen Caroline, the girl had struck her. Marion understood the outburst for what it was: fear and vulnerability and disappointment. The poor child felt abandoned. Again. And Layton? He'd said the afternoon before that he was beginning to find some measure of peace in his life, and yet he'd looked so troubled. In her distress, he had held her and offered the comfort she'd needed. In that moment, she'd felt home again for the first time since her father and brother had died. He had eased her burdens, but she was helpless to lift the weight off his heart. After she left, would he return to his isolation and unhappiness? Would he ever truly find the peace he needed? How she ached to stay there, to simply be near him.

She walked up the narrow path to the church with Roderick and Adèle and Cousin Miles, trying to feel some joy in the crisp, clear winter morning.

Only halfway to the church doors, something collided with her legs. Cousin Miles barely managed to keep her upright. Marion twisted to see what had nearly knocked her down.

Caroline, face buried in Marion's skirts, stood with her arms wrapped around Marion's legs. "I'm sorry, Mary! I'm sorry!" her muffled cries repeated.

Marion managed to detach her enough to lower herself to Caroline's eye level. "Caroline, dearest," she said gently.

Caroline looked up at her, tears streaming down her cheeks. "I hurt your face," she wailed. "I'm sorry!"

"My face feels much better now." Marion stroked the perfect ringlets framing that darling face. Caroline sniffled loudly. "And I think I know why you did it."

"You do?" Caroline's voice shook with emotion.

"We are going to miss each other, aren't we?" Marion asked quietly, forcing a smile to her lips. She would miss them both desperately.

Caroline nodded.

"Perhaps someday you could come visit me at my home," Marion tentatively suggested. "We could sit under my golden tree."

"Do you think Papa will let me come?" Caroline asked, her tears slowing a little.

"I don't know," Marion answered honestly. "I hope so."

Caroline nodded and took a shaking breath.

"And I promise to write to you."

"I don't know how to read."

"Your new governess will teach you," Marion said.

Another nod, but Caroline's chin had begun quivering again.

"We should keep moving, Cousin Marion."

Marion looked up to see something of a crowd waiting just behind them on the narrow path. Lady Lampton stood at the very front.

Marion rose to her feet. "Your grandmother is waiting for you, Caroline. You'd best go with her."

"I want to sit with you." Caroline took a fistful of Marion's skirts.

"You need to sit with your family, dear."

"Yes, come, Caroline." Lady Lampton held her hand out to Caroline.

"No, Grammy." Caroline pouted. "I want to sit with Mary."

"Lady Marion will be sitting with her cousin," Lady Lampton explained. "And you will be sitting with your family in our pew."

"I want to sit with Mary." The pout grew mutinous.

"Caroline," Marion gently reprimanded. To have her time as a governess end with this display was almost as depressing as actually leaving. Perhaps she hadn't achieved anything at all.

"I want to sit with you," Caroline demanded, stomping her foot.

What had come over the girl lately? Marion looked across at Lady Lampton, unsure what to do. A scene in the church courtyard was unthinkable.

"Caroline, please, dear," Marion implored.

"I . . . want . . . to . . . !"

"Caroline," Lady Lampton loudly whispered.

"I—" But Caroline began to sob, her words inaudible.

Marion and Lady Lampton watched each other in mutual confusion. The rest of the Lampton Park party watched the scene, equally baffled. Just when Marion didn't think the situation could grow any worse, Mr. Throckmorten descended upon them with his usual look of disapproval and superiority.

"Is there a problem?" He eyed the assembly, lips pursing as his look fell upon Caroline.

"No, there is not," Marion insisted.

He looked down at Caroline with much the same expression one might reserve for the mangled remains of a spider recently introduced to the heel of a boot. How could any man of the church look on a child that way?

"I suppose there is little to be done with a child destined to be a heathen." Marion's jaw tensed, even as her hand tightened around Caroline's.

"Her father is so far fallen from what is good and right that he's not darkened this door in years. One can't expect the offspring of a hopeless sinner to be anything but that herself."

"How dare you," Marion ground out, heat creeping up her neck. "You should care for your congregants, not condemn them."

The vicar spoke across her words, not hearing them in the least. "If you cannot bring this child in to some semblance of good behavior, I suggest you remove her at once." He watched Marion with utter distaste. "Such an ill-behaved display is hardly welcome, Miss Wood."

"She is *Lady* Marion Linwood, *Mr.* Throckmorten," came a familiar voice that stopped every noise and every conversation in an instant. "It was my understanding that all people are welcome in a place of worship, even a 'hopeless sinner.'"

"Bravo," Marion heard Cousin Miles say under his breath.

But Marion was too busy staring to do much more than register it as a passing remark. Layton, pristinely turned out, stood beside Caroline. He looked decidedly uncomfortable but with a determined lift to his chin.

"Come, Caroline." Layton held his hand out to his daughter. "It doesn't do to keep the Almighty waiting."

Caroline's surprise gave way to a tremulous smile as she laid her tiny hand in his. "Will you sit by me, Papa?" she asked with obvious uncertainty.

"If you will share your prayer book with me," Layton replied with an equally uneasy smile. "And nudge me if I forget something."

Caroline nodded mutely.

"Perhaps if you had stepped inside a chapel even once in the past five years or more, you would not require the guidance of a child," Mr. Throckmorten answered at his most top-lofty. He was enough to turn even the most devoted of believers into cynics. Marion herself had heard him humiliate members of the parish each Sunday for weeks. Those who toed his chosen line escaped the most scathing denunciations, but the rest were treated with such contempt that it often left worshipers in tears. It was little wonder Layton had stayed away so long. If he had lived in Mr. Martin's parish during the past five years, the outcome might have been quite different.

"I seem to recall," Mr. Harold Jonquil said—Holy Harry, as the brothers had dubbed him—watching Mr. Throckmorten with something like pity on his face, "reading somewhere . . ." His face turned in a look of mock confusion that brought the earl immediately to mind. "What was that phrase?"

Layton watched Harry, a smile nearly emerging. The earl grinned full out.

"Ah, yes. 'And a little child shall lead them.' And I do believe this was a pleasing turn of events." The usually even-tempered future cleric skewered his would-be contemporary with a look of fierce accusation. "I wonder, sir, if you have ever read the book in which that particular passage is found. If you have, I doubt you have understood a word it contains."

"Bravo," came the same whispered observation from Cousin Miles.

Mr. Throckmorten sputtered and turned several shades of purple.

Layton had apparently had enough. Holding Caroline's hand, he stepped around the gathered assembly and walked toward the church doors. He kept his eyes firmly fixed ahead, his hand clasping Caroline's as if his survival depended on it. Behind him, the assembled churchgoers were entirely silent.

"Please continue inside," Lord Lampton instructed the crowd in a voice that brooked no argument. They obliged, looks of smug satisfaction on each and every face. Mr. Throckmorten obviously hadn't won many allies. Only the Jonquil family, the Kendrick sisters, Marion, Cousin Miles, and the Duke and Duchess of Hartley remained.

"I say, Throckmorten," the earl said, swinging his quizzing glass, "you do not look at all well. Perhaps you should have a lie down."

"*I* am to deliver a sermon this morning," Mr. Throckmorten said, very much on his dignity.

"Oh, I believe your message has been most effectively delivered and far too many times at that. More than ought to have been allowed, in fact." Lord Lampton drawled the observation, but his eyes were chilling. "And I have a message of my own I would like to relay to you." He studied his fingernails with a casual air that didn't fool a soul, Marion would wager. "But I suggest you not risk receiving it if your health is at all fragile."

Miss Sorrel Kendrick seemed to barely hold back a spurt of laughter.

"A message, my lord?" Mr. Throckmorten looked at him warily.

"Perhaps it would do to remind you, Throckmorten," Captain Stanley Jonquil jumped into the fray, "that Lord Lampton has the giving, and *taking*, of this living."

The purple hue of Mr. Throckmorten's face almost immediately turned ashen. "What about my sermon?"

"Did you mean to wax long and eloquent on the shortcomings of your parishioners or read your usual list of local sinners?"

Though Mr. Throckmorten didn't reply aloud, his face gave his answer.

Lord Lampton raised an eyebrow to his brother Harold and received an almost pontifical inclination of the head in return. "I do not believe your words will be necessary," he told Mr. Throckmorten. With a rather condescending look of concern, he added, "Go have that lie down. You'll need it."

The earl bowed so slightly that it was more of an insult than an acknowledgment. Mr. Throckmorten took himself off, looking more than a little flabbergasted. Miss Kendrick offered her betrothed a round of silent applause.

"I haven't taken Orders yet, Philip," Holy Harry reminded his brother.

"I sat through a long, tedious ordination not a year ago." Lord Lampton smoothed the front of his unusually somber waistcoat.

"A deacon cannot—"

"God *can* be merciful, Harry," Lord Lampton replied with a shrug. He took his fiancée's arm once more. "And not having to listen to Throckmorten extol his own virtues while throwing his harsh and poisonous barbs at everyone else in attendance will be merciful indeed. Just make it a short service," he added.

"It will have to be" was the grumbled reply, but Marion thought Mr. Harry Jonquil looked at least a little excited at the possibility. His step picked up speed as he too made his way inside the church. No doubt, his mind was spinning at the task ahead of him.

"Come, Cousin Marion," Cousin Miles whispered at her side. "We too should be finding our seats."

She nodded and walked almost numbly into the impressive edifice of the church. Throckmorten was about to lose his position, Marion had a feeling, and not a day too soon—probably a few years too *late*, in fact. But Mr. Throckmorten's situation completely fled from her thoughts as she walked up the aisle to the pew Roderick and Adèle already occupied. Ahead, in the Farland pew, sat Layton, Caroline at his side, apparently explaining her prayer book to him in astoundingly acute detail, considering she couldn't read. Layton listened with a fond smile on his face, though his posture was anything but at ease.

It would take time, Marion reminded herself and hoped he understood that as well. For so long, he had considered himself beyond redemption, hated by a God she knew he revered. But this was a step closer to peace of mind. If forgiveness for what he saw as grievous sins had been less important to him, Layton would not have been as unhappy as he had been and this return to a way of life he'd always embraced would not have meant as much.

Lady Lampton pressed up the aisle just as Marion seated herself in the row behind Layton and Caroline. Rather than take her customary seat in the Lampton pew, the countess sat beside her son, laid a hand on his cheek for the slightest moment, and smiled a little tearily before shifting her attention ahead.

Marion felt tears trickle down her own cheeks as she watched the Jonquils enter. They couldn't have all fit on the Farland pew but looked very much like they would have liked to make the attempt. Lord Lampton, Mr. Jason Jonquil, and Captain Stanley Jonquil sat with the Misses Kendrick, and Mrs. Kendrick sat on the Lampton pew across the aisle. Mr. Corbin Jonquil joined his mother and, Marion noted, held her hand as the congregation settled in.

"He came, Mary!" Caroline whispered over the back of her pew.

"Yes, dearest," Marion whispered back.

"And he will sit by me every week." All signs of her tantrum of minutes earlier had completely disappeared. "He said so!"

Two more tears escaped Marion's eyes. She leaned farther forward in order to address the girl without her words being overheard. "Do you think your papa will be happy now?"

"Oh yes," Caroline answered, her whisper a touch louder than it had been. She wrapped her arms around her father's neck. She smiled lovingly at Layton then kissed his cheek. Layton turned to smile at his daughter after her unforeseen gesture. His gaze met Marion's. She loved his beautiful blue eyes and the depth of feeling she always saw there.

His forehead creased with concern. "Tears, Marion?" he whispered.

She shook her head, waving off his worries. These were tears of joy as much as sorrow.

Layton pulled from his pocket a folded bit of linen and passed it back to her. Marion accepted it but not without a flip in her heart. She would never be able to look at a handkerchief again without thinking of the evening she'd spent with Layton and Caroline laughing over handkerchief etiquette.

She dabbed at the tears hovering on her lashes.

Caroline pressed her tiny hands to either side of her father's face, turning his head until he looked fully at her once more. She didn't speak, only smiled broadly.

"Services are beginning, Caroline," he whispered kindly. "We'd best sit and listen."

"That's not Mr. Mockportant," Caroline said full voice, noticing her uncle Harry in the vicar's usual place. No doubt the entire congregation was thinking the exact same thing.

"No, it isn't," Layton answered so quietly Marion could hardly hear his words.

"I think we shall like church far better without him, don't you?" Caroline looked to her father for confirmation. "He always looks mad—mad and sour."

Layton smiled at her and nodded. Marion watched his arm slip around Caroline's shoulders and pull her closer to him. "I love you, poppet," he whispered to her.

Her tiny head rested against her father's shoulder. Marion saw Lady Lampton wipe another tear from her eye.

They will be happy now, Marion thought, bowing her head as the service began. *They will be happy.*

CHAPTER TWENTY-SIX

THE CHURCH ROOF HADN'T CAVED in or been struck by lightning. Layton took that as a good sign. He had come to church in an attempt to find some of that peace he'd told Marion he was beginning to discover in his life. Bridget's death had been a tragedy, one he wished he'd done more to prevent, but he felt her soul was at peace, and his ought to be as well.

"Farland."

Layton spun around, knowing only one person who insisted on addressing him by the title that was not yet his own. Mr. Sarvol. Bridget's father.

Layton had seen the man a handful of times over the past five years but not at all in the previous six months. Those months hadn't been kind. Sarvol weighed several stones less than he had, his hair nearly as thin as his face. His complexion was a study in contrasts, pale but blotchy. His eyes were still as coldly assessing as ever.

"Mr. Sarvol," Layton acknowledged, guiding Caroline a little behind him. Sarvol had never made any attempt to grow acquainted with his granddaughter, and Layton didn't entirely trust him to be civil.

"I want to talk to you," Mr. Sarvol barked, his usual mode of speaking. It was a miracle Bridget had been a kind, likable person with such a father.

"Mater," Layton called softly as she passed. Her eyes flitted between Layton and his father-in-law, a tinge of alarm in her look. "Will you take Caroline back to the Park? I will join you there."

"Of course, Layton." Mater reached for Caroline's hand.

"Papa?" Caroline asked uncertainly, watching Mr. Sarvol with wariness.

"Everything is fine, poppet. I'll be along soon enough."

She still seemed unconvinced.

"Maybe Flip will let you play with his fobs."

Caroline's face lit up, and she took Mater's hand. Layton breathed a sigh of relief as Caroline walked farther down the path from the church.

"Who was that man?" he heard her ask Mater.

Layton didn't hear the answer. He eyed Mr. Sarvol nervously. What did the man want after so many years?

"The child doesn't know me?" Mr. Sarvol seemed genuinely pained by the realization.

Layton could not summon much sympathy for him, despite the uncharacteristic flash of regret in the man's face. "That is your doing, sir. I brought her to Sarvol House any number of times that first year. You refused to see her. You will recall I informed you that should you wish to make the acquaintance, you knew where she was to be found."

"I am a busy man," Mr. Sarvol said gruffly.

"As am I."

Mr. Sarvol seemed to redden at the reference to his ill-mannered behavior. Layton had never known Mr. Sarvol to be the least bit discomposed by anything said to him.

"You attended church today," he said, bushy brows furrowed.

"As you can see."

"Ain't seen you here in years." It sounded almost like an accusation.

"Perhaps I am turning over a new leaf."

Mr. Sarvol nodded slowly. "Comes a time when a man has to reevaluate things." He continued nodding. "Starts to rethink the way he's lived his life."

Layton watched silently, wondering what had come over the man who had accepted Layton's request to marry his daughter but had never been remotely friendly.

"I've been rethinking some things," Mr. Sarvol said, obviously uncomfortable with the admission, though he had said as much a moment before. "When I saw you were staying for services, I sent my man back to Sarvol House."

Layton listened in wary silence. He had no idea what his father-in-law was getting at.

"I had him get this from my desk drawer." Mr. Sarvol roughly pushed a folded piece of yellowed parchment into Layton's hands. "Ought to have given it to you years ago. I knew you were weighed down by everything that happened, but I . . . I liked having it. It made me think of her. But I ought to have given it to you. I almost did a couple times the last few years, but . . . couldn't . . ."

As his words trailed off, so did he. Mr. Sarvol wandered from the church-yard without a backward glance, climbed into his antiquated carriage, and rolled away.

Layton looked down at the paper in his hand, turning it around to try to make sense of it. He realized he held a letter. One addressed to Mr. Sarvol at a London address, written in handwriting he knew he'd seen before.

The seal had long since been broken, the wax completely gone, leaving behind only the slightest stain. Layton opened and unfolded the letter, letting his eyes drop to the signature. His heart thudded against his ribs.

Bridget Jonquil.

Layton hastily refolded the missive and stuffed it into the inner pocket of his jacket. He wasn't prepared for a letter from Bridget.

"The Meadows," he instructed James Coachman as he climbed inside his rig. The door closed, the carriage began bowling down the lane toward home.

The letter seemed to burn in his pocket. What might she have written to her father all those years ago? They were obviously married at the time it was written. Had she mentioned him? What would she have said?

Though he couldn't see the road well for the condensation on the windows, Layton knew the way by memory. He knew the very moment the carriage turned from the main road, could picture with little effort the canopy of barren trees the carriage would even then be passing under.

He needed someplace quiet, isolated, to read, for he *had* to read the letter. He had to know what she'd said to hopefully gain some idea of how she'd felt during their brief marriage. He tapped the roof of the vehicle, and it came to a skilled stop. Layton opened the door enough to lean out and address his driver.

"Let me off here," he instructed. "Then continue on to the stables. I will no longer be needing the carriage."

James pulled his forelock respectfully and did as instructed. Layton didn't watch to see the vehicle disappear up the lane but made straight for the place he had in mind. His heart pounded so loudly in his ears that it drowned out his footsteps.

He reached the riverbank sooner than he would have expected. He sat down on an overturned log, knowing his pantaloons would be hopelessly stained. He took a few deep breaths and listened to the sound of water lapping against the bank. Slowly, some of the tension drained from his shoulders. He'd known, somehow, that this place would work its magic.

Here it was that he'd listened to Marion's stories. He'd told her about Bridget, about himself. She'd charmed Caroline into smiles and giggles, and they'd fished sodden leaves from the river with all the enthusiasm of treasure hunters.

Layton sighed. He pulled off his gloves and reached into his jacket. The parchment felt almost soft beneath his fingers. It opened silently, the creases worn nearly all the way through in places. Mr. Sarvol had apparently read the letter several times over the years. What could have been so important to warrant saving a letter for half a decade?

He closed his eyes for a second before forcing himself to read.

Sept 23 1809

"Five and a half years ago," Layton whispered. Before Caroline was born.

Dearest Father,

My condolences on your poor luck at Tattersall's. Layton's brother Corbin is considered something of a hand at choosing horseflesh, and he too has recently lamented the lack of options at Tatt's. Perhaps the coming weeks will prove more profitable for you both.

How pleasant you make the Little Season sound, and how pleased I am that you are enjoying yourself. Alas, my condition does not permit me to join you as you have requested. Do not, dear Papa, think for a moment that I resent missing the delights you write of. I could not possibly be happier anywhere than I am at Farland Meadows.

My Layton is everything attentive, seeming every bit as eager for our coming arrival as I am. He quite adamantly declares that this child will be a girl. And though I am of the same opinion, I find I am enjoying asserting otherwise if only to give myself the pleasure of watching him debate his point. In the end, he shall be proven right, of course.

Oh, Father! Was ever a woman so lucky in her husband as I? And for that I need thank you for agreeing to my Layton's suit. When I think I might very easily have been shackled to a boorish or unkind man, I can scarce countenance the thought. I could never do without my Layton!

He shall be a most attentive and loving father, of that I am certain. Is it possible for a man to possess a talent for being a father and husband? I am convinced there must be, for my Layton, having no prior experience, seems remarkably well suited to the roles.

Any woman would count herself excessively fortunate to have such a husband!

I send you my love as always. And I am sure Layton would too if he knew I was writing this letter. Do not worry your- self over me, Father. I could not possibly be better cared for!

Your happily contented daughter,

Bridget Jonquil

Layton read the letter again and again. There was no doubt as to its author. Layton fancied he could almost hear her speak the words written there, so much did they sound like his late wife. Yet these were thoughts she'd never expressed to him.

I could not possibly be happier.
Was ever a woman so lucky in her husband as I?
Any woman would count herself excessively fortunate to have such a husband!

Was it possible she actually felt that way? That she was not only content but, from the excessiveness of her praise, quite happy? And that he had, at least to a degree, been a good husband to her?

The tone of this letter differed so drastically from the encounters they had after Caroline's birth. The ceaseless sobs and constant sadness.

"Perhaps it was only the madness that made Bridget feel that way," Layton muttered softly. "And if not for that, she would have been happy."

"Undoubtedly."

Layton's head snapped up. Philip stood not far off, watching him.

Layton hastily refolded the letter and slipped it inside his jacket. "I was just . . . thinking . . ."

"Something I never bother with." Philip shrugged. "Far more effort than it's worth."

Layton smiled, even chuckled a little, in response. Philip picked a rock out of the snow and flung it expertly out at the cold Trent. They both watched it skip, one, two, three, four times.

"You knew about Bridget?" Layton asked. Philip hadn't seemed surprised or upset at overhearing Layton refer to Bridget's madness.

His brother looked back at him over his shoulder. "I didn't, until recently," Philip admitted, shrugging and looking back across the river. "You didn't bother telling any of us."

There was no response to that.

"But a remarkable young lady told me a story," Philip continued, still not looking back.

A lady telling stories? Philip had to mean Marion. No one told as many stories as she did.

"She gave me no names, but I began to recognize something in the gentleman the story was about," Philip said, "something that reminded me of you."

Frustration rose in him. He'd told her his history in confidence. "She wasn't supposed to say anything to anyone."

"She did the right thing, Layton. She told me just enough for five years of seeing you in pain to finally make sense. I could see in her eyes the argument she'd had within herself at sharing a secret, even disguised as it was. But she couldn't bear to see you in pain. She wanted to help but didn't know how else to do so. She told me what *you* should have told me years ago."

His tone held a hint of accusation. Layton felt himself tense. "I know I shouldn't have lied," he admitted, rising to defend himself. "But—"

"Layton." Philip turned back to face him fully. He was Philip again, no dandified mannerisms, no brainless posturing. Layton was face-to-face with his brother, the real man behind the mask he'd worn for so many years. "Do you know something? I would have lied too. If it had been my Sorrel, I'd have done exactly the same thing. Except it wouldn't have bothered me so much. Not that I care to incur the wrath of God or anything, but . . ." Philip took a deep breath. "You didn't have to go through this alone, Layton. Don't you think I would have stood by you?"

"I couldn't ask you to be part of it." Layton shook his head. "Knowing that I'd . . ." Suddenly, Layton just felt tired. The tension drained more every minute. And he was weary.

"I know now." Philip dropped his hands onto Layton's shoulders. "And I am proud of you, brother. You were good to Bridget. In life and in death."

"But—"

"And you know something else?" Philip's look became almost fierce. "I think it isn't God's forgiveness you are struggling with most. I think it is *your own*."

"Mine?"

"You are a Jonquil." Philip stepped back but kept his eyes firmly locked with Layton's. "We have this inborn need to save people."

Layton leaned back against the trunk of an obliging tree and thought about that. He had to admit there was truth in it. Even after accepting that God might not have condemned him, he'd continued to condemn himself, berating himself as a failure. "I couldn't save Bridget."

"I think, Layton, the one you were meant to save was Caroline."

"Caroline," he whispered.

"She could have suffered enormously at losing her mother." Philip flung another stone across the river's surface. "Instead, she is happy and loving and *loved*. You saved *her*, Layton. You saved *her*."

Saved Caroline. He hadn't entirely failed his daughter. In fact, she seemed quite happy, especially since Marion had come to them.

"I hope we will see you in church every Sunday." Philip wandered toward the water's edge. "Throckmorten has decided to retire to some other county. I am thinking of offering the living to Harold after he takes Orders."

"I think you had planned to all along," Layton said.

"I should have replaced Throckmorten long ago." He shook his head in obvious frustration with himself. "I knew he was cold and uncaring, but I told myself things weren't bad enough to warrant letting him go. If I'd been here more often, I might have realized how vicious he had become, how unpleasant and hateful a place he had made the church. Father would not have allowed things to go on this long." Philip's shoulders dropped. He rubbed at the back of his neck, his posture one of disappointment. "I should have dismissed Throckmorten years ago instead of waiting for Holy Harry to grow up."

"Harry will do very well."

"Yes, he will," Philip answered with a hint of pride in his voice. "Does that mean I won't have Caroline climbing all over me during the sermon from now on?" A certain urgency in his tone belied his casual choice of words.

"I always did like attending services," Layton remembered wistfully.

"You were the only one of us brothers who actually read your prayer book outside of church."

"Harry did," Layton reminded him.

"Harry preached from it," Philip corrected, flashing a grin over his shoulder. "Entirely different matter."

"Holy Harry." Layton laughed as he shook his head. "I suppose I should show up for a sermon or two. Support the family, you know."

"I would appreciate that," Philip said. "Without the benefit of Lady Marion's calming influence, Caroline would wreak havoc on the masterpiece my valet makes of me every morning."

Layton knew he was supposed to laugh, but his brain was caught on the first part of that sentence. Marion was leaving. He'd almost forgotten. She would be gone soon.

"Caroline was quite beside herself when she said good-bye in the church-yard," Philip said.

"Good-bye?"

"Lord Grenton and Lady Marion left for Derbyshire immediately after services. You weren't there. It's one of the reasons I came looking for you. Perhaps it was only my imagination, but I thought you would have wanted to at least say good-bye."

"She's gone?" Panic swelled in him.

"She'll be miles from here by now. They've been on the road at least two hours."

Two hours! How long had he been sitting on the banks of the river?

"Have you ever seen anything quite like that before?" Philip asked, pointing toward the river. Layton barely registered the rhetorical question. Would Marion come back? Write, at least? "End of February, and we have a whole assemblage of autumn leaves holding court right there in the river."

"Leaves?" Layton came to stand beside Philip.

At least a dozen leaves, the golden brown of late fall, swirled amongst the roots of a tree growing close to the water's edge.

"Drops of Gold."

"Drops of Gold?" Philip replied incredulously.

"Marion." Layton half sighed the name as he fished out a handful of damp leaves. "What have I done, Flip?" There was no answer. He didn't need one. "I have to stop her."

"Take Devil's Advocate," Philip immediately offered. "He's tied to a tree back a few yards."

"You rode here?" Layton asked, hardly believing he'd missed the sound of a horse's approach.

"I led him. I figured you couldn't chase down your lady fair without a daring steed."

"But how did you know . . . ?"

"Sorrel told me." Philip shrugged. "And I always listen to my Sorrel. She is by far the more intelligent of the two of us."

"Thank you, Flip," Layton said, clasping his brother's shoulders. "Thank you!"

And then he ran.

CHAPTER TWENTY-SEVEN

MARION HAD CRIED ONLY FOR the first half hour and only a few stubborn tears at that. She continually told herself that Layton and Caroline would be fine. She'd watched them interact all through the sermon that morning: smiling and affectionate. Layton had his family now; he had them to share his burdens and support him. She wasn't needed any longer, so it was fitting that she was leaving.

"And I have missed Tafford," she told herself for probably the hundredth time since she'd left the neighborhood of Collingham some three hours earlier. "It will be good to be home."

But somehow she felt more like she was *leaving* home than *returning*. In all fairness, Cousin Miles had gone out of his way to make her feel welcome. He was kind and generous and already treated her like a close member of the family. But it would be different. Perhaps if she hadn't grown so attached to Caroline, she wouldn't be feeling so ridiculously lonely.

"Who are you trying to fool?" she demanded of herself. "Caroline isn't the sole reason for these dismals. You are pining for *him*!"

Marion closed her eyes and tried to picture herself a tragic heroine in some gothic novel, wasting away for the love of some dashing gentleman. The image came far too easily. There she sat in a lumbering traveling coach, the windows so fogged she couldn't see out, on her way to a life of loneliness without the man she loved. Tragic did not begin to describe the situation.

Adèle had quite broadly hinted that she would enjoy sponsoring Marion for a London Season, what with her dowry established and their friendship further firmed. The very idea made Marion want to weep. How could she consider throwing herself on the "Marriage Mart," as it was termed, when her heart already belonged to another? To a gentleman who hadn't even bid her farewell?

She wiped furiously at a tear with Layton's handkerchief, which she had no intention of sending back to him, and told herself to be sensible. Layton had probably appreciated her efforts as a governess, perhaps even felt some gratitude for the ear she'd lent to his troubles. He simply hadn't loved her the way she had loved him. And why should he?

Marion knew her worth quite well. She was rather plain, with hair far too red, and a tendency to make a blundering wreck of any attempts at social niceties. She was too inclined toward the fanciful and not nearly accomplished enough to gain a gentleman's attention.

Layton was improving a little every day. Soon he'd be in a position to consider marrying again. He would be happier, Caroline would be cared for, and she, Marion, would be . . . devastated.

She moaned and dropped back against the leather upholstery of the Grenton traveling carriage. She was grateful not to be afforded a view of the passing scenery through the fogged windows. She couldn't bear to see Nottinghamshire slip away. Marion closed her eyes, reliving that glorious moment so many weeks ago when Layton had opened up to her, shared his heaviest burden, and trusted her with his secrets. The memory was followed quickly by the recollection of a bone-melting kiss, the moment she'd been so certain he'd loved her.

Marion forced her mind to stop there, to not float to the next memory: one that still hurt and ached in her chest. She felt as though she'd lost every ounce of happiness she'd possessed in that one morning when he'd so completely and painfully rejected her.

She became conscious of the carriage coming to an abrupt stop. Marion sat up straight and pressed her face to the glass window at her side. She could make out nothing but the hind half of Cousin Miles's horse dancing around at the unexpected stop. Muffled voices raised in a hurried conversation made their way inside the carriage, but she could make nothing out.

Highwaymen? she wondered briefly. As a child, she'd often imagined herself beset by a desperate highwayman, only to be saved by a dashing hero. Sitting in the cold, lonely carriage, the idea wasn't so enjoyable.

Someone outside moved toward the carriage. She couldn't see through the window to make out much more than a broad silhouette. Suddenly panicking, Marion pressed herself against the opposite side of the carriage and watched the door with alarm.

The door rattled. Marion held her breath. Slowly, it opened. Where was Cousin Miles? She could scream if she needed to. But who would hear? The stranger stepped inside, and Marion nearly fainted.

"Layton!" she managed to whisper as he pulled the door shut behind him. She'd never seen him look more determined. Something in his eyes made her heart turn over in her chest.

"Don't leave me, Marion." He took her face in his hands, his eyes boring into hers. "Promise you won't leave me."

She had no chance to reply. In the very next moment, his lips brushed over hers. His hand slipped behind her neck, holding her fast to him. She clasped the front of his coat, desperate to keep him there, willing herself to believe she wasn't imagining him there.

"Marion," he whispered against her mouth before kissing her more deeply.

The moment absolutely had to be real. Even in her most fanciful moments she'd never conjured a kiss as heavenly as this. The feel of him there, his masculine scent that she'd memorized but couldn't quite describe, the warmth of him so near, all made the moment as close to perfect as she could imagine it being.

Layton pulled away enough to rest his cheek against hers. "My darling Marion," he whispered. "Tell me I haven't lost you completely."

She couldn't even force a reply. He must have cared for her to have come after her. She turned her face up toward his, studying his expression, every nuance of his look. *Please*, she silently begged. *Please love me.*

"I have found every excuse imaginable to convince myself to give up the idea of—" He brushed his fingers gently along her cheek. "I was so afraid I would make you unhappy, would fail you, that you would be miserable with me."

Like his first wife had been. Surely he knew that was illness, a mind ravaged by madness, and nothing he had done.

"I cannot promise to get everything right, but I swear to you I will try." His eyes were pleading with her, begging for understanding. "Won't you please give me a chance? At least come back for Philip's wedding. Give me the opportunity to show you I could do better, that I—"

Marion pressed her fingers to his lips, which brought back that old, familiar fluttering in her heart. "A trial period?" she asked.

He nodded his head without speaking, her fingers still pressed to his lips.

"To decide if I love you enough to take a chance on you?"

Layton nodded again, the vulnerability in his eyes all but undoing her.

"Can I ask you something before I give you my decision?"

"Of course, Marion," he replied, removing her muting fingers by taking her hand in his. "Anything."

"Why did you—" This was harder than she'd expected. "The morning after you kissed me the first time." She felt herself blush. "Did I do something to—You lectured me. Chastised. All but said you found me and my kisses"—another blush heated her cheeks—"horrid. I don't understand."

Especially in light of the fervid kiss he'd only just given her.

"I was afraid," he said quietly. "Between what I saw as the difference in our stations and the gossip that still occasionally surfaces in reference to Bridget's passing and my guilt over her suffering and the lies I'd manufactured during the course of it all . . . I couldn't ask you to share that burden." Layton stared at their clasped hands. "And I was afraid you wouldn't. That you didn't, couldn't—"

"Love you that much?" Marion finished for him, smiling for the first time in far too long. She didn't think it possible to love him more.

Layton nodded without speaking, his fingers playing with a lock of her hair that had come loose. Tiny, tender gestures like that were among the things she treasured most about him. They were evidences of his thoughtfulness, reassurances that no person he cared for would ever be neglected.

"If you doubted my love for you, what sent you chasing after me?"

Layton reached into the noticeably wet outer pocket of his coat and pulled out what at first looked to be a mess of river junk. But on closer inspection, she recognized the pile as sodden leaves, no doubt fished from the River Trent.

"Drops of Gold," she whispered.

"There were twice this many, Marion." Layton let them drop to the floor, wiped his hand on his coat, and took her hand again. "Three times, perhaps. I remembered what you said about the river bringing the Drops and the Drops bringing joy and happiness. And I realized . . ."

"Realized what?" Marion knew she clasped his fingers a trifle too tightly, but she had to know, had to hear him say the words.

"The river brought me you, Marion Linwood." He pulled his hands free and wrapped her in his arms. "You and your stories. Your eternal optimism. Your refusal to be cowed by what I now realize was a suffocatingly unhappy household. You came. And you saved us. And I fell hopelessly, completely, in love with you. It scared me, Marion."

"Does it still?" Marion asked, though she was smiling.

"Absolutely," he answered. "But I am far more frightened of losing you." He kissed the top of her head. "Say you will come back, Marion."

She closed her eyes, savoring the moment. "I want to go home, Layton."

"Oh." He sounded completely deflated. Clearly, he'd misunderstood.

"No, Layton. Home to Farland Meadows."

"The Meadows?"

"I could not imagine being happier anywhere else in all the world than I would be there." Marion looked up at his face. "Promise you will never make me leave."

"Marry me, my love?" Layton whispered.

No words could possibly have been sufficient in that moment. She pressed a kiss to one corner of his mouth then to the other. "I love you, Layton. I have for so very long."

A look of contented peace filled his eyes even as a grin split his face. "We didn't make this easy for ourselves these past months, did we?"

Marion shook her head. How they'd both suffered in silence!

"I told your cousin that if I wasn't out in ten minutes he was to turn the carriage around and head back to Collingham." Layton held her as closely to him as she imagined she could possibly get. He tucked the carriage blanket around her legs.

"We're going home?" Marion laid her head against his shoulder.

"Will you help me make it a home again?"

"It only needs a little cheering." Marion felt warm for the first time all day, all month, perhaps. "And a great deal of love."

"And heaps of soggy leaves," Layton added with a laugh.

"Oh, Layton." Marion fairly sang. "What a story this will make."

"What a story, indeed," Layton muttered, kissing her once more for good measure as the carriage began to slowly roll back along the road toward home.

ABOUT THE AUTHOR

Sarah M. Eden is a *USA Today* best-selling author of witty and charming historical romances, including 2019's *Foreword Reviews* INDIE Awards Gold winner for romance, *The Lady and the Highwayman*, and 2020 Holt Medallion finalist, *Healing Hearts*. She is a two-time Best of State Gold Medal winner for fiction and a three-time Whitney Award winner. Combining her obsession with history and her affinity for tender love stories, Sarah loves crafting deep characters and heartfelt romances set against rich historical backdrops. She holds a bachelor's degree in research and happily spends hours perusing the reference shelves of her local library.

www.SarahMEden.com